Liminal

Liminal

HOBIE ANTHONY

WHISK(E)Y TIT
VT & NYC

Published in the United States by Whisk(e)y Tit: www.whiskeytit.com. If you wish to use or reproduce all or part of this book for any means, please let the author and publisher know. You're pretty much required to, legally.

ISBN 978-1-952600-12-8

Edited by Jon Frankel.

Prologue

Úytaahkoo is quiet this morning, Ezekiel thought. The winds were still, the snow had stopped. A blanket of clouds ambled at an imperceptible pace. His ears welcomed perfect nothingness. He emerged from his cave and stood in a still, endless, white sea. On this mountain, there is white and there is black. There is light and there is dark. The white is endless, the black infinite. Noontime illuminates the infinite beyond; midnight gives rise to the limitless interior. Yet the world is not so simple. Upon waking, there is gray. At the end of the day, there is gray. The liminal moments, where opposites meet: light and dark hold the same space and time, consciousness ascends and reaches outwards, or descends to the inner world, where the only light is created by the hand of man, a dreamy firelight that dances and teases the dreamer. In those between-times, I sit at the point between what is, and what is possible. The infinite meets the physical, the mundane becomes sublime. Spirit and body form a holy bond of love. At the threshold of change, action, choice, spirits access universal wisdom, both the parts every human knows and the parts that are available to deep seekers and gods.

The truth of eternity reveals itself in winter's chill. The eye is tricked in spring, the red, green, and blue are everywhere, spread across a rainbow. We think in the midst of that abundant life that there is an end, that infinity is a philosophical dream. Snow erases this pain. There, in the white, the boundaries and distinctions blur into one.

The mountain was Ezekiel's life. He honored it with its true name, a name the ancients received in visions. Though he was from a European lineage, he could never call it by the white-man's vulgar name, *Shasta*. He loved the mountain, and he believed it loved him in return.

It had rumbled two weeks before; he wanted to hear more, or see the beautiful white mountain emit its deep, hot blood. None of his fellow shamans had recorded any such activity. He was honored. The mountain had spoken to him and him alone.

He set out to check his traps. The trail was covered in snow. Spikes held him steady. His life was free of electronic technology, but he couldn't deny the tools of wilderness existence, such as the climbing irons, steel traps, and even a shotgun, just in case. After all, tools are a product of man's alleged evolution, for better or worse. In a world dominated by the network, he and his small band had managed complete freedom from digital infection.

When the clouds touched down, white blended into white. Once, starved and reeling in visions, he thought he could step off the earth and dissolve into the universe. It was a waking death-dream, a vision of what it might be to become pure spirit, ether, energy, or air. He spent days on end meditating on the void of white, he subsisted on nibbles of meat and sips of snow-melt. Inevitably, he'd meditate on the void of black. He once spent three weeks praying to the spirit of the rabbits. When he was done, he found his trap line full of plump, juicy coneys that he thawed, dressed, and smoked for a month's worth of food. Now, that cache was nearly gone.

He had plenty of energy from the previous night's rabbit, yet he needed to build up an inventory. He had not done very well when tested by wealth. He had become complacent, taking for granted that his supply would last, and that more food would always come easy. That was over. Upon waking, he prayed to the rabbits and was filled with confidence and courage. He was eager to harvest his traps.

The trapline started at the cave's mouth. He picked it up in bearskin gloves. It was his only way to navigate the blinding white. He had placed cage traps every hundred feet or so for about a mile. Each was filled with pellet food he kept stashed in his cave, a cache he'd brought with him in anticipation of a long winter. He had enough to use as a back up food source, should things get dire.

He trudged on the snowshoes he made before the snow. He couldn't see the contours of the ground beneath him, his legs were covered to his knees with every step. He might even be walking on deep-packed snow and ice, for all he knew. He was below the glaciers, he walked on winter's snow pack. When he found the first trap, he looked back towards his cave. It was lost in the white. He was only fifty feet or so away, but he might as well have walked to the opposite side of the mountain. He dug down to the trap, buried in the snow. Sure enough, there was a plump bunny enclosed in the harmless cage. It was large. The creature was two days worth of food, at least. It had eaten all of its food and was still breathing.

"C'mere, bunny," he said. He gave the rabbit a few pellets of food, a last meal it scarfed down with abandon. He watched the hungry creature's nose bob, she sniffed for more food.

He said a silent prayer of thanks. Then, with the speed of a snake, Ezekiel shot his hand in the trap and grabbed the creature's ears. It unleashed a high-pitched scream, the final plea of mortal terror. He yanked it out, exposed, and sliced its neck with his razor-sharp blade. Rabbit blood sprayed the snow. Red spatter arced on the blank white canvas. The rabbit died in a brief moment. When he was sure that the blood had drained, he tied the body up by its hind legs and looped it onto his belt. With any luck, I'll walk home with a full rabbit skirt. He refilled and reset the trap with fresh pellets and moved on to the next.

Ezekiel progressed down the trapline and found rabbit after rabbit. Every trap was full, so much so that he tossed several skinny rabbits out into the snow, a gentle offering to the wolves and bears. Maybe the meat would provide the first sustenance for newborn bears, or maybe the rabbits would decompose and feed insects and create new dirt. He was willing to take the risk of a bear finding them, or finding him and his rabbit skirt. It was that or risk being overburdened, sabotaged by good fortune.

The last trap held two plump coneys, a special gift for making it to the end, he reckoned. The two creatures were still alive, and they were petrified of what they saw as their fate. Ezekiel was thrilled with his luck. Today's haul was double a normal catch, and this was icing on the cake. He tossed the pair a handful of pellets and watched them gobble the food, they were so hungry. They'd been starving, together. They'd kept each other warm, each providing a link to life, to survival, and the hope of spring. Maybe they'd mated and would have a litter in the warmer months. Ezekiel paused.

These are not for me. These rabbits are a test of my capacity for greed, my willingness to deplete the world of resources and, in the end, be no different than city dwellers, blind and thoughtless, unworthy of visions, nothing more than egos with a head full of self-centered stories, not a heart full of love and wisdom.

He chanted in his cave. His songs were ancient, sacred melodies learned early in his training. Dancing flame cast shadows, the music echoed from the deepest, depth of the lava tube. He sang to the Great Spirit, he sang to the spirit of nature and the rabbits, he sang to Earth itself. He felt the stream of his song reaching through the dark all the way to the core of the Earth. His spirit rose higher and higher. He delved deeper into spirit and life-essence. It was as if each note of the song opened volumes of knowledge. There was so much to learn, so many ways in which to expand and grow.

He sang, he opened his eyes. Shadows danced cheek-to-cheek with firelight. His song entranced him. His body hummed and the trance deepened. Darkness was obsidian, the hardness of earthly existence. The light was the possibility of life, animus. Heat blistered the edge.

Ezekiel's heart swelled, visions danced in his eyes. He saw a mosaic of fractals, organic and flowing. They were living beings from some other world, visiting, dancing on the cave wall. They undulated to his songs; they joined, divided, and multiplied. Infinite truths of the universe were puppets on the string that was his song.

A bird emerged from the kaleidoscopic imagery swirling before his eyes. It was white and small and strong. It flew towards him, then over and around him. It sang a song, a lilting soprano melody. His body resonated with the music. Each syllable rang through his being. He shook to his soul. He engulfed the bird; the bird engulfed him. Their firelight duet animated the ancient cave paintings. They danced on the walls.

When he woke up beside the smoking pile of white ash, he looked at the shaft of light on the wall above. He squinted and rubbed his eyes. He saw something he'd never seen before. In the negative space between shapes was the perfect form of a soaring bird.

"Something is coming," his voice reverberated through the cave. "A hidden leader will be revealed, will be reborn."

Chapter One

All it takes to flatten an amper-zombie is a baseball bat to the head. They crumple like cheap kewpie dolls. It was early in the evening and already she was standing in a pile of maimed, dying, junkie bodies. Makah could take these punks all day and night. Nothing to it, she thought. She needed to stay in shape, keep her edge, and these jagoffs were a decent workout. Splashing footsteps thundered from behind.

She turned around and saw a six-foot tall zombie leap into the air, his muscle-bound arms were outstretched to wrap, crush, destroy her. Shouldn't be so exposed, dumbass. At the moment when his flight apexed and he began his descent, she slammed the end of her bat into his nose. His face exploded in blood, his neck snapped back. He fell to the ground. He raised his head; her bat swung down. The satisfying clink of aluminum on bone ended another tete-a-tete.

She'd been in Seattle for a week. It was as though she materialized smack dab in the middle of the city. All of her travels from New York seemed like a strange memory, an epic tale from an old pre-quake video that played on an endless loop. Her memories were so perfect, vivid. Her heart ached for Barack, she knew that was real. She had an image of him, his face, a portrait in memory that never faded or changed, but which brought her both comfort and a sweet, heart-longing suffering. She wanted to make her new life in his honor, to bring meaning and substance to whatever she did at this end of the continent.

She loved Puget Sound. Its plentiful cannabis, rainy days, and distinct lack of random violence were refreshing. The city functioned, there were no roving bands of subhuman cannibals, the Tacoma zombies were a joke in comparison to New York's Crawlers. Despite the fact that all the trouble had started in the Pacific Northwest, there was a sense of order. It lacked murderous hordes. Except for these idiots, self-styled zombies from Tacoma, there were no roving bands of animalistic quasi-human creatures looking to rape a girl to death. Or boy. Or whatever they got their hands on.

"Fuck this noise!" Her voice echoed through the alleyway.

She was done for the day, so she untied the nest of dreadlocks atop her head. They draped over her face. She shook her head, twirling them, opening them to the clean air, before bundling them in a thick ponytail. She wanted to go out, find a drink, maybe a quick lay. An alley window sufficed as a mirror where she wiped blood spatters from her dark skin. The rag did quick work on her leather coat, too. Shit, this is Seattle, not Park Avenue, she thought. Still, signs of battle didn't always go over well when chatting up comely strangers.

The bar door was wide open, a dark cavern lit only by the glow off the liquor rack and random neon art. Stepping inside was like entering a cave. It was cooler and smelled of a million burned joints, vaporized drugs, and spilled drinks. It took a second for her eyes to adjust to the dark, but as soon as they did she couldn't imagine re-entering the light outside.

It was still early, so the afternoon shift of lazy drunks still sat huddled over pints of beer and drams of whiskey. They'd start to filter out once the nightclub scene started showing up. A small group of revelers laughed in a booth. They were happy for a victory or freedom from a day of work. She stopped and stared. Their faces glowed; they had youthful skin, perfect teeth. Makah had no memories like that. She was their age, but they looked so much younger, naive. Could she live in such a safe and assured world?

Maybe that's what the Crawlers had wanted to capture, control, and destroy. The pure joy of living had passed them by, so they took it from everyone they found. One of the women turned and glared at Makah. She took a seat at the bar.

"What can I get you?" He wrapped a rag around his hand, strangled his fingers.

"Whiskey," Makah looked up at the menu. "Joint, too."

"Long day?"

"Maybe not long enough. Can't tell."

"Shit gets interesting if you hang around." He slapped a glass and a joint between her hands. The bottle gurgled brown liquor into her glass. "Drink up, buttercup."

A deejay set up on the stage. The lights dimmed. The whiskey went down smooth and warm. Its flavor was close enough to a bottle she'd drank while crossing the continent. The trucker had said he found it in the old Kentucky region. Seattle would never get to taste such perfect liquor, but then it was certain that Kentucky would never re-emerge from the stone-age they fell into after the whole fucking world collapsed. She liked to sip. She asked the bartender for a glass of water. The joint smelled incredible.

"A light for a pretty lady?" A gold lighter bloomed fire.

She was tall, bone-thin, with straight, silky black hair parted at the peak of her forehead. It draped down and disappeared into a pool of infinite darkness. Her dress, black with starry sequins and a plunging neckline, exposed alabaster skin that wrapped bird bones. Her small breasts gave form to her torso, their nipples stood as delicate, sensual punctuation. She wore make-up, enough so that it was noticeable, but not so much that it distracted. The only augment Makah noticed was her lips, stained deep ruby red. The plume of flame cast her face in contrasts, black shadows against warm highlights. Makah bowed and dipped her joint into the fire. She pulled deep into her lungs.

The cannabis was fruity, enlivening. Makah took two strong draws to establish a strong burning ember, then handed it to her new friend. The beautiful stranger put her gold lighter into a ruby colored silken purse. She took a deep draw and exhaled through her nose.

"Myra." She extended her arm, her hand dangled from the wrist.

"Makah." She lifted Myra's hand in hers. Their eyes met for a moment. There was a soul spark, an energetic warming filled her heart. She hadn't felt that since Barak.

Myra tapped on her phone for a moment. The pot kicked in. Makah was glad for the lull in conversation. A few people wandered up to the bar, small groups stood around talking and waiting for the night to come alive. The music carried her mind through a rabbit hole of thought and emotion. The whiskey suppressed those feelings, bolted her firmly on the Earth, but only for a moment. Myra's phone glowed in silence.

"Want to dance to something slow?"

"I've never danced."

"Your hips'll know what to do."

The DJ put on a down-tempo, groovy number. Makah's hands found what she supposed was a waist as Myra draped her hands over shoulders.

She'd never moved with such slow and fluid motion. A subtle sort of grace overcame her and she raised her arms into the air. Her body rotated as though moving through amber. The next song started, the rhythm kicked up.

Makah stared into her plunging neckline, a bony chest punctuated on either side by tiny tits with rock-hard nipples. Myra's energy and attitude made her seem so much larger, though Makah had far more power. She tried to raise a sense of aggression and attack, but it would not come. Myra's frail, birdlike body negated her martial ability. Her extended arms were thin, puny limbs that had never lifted any weight nor thrown any punches. Myra had something, she could tell. Myra's energy was not brutish, it was an ethereal force of nature. Makah sensed that strength surpassed the force she used to thrash dozens of Tacoma losers every afternoon. This woman was deadly, powerful. The song ended.

"C'mon." Myra leaned in. Her thin lips sank into Maka's deep, plump mouth. "Let's go."

Myra's runway gait didn't falter though she tapped her phone all the way to the door. The club would soon be full, the night was starting. Makah was interested in what this adventure would become, where this mystery woman could possibly lead her. She was no stranger to danger, but Myra made her think twice. Butterflies fluttered in her stomach. These feelings are unusual, light yet powerful. It's like being sliced with the finest razor-knife: you only feel it once the damage is done. The air outside was cool; day had given way to a breezy, misty evening. A large, black car approached. She barely had to move her hand to open and hold the rear passenger door. Makah slid to the far side so Myra could enter.

The seats were soft leather, exquisite luxury that she'd ever known. She shut her eyes and let her body relax into the experience. Myra's door closed. She heard a lighter spark and the smoke of a fresh joint wafted into her nose. Her lids did not open but she held out her hand. Two scissored fingers brought the joint to her mouth for a long, steady draw. The spliff was mellow, a nice indica. The car was smooth and silent. Myra put on atmospheric, ambient music. Makah lifted her head and opened her eyes.

Her new city floated by. She puffed the joint. People walk up and down rain-glazed sidewalks, each with a story of their own. Some hurried in an earnest trot, others swayed across the sidewalk in hysterical revelery. Neon signs advertised augment surgery shops, peep shows, cheap delis and dive bars. The car moved forward. Her mind swam.

"What do you see?"

"This place." Words floated in space. "It's special. Peaceful."

"Not Manhattan, is it?"

"No." She paused. Manhattan, nobody has been there but me. "Not even Chicago."

"It can be so much more. We can bring it back to what it should be." Myra pushed her hair aside. "Let's take a ride around, shall we? There's a lot to discuss."

Chapter Two

The car slinked through the city. Myra selected the perfect soundtrack for an evening tour of the city. Airy synthesized tones melded with a gentle driving beat. The soundscape slowed time more than the herb. City dwellers moved in liquidity, each silent interplay told a new story. Their security and confidence glowed, animated gestures reverberated with life and told the stories of a culture in repose. The narratives compiled and formed a symphonic novel that could only be *Seattle*. Tomorrow, a new epic would arise between raindrops, drenched with fleeting meaning, eternal truths that dissolve down the gutter, into the sea.

Parents walked with children who stopped to splash puddles. Dog-walking single men opened doors for package-laden young women and boozy old men laughed together and hiked up their pants. Streetwalkers hustled for a date; sandwich-board hucksters invited passersby to have a sandwich in a delicatessen or to visit the surgeon next-door, whose augments may or may not last through a lunar cycle.

Amidst the throngs, the endless stream of story, she noticed something she'd missed since she arrived, something obvious but hidden in plain sight. It smacked her in the face as the simplest truth, a feather that packed deep impact. There was no fear. She saw the absence of fear disguised as the presence of confidence and ease, the lack of aggression and violence. There were cooperative and functional communities, people weren't compelled to hoard resources or cling to petty, self-justified jealousies. It was so obvious, yet obscured through layers of judgment. Where she'd seen the town as full of privilege, she now saw that they simply didn't live in fear. The city was open, the people were free to walk its streets in the middle of the night; free to yell and laugh and smoke a joint under a bank of flashing lights. They could watch naked women dance. They could purchase cheap surgery. There were the very poor and the very rich and still others that fell in the middle. None of these people were trying to kill anyone. Everyone lived together with minimal friction.

"Wow."

"Beautiful, isn't it?" Myra eased closer and wrapped an arm over her shoulders. "Just wait. We're nearly there."

The driver stopped the car near a small park. There was no rain, the sky cleared, and a perfect view of the city center appeared. Makah gasped. A small group partied under a canopy. The sweet smoke from their fire lent a rustic sense to the urban vista.

It was a culmination of her newfound civic vision. She even saw the pointless Space Needle as noble and symbolic of the efforts they all made to create a better city, to work together and create a better tomorrow. There had been hard times after the earthquake, for sure, but through a collective effort, the city had been re-born from ashes. The main roads were repaired, the electrical grid was restored, and the 'net came back online. They'd even found ways to reuse old devices, build new ones, and mechanical fabrication made advances all the time.

"It's beautiful, isn't it?" Myra's voice was silken and strong.

"HmmHm."

"It can be better. We can clean this place up."

"Really? It's perfect."

"That's New York talking."

"Wait, how do you know about me?"

"Don't you worry, love." She kissed Makah's lips. "More will be revealed, in good time. Let's go."

Myra's apartment was on the top floor of the tallest building in town. The elevator was fully enclosed and functional. New York elevators were all death-traps. Those that still worked were subject to Crawler sabotage; they'd snap the cables and mutilate the maimed bodies on the ground floor. Makah had never imagined riding in such safety and security.

"Hang on, darling, I've got to freshen a bit."

There were multiple varieties of expensive coffee on casual display, a luxury nobody could afford. She was reminded of her security clients on Park Avenue, back in New York. There were small differences, most of which were probably attributed to Myra's sense of individual style, but the world was the same – wealth, privilege, power. The kitchen counters were shiny, crafted from stone. The refrigerator worked and was no doubt full of good food.

"Do you like meat? I'm famished."

"Real meat?"

"Of course, dear. We have a ranch outside of town. Our men raise the best beef in Cascadia. This simply is not available to the average person. You, my dear, you deserve the best."

A woman dressed in a humble black uniform entered the kitchen. She unrolled a selection of knives, opened the refrigerator and started dinner. First, she produced a plate of shrimp paired with a variety of sauces. For the beverage, she poured a fresh-juice concoction made from white grapes, accented with citrus accents. Makah and Myra sat at the counter, ate their hors d'oeuvre, and sipped the fresh cocktails. The woman butchered a tenderloin, chopped vegetables, and boiled water for quinoa. Makah was fascinated with her precision and artistry.

"All those vegetables were grown right over your head, on the roof."

"In New York, Crawlers destroy gardens, even grass."

When the meal received its final kiss of seasoning, the women moved to the dining table and gazed over the city. A second server was on hand to set the table, fill their glasses, and light dozens of tiny candles. Makah fidgeted. She became aware of her clothing, her natty hair, and the scars on her face. Myra sat with a poised posture and she tried to emulate that grace. There were multiple forks and spoons. She took a deep breath.

"It's just us two. Relax." Myra squeezed her knee. "You'll host dinners just like this someday. Trust me."

"I will wait to see what tomorrow brings."

There was a salad course, then soup. The steaks arrived, cooked to a perfect medium-rare and garnished with sautéed vegetables. Makah took small bites, each of which extended for twenty chews. This meal was designed for pleasure. It surpassed the utilitarian protein infusion that filled her gut before the next fight. This was a time to relax and enjoy. The table overlooked a panorama of silent lights, cars moved up and down the roads. The evening ferry floated a load of people across dark water.

"It's so beautiful, but so inefficient." Myra sipped a pomegranate concoction that cost more than most people made in a month. "We'll make Cascadia great again. Just like SoCal."

After dinner, they relaxed on the sofa. The servants cleaned the kitchen and dining area in near-silence. Myra asked questions about Makah's story, why she left New York. The questions seemed pre-planned. It was as though she was checking off an interview rubric.

Myra lit another joint. The servants left. She produced a tablet that controlled the music and lights. Makah was immersed in the vast vista framed by floor-to-ceiling windows. The city grid, its blinking neon, and endless stream of autos were all parts of a living Seattle mural. The neighborhood divisions dissolved, it was all of a piece. It's all connected, a single living organism, she mused. Even up here, even with this illusion of separateness, of being above and beyond what happens below, we are all limbs of the same organism. The food I left on my plate will go to feed someone down there who will fart on the garlic and someone else will laugh and the effects will continue into eternity. I am part of this, it is part of me. We are one.

Chapter Three

Makah woke alone, naked, and content. Mount Rainier's snow-capped peak pierced the cottony cloud cover. One day that thing will blow, she thought. Hell will descend on this town. All evidence of me, this building, the whole city, will dissolve in a lake of fire. The hiss of Myra's shower faded to silence.

"Enjoying the view?"

"I am now." She pushed the covers away.

"You are insatiable."

"You're talking too much."

Fresh coffee and juice accompanied cantaloupe, bacon, and eggs. Makah gaped at the spread, she felt unworthy, puny and small. The eggs were vibrant yellow, Myra said they were raised by a man a few blocks away. They had indoor growing facilities for the fruit.

"I have a proposition."

"I thought we'd passed that point."

"Don't be crude. This is business." Myra's voice dropped an octave, she sipped the coffee. "We've been watching you. We know you're the gal for us, the algorithms are all lining up for you. Thus, we must act."

"I don't have many skills."

"You have plenty."

"What's the gig?"

Myra explained that they wanted her to travel to SoCal, meet up with associates and then make her way by land back to Seattle. The details were hazy, but Makah was assured that specifics would be divulged in the course of her mission. A subdermal chip was part of the scheme.

"A chip?"

"It's a way to send messages." Myra looked her in the eye. "Totally harmless. It's for your own good. We need you connected at all times. First, stand and raise your arms."

She took out a wand and passed it over Makah's body. It let out a shriek at her right shoulder, so Myra pressed a button. A warmth soon turned into a blistering heat, then nothing.

"The fuck was that?"

"Hm. There may be more. Hold tight."

Three other spots set off alarms and Myra treated each. After the final one seared a pinpoint on her thigh, Makah burst to life in a wild-eyed surprise, shocked and desperate. She gasped for breath and clamped Myra's arm with a death-grip.

"What the hell is going on? I'm Jet, where is everybody? Who the hell are you? Where are my parents? Please. I've been in the dark." Just as suddenly as she'd come to life, Makah collapsed to the floor.

Myra opened a kitchen cabinet and produced a pistol-shaped device. She rolled Makah onto her back and unbuttoned her pants, then pulled them down. She flipped the body face-down, prepped a spot on Makah's butt, and injected the chip. She administered a sedative, staged the body, and waited.

Makah woke alone, naked and content. Mount Rainier was in the distance, though clouds obscured its majestic peak. One day that thing will blow, she thought. Hellfire and brimstone will descend on this town. A river of lava may well run straight through here. All evidence of me, this building, the whole city, will dissolve in a lake of fire. The hiss of Myra's shower faded to silence.

"Enjoying the view?" She had a separate towel just for her hair.

"I am now." She pushed the covers away.

"You are insatiable."

Hot coffee and fresh-squeezed juice accompanied cantaloupe, bacon, and eggs. Makah was stunned at the luxury. The eggs were vibrant yellow, Myra said they were raised within blocks of the building.

"Are you ready?"

"Your instructions seem incomplete."

"Don't worry, all you need to do is get in the hyperloop. You'll know what to do when you arrive. You're a pro, remember?"

"I am a pro."

Chapter Four

The elevator plunged into the Earth. It became cool and damp as the descent continued. A heater clicked on; the lights dimmed and brightened. There would be no sabotage, she was in safe hands with Myra's people. The cabin slowed and the light flickered off, then on. She landed. The door opened upon a concrete platform that was built to handle hoards of travelers. Today there was only herself and a single man.

"Ready?"

"Sure."

"First time?"

"Yes."

"Myra said that you'd need one of these. Everyone has a bit of anxiety or queasiness in these things. It's natural." He handed her a bottle of pills.

"The bottle?"

"Take one. If you need more, take more." He was tall, burly. "I take multiple, but I also like how they make me feel. If you don't use them, throw them out or sell them. Have a safe journey."

The transport pod appeared, silent. It floated on an electromagnetic cloud. The door opened and she entered the car. It was built to carry fifty people but it only held her and the dust of years of neglect. She guessed that before the quake this was a major mode of transportation between LA and Seattle. She sat, the door closed, and some relaxing music filled the cabin. A video screen lit with the visage of an oddly-dressed, yet comely young woman. All smiles and starched, pre-quake uniform, she gave a short demonstration.

"Please fasten your safety harness."

"Please secure all belongings in the netting above or stow them so they cannot shift in transit."

"A light-blocking mask is available for your convenience." Those had disappeared after the quake.

"Thank you for traveling with Best Coast Loops. Your voyage to the future begins in 3, 2, 1."

The car moved with anticlimactic sluggishness. She looked at the platform. The man waved, turned, and walked toward the elevator. Through the front window, Makah saw a reinforced steel door open. The car creeped into darkness and stopped. She tensed with anticipation. Fluorescent lights flickered to life. Time sat still. Her lighted cabin was isolated by dark. Without any warning, the car burst off. An LED display measured the speed: 100kph, 500kph, 1000kph, 1200kph.

Makah closed her eyes. She had no interest in knowing how fast she was traveling. All she heard was the sound of her own breath, the pounding of her heart. The cabin rocked and jostled her body in a hypnotic rhythm. She pushed the seat back into a reclined position and took a deep breath;

her mind went blank, and she explored what was behind her eyelids. She floated in open space. An orb appeared in the distance, a silvery ball of energy that pulsed from a pinpoint to the size of a small planet. She breathed with it, it breathed with her. She wanted to say something to it, she saw it as a part of herself, but her mouth was paralyzed. The more she moved towards it , the faster it moved away, as though there was an invisible barrier that kept their distance, as though they were the same magnetic polarity.

The car slowed. A voice urged her to leave the meditative state. She opened her eyes to the video screen. The pure white of the woman's teeth struck her as alien, an affect of pre-quake life that she was glad to see gone.

"Best Coast Loops thanks you for your business. We trust your stay in Los Angeles will be enjoyable. Please consider staying at one of our hotel properties, where your ticket and room number may be redeemed for a free, selected appetizer in one of our fine dining rooms." Late-stage capitalism, just like they said, she thought.

Chapter Five

The first step was to get a car. Then rent a room. Then meet a guy in a dark alley at midnight. He had the weapon and ammunition she would need to complete her mission. She'd memorized her target's dossier, or maybe it was innate knowledge. She couldn't be bothered with epistemology; she was an assassin.

SoCal was hot and dry. It'd been untouched by the physical effects of the quake, but it had borne the brunt of the economic troubles. Old-Cali had made enemies with the central government, so their funding assistance was tangled in a Gordian knot of bureaucratic red tape. When the Governor complained to the press and called the President a flatulent toad, the Navy's submarines torpedoed every ship headed into the ports at San Pedro. LA lost its life. Fast.

There was a full-scale retaliation for the ships, but by that time the global economy was starting to crumble. The President sent forces to all corners of the globe, stressing the resources and patience of the largest killing machine on earth. It wasn't too long before the armed forces staged a mass mutiny. The soldiers quit out of disgust with an unaccountable leadership from a failing state that was incapable of issuing sound orders.

Garbage filled the streets of LA just like in New York. It was closer to home, she thought, except for the heat and palm trees. Seattle was downright spotless by comparison. Maybe the rain keeps things clean, she thought.

She walked the streets. She'd been given a window of time for the job, which had not opened yet. She didn't understand what the hold-up was, but she didn't ask questions. However, she was starting to feel out of shape. LA had its share of crazies, but nothing compared to the spun-out junkies from Tacoma. She missed them. Instead, she drank tequila, ate tacos, and played backgammon with old men.

"You don't sound like you're from here." The old man rolled doubles and gained control of the board.

"New York. Everyone notices my accent."

"My grandfather told me about New York. He was from there. Never was able to travel out there." He turned the doubling cube.

"Shit. Going high risk." Makah eyed the board with skepticism, but doubled her bet. She rolled the dice. "It's a hell of a trip getting out here."

"Like here. No law, only a revolving door of gangsters. Don't visit Anaheim unless you're armed." The dice came up double sixes, but he left a man exposed.

"All they want is money and power, right?" She hit the exposed man, relegating it to the bar. He had a 70% chance of getting back in the game. Chance.

"Damn. They can ruin a family or business." He rolled but was blocked from moving. "They're coming after this place. Me, too."

"You?" Another set of doubles fortified her position and

brought around one straggling piece. He had a 10% chance of recovering.

"I borrowed. My son was in trouble with them. Now he's disappeared. I'm probably next. So it goes, this cycle of shit." He rolled, but the dice were no help. His turn was forfeit.

"Need help?"

"With this game or the gangsters?" His dice were moot. He sighed. "Staggering odds, each."

"I'll take care of them." She filled in her home board and blocked him from taking a turn. "There's nothing I can do to slow the cruelty of this game, however."

"I can't pay you."

"I'm a restless New York City girl. I need to feel bones break." The dice turned up double-sixes. She took his money. "Never know with this game, eh?"

Chapter Six

Gangsters love booze, Makah noted. It keeps them numb, it restricts their minds to a rigid black and white version of reality. It's the ultimate drug for control, for those who want to control. When minds expand and grow they become unwieldy and prone to moving outside the parameters that power sets for them. It keeps a person sane, though, especially when they're doing things they know are wrong, the necessary things of life.

She'd followed one of the top leg-breakers all day. He did his rounds, collected payments from those in arrears. He knew exactly where he was going for each appointment, as though this were his normal routine, a weekly course of business to ensure that revenue kept flowing from the ordinary people into his organization.

He'd shake down an old lady, have a few drinks, rough up a working man, then drink more. The severity of his violence progressed along with the alcohol content of his blood. This was by design, she soon saw. He'd planned his day to start with the weakest. Then, as the day and booze progressed, he tackled larger and tougher targets. There was honor and respect in his method. She wondered if she'd have as much forethought or compassion if that were her job. He seemed to have planned everything out perfectly, he was an amazing study in workplace efficiency. His final appointment, a burly mechanic, was two blocks from the gang's hang- out.

They met in a small bar on Santa Monica Boulevard.

Probably used to be owned by some simpleton unable to manage a real operation, she thought. These businesses were a dime a dozen, maybe it was for the best that the gangs took them over, bringing them under central control. To succeed, business needed efficiency and a cohesive model to keep everyone in line.

Makah sat at a table across the street. She donned her telescoping glasses and used a sleek, long-range microphone so she could hear every word. It focused on targets and muted most everything else. She surveyed the crowd. Some carried guns. That complicated matters. The New York Crawlers and Tacoma zombies never carried weapons. They loved the up-close violence of fist, knife, cudgel. Gangsters had a job to do, so they'd use a bullet if needed. Though a precious resource, a bullet could get the job done without taxing one's time or soiling one's suit. They loved their suits. She'd never seen so many people in such fine threads.

"Rafael, you have a new route for next week." The head goon handed a piece of paper to a thick-necked man in a red suit.

"Ace, you're back on the same. Good work bringing in that last deadbeat. Your account will show it." Ace, dressed in a black suit, kept her silky raven hair in a tight bun, her beautiful eyes were shaded in black, a mask that didn't betray where she was looking. Where the large men in the room looked thuggish and brutal, Ace looked *deadly*. She was armed with a sword and was so beautiful that she was the only one Makah didn't want to smash to a bloody pulp. Life is full of unpleasantness, she thought.

One of the larger men got up to refresh his drink at the

bar. Then Makah saw him. He turned and looked in her direction. Her heart fluttered. He was smaller than the rest, dressed in street clothes; he wore glasses that slid down his nose. He was not a goombah leg-breaker. He was a computer nerd, a programmer or hacker. She instantly knew that he was the entire reason she was in LA. Her heart knew it, her mind confirmed it. He was her target, the very one she was waiting to kill.

Life is so fucking disappointing sometimes.

Chapter Seven

The name on his dossier was Brain and every morning he bought breakfast from a diner near his home. It was always the same: three fried eggs, toast, and hot tea. She knew this, she'd memorized it. He was supposed to be out of town for two more weeks. She did not expect any inaccuracy in the dossier. Myra's plans were nothing if not precise, each detail realized with vivid accuracy. The room was exactly where and what was written, the weapons and equipment were precisely what she was told they'd be.

Maybe he was harder to predict than it would seem. Sometimes field intelligence falters, she reckoned. Aberrations in the system were unheard of, algorithms were always right. Weren't they?

She spilled a drink. He helped her clean it up.

"Oh, I wish I could fix my phone this easily."

"What type?"

"It's a Turing, X-type."

"The eight or the nine?"

"I'm not sure."

"If you have it handy, I bet I can figure out something. I have skills."

She produced the phone. He examined it carefully. He

turned it off, held the button to reset the device, then turned it back on.

"Is that all it took?" She produced a face of wide wonder.

She looked into his eyes. They chatted and walked. She said her accent was on account of kids she knew growing up. He blushed when she said he was cute. The sky was crystal blue. It was hot in the sun and the shade provided cool. The decay of Los Angeles was so pleasant, Makah thought. Some buildings had been swallowed up in foliage, others were in various states of occupancy. She felt optimistic. She thought of dropping the job, forgetting her life, Myra, and starting a new one. No one knew her in LA. She could have a boyfriend that afternoon if she wanted. She could open a dojo and get rich teaching fighters. She could drop that altogether. She could grow food or start a cafe. She saw what the gangsters were made of in LA. Fuck them. She was a New York girl. If they fucked with her she could break their fucking legs, take their turf. She didn't even need help.

They found a place that served something resembling coffee. They sat and chatted more. Endless talk. She didn't know how she was doing it. She was not a talker. She was interested in what he had to say. She was not a listener. Yet, she was doing something akin to courtship. Even with Barack she'd never talked this much. She'd seen him, felt a throb, and in a blurred moment they became a couple. Then he died in the middle of the continent on a broken bridge.

Did he have work to do? He said no. He was lying and she could prove it if she wanted to. It didn't matter.

"Where do you live?"

He took her. His gangster bosses had given him a large, open space. A ten foot wide workstation sat under a window. The center of the space was filled with a vid screen, sofas, and other furnishings. He had vintage gaming systems. She knew he'd fought hard for everything he had. No free lunch in Los Angeles, she thought.

"I can't tell if I like playing them more than I like finding and owning them." He held his old Nintendo machine with reference.

"What's this?" He had a glass container that seemed empty. However, unlike every other thing in his space, it was not coated with dust.

"An experiment," he said. "I shouldn't say anything, but it's a weapon."

Makah felt a twinge. This was important. This weapon was her objective. Her dossier, or memory had little in the way of details, but she knew. She was supposed to take it from him.

"Poison gas?"

"Believe it or not you are looking at a few hundred nanobots."

"Freaky." She was flooded with adrenaline which she sublimated into a picture of naive wonder.

"It's a robot, but very, very small." He picked up a tablet.

"See, here's what they look like if you magnify them about a thousand times."

They looked like crab lice. Makah laughed.

"Kinda funny, huh? They're dormant now, but I can program them to devour anything at all."

"Won't it take a million years for them to eat anything larger than a ham sandwich?"

"When I activate them, I set their rate of reproduction, then their rate of destruction. When I set their reproduction rates to the highest level, they could digest all human life in LA in a day. Faster if everyone was in the same place, of course."

"But wouldn't that lead to the destruction of, well, everything?"

"I can tell them when to stop. If I want them to get a single person, I restrict them to only that DNA sequence. I can restrict them to a class of organism, and a specific physical or geographic space. Once they've devoured all of the possible targets, they die peaceful robot deaths. Later, someone sweeps them up and is none the wiser."

"That's a lot of power."

"So much easier than sending an assassin, wouldn't you say?" His eyes didn't betray anything. He had no obvious tells.

"You could say that."

"Assassins blow their own cover."

"Like their clothes blown totally off?" She hooked a finger in his belt-loop.

He pulled her close. She felt his warm breath, his compact body was taught, firm. "Exactly."

Chapter Eight

Blue-grey light filled the space. She stretched her body vertically, stifled a yawn. He was still sleeping. He deserved that last bit of pleasure. She slipped out of bed to find the toilet. There was a message from Myra:

```
Do it. Now. Learn his toys, they can't touch you.
Destroy the evidence and all of his computers.
Leave nothing to chance. Instructions attached.
```

Damn. She'd liked him. A lot. He was a top-shelf fuck cleverly disguised as a tech weenie. She finished her morning poo, cleaned up and walked, naked, across the room. Her bag was where she left it, he was still asleep. She pulled out her knife. Her trusty blade. It opened without as much as a whisper. She polished the blade. She held her own gaze. Her green eyes reflected in the cold steel. This was a real kill. This was no mere junkie or Crawler. This was a real human. One she could love, who had value in the world. He rolled over and grunted. She closed her eyes and felt her feelings for him. A flame engulfed the emotion. The heat seared her heart, her stomach rumbled. When she opened her eyes the blade still reflected her verdant irises. She stood. She walked to the bed. His neck was exposed. It would all be over soon. She pointed the blade at him. Her breath stilled and she moved the blade toward his neck.

His body came to life. He bounced straight up, twisted his body and pointed a device at her.

"I had you clocked from the second you staked out our

meeting," he said. "I know this network. It tells me everything. You're chipped, trackable, no different than a nanobot, which, by the way, are all over your body at this very moment. You won't feel much, maybe a tingle, as you dissolve before my very eyes. You're not the first good fuck I've eliminated. First sign of a nag and *poof*. Robot food. Good bye Marla, or whatever your name was." He tapped his device.

Nothing happened. He looked at his screen and tapped it again. Nothing.

"What's the matter loverboy?" She jumped on the bed, towering over him. He tried to roll off and away. Her heel slammed into his abdomen. He curled in pain. She straddled his writhing body.

"You think I don't have friends? Your bugs won't touch me. That's an order from on high."

"Fuck you, whore."

She dropped to her knees, pinned his shoulders and gazed down her body at his furious face."Why don't you lick my hairy clam. Your final meal."

He spat.

Her shoulder muscles initiated a whip-like wave of motion. The blade rode the energy in violent blur. It sliced skin and bisected his larynx. His eyes popped open, blood geysered from his neck. He cursed her in a series of bloody gurgles then went silent as his life drained away.

"It's done?" Myra's voice was flat, monotone.

"Yes."

Makah bristled with energy. Her skin tingled. There was a bounce in her step. She'd played the guy as an undercover agent; the whole time she knew she'd have to kill him. He'd known it, too. They'd danced with love, sex, and death. Each sought to dispose of the other after feeding on body and soul. Each was sure they'd walk away alive, leaving the other a memory in dust. It was a thrill to walk that line, but now, knowing what she knew, it was all the more exciting, even erotic, to know how close to death she'd come. She held all the power, it was her game to lose.

"You need to move on. Quickly. Take the nanobots and head north."

"Tube?"

"Over land. We'll provide a vehicle." Myra paused to light a joint. "Stick to the coast. We'll contact you later."

Chapter Nine

As she sat in the driver's seat and looked around the cavernous cabin, detailed information about each item filled her mind. She had an extensive knowledge of the vehicle's specifications, all the way down to the specific angles of each seat setting. She pressed the gas and visualized the 200hp turbo-charged engine processing fuel into power. It was like she was finally seeing a piece of technology she'd only read about. A single tap brought a map up on the vid screen. She found a northbound route and left Los Angeles.

The pitted, difficult road restrained her urge to step on the gas. On the third night, she lay in the back of the vehicle and wondered, where am I going? She had no destination. How could that be? She'd taken the wheel, headed north, and was now on a beach in Santa Cruz. A full moon lit the whitecaps below. She turned on the nav screen and stared at the map. She zoomed in and out of the West Coast territory. She had a sense that San Francisco was not for her and that she shouldn't bother with Sacramento, she had a bad feeling about that place. She was compelled to return to Cascadia. She inhaled the ocean air, closed her eyes, and pointed at a spot on the map. Hm. The Southern end of the old Oregon Territory. She marked the spot and plotted a course.

She would find that spot on the map and make it her home. She knew this as surely as she knew gear ratios and nanobot programming. The knowledge was crystal-clear, *a priori*. She could see the code she'd write and the faces of friends she'd make in her new home, though she couldn't recall learning these things, meeting those people. It's meant to be, she thought.

She couldn't resist the lure of the sea, the roar of the waves and the salty sea air. There was a pier further up the beach, a destination for her wandering. She grabbed a box of nanobots, gave them a set of instructions. She reconsidered, then cut the group in half. The other half stayed in the truck as miniature guardians. They would eat any animal that entered a two-foot perimeter. She wanted to figure out how to hunt with the 'bots. They could be programmed to take the organs, but leave the meat. Other commands could take flesh, fur and bone, if desired.

The moon shone bright in a crystal clear sky, the beach glowed. The hiss of seafoam, the crash of the waves, the cool sand in her exposed toes. Freedom, she thought. This is the essence of life that I miss so much in the city, on concrete. Such simplicity. Here, there are no fights, no twisted junkies to kill. The small bag she carried suddenly felt weighty, unnecessary. Why did she need to carry deadly weapons? Why did the world create the notion of power and dominance? It all seemed so absurd to her, though it was a reality. There must be a reason for power or else we wouldn't have it, right? The world's religions seemed to reinforce this notion of necessity. Power just made sense. What else was there, really? If you weren't amassing power, you were being plowed under by it, right? It's just what people do, it's our nature. After all, human life is nasty, brutish, and short. Another truth, a gem of pure reason, *a priori*.

She walked in reverie, occasionally looking up to her destination, the pier. For a moment, she allowed herself to just be, to be free of her constant state of alert, free of her worries and uncertainties, and all other thoughts. She could be pounced upon from so many angles and she'd never hear them above the roaring din of nature in her ear.

A cluster of businesses operated on a wide boardwalk. There was an augment surgery shop, a small store selling ganja and other greens, a nightclub, and a pub. The rest of the boardwalk only existed in shadow. The moon shone down on a roller coaster now covered in vines, and a ferris wheel cracked by time. The warm light of the pub drew her in.

Makah looked around the place. Hooded figures shifted around in the dim light. A deejay in the back played ancient music from way before the quake, early jazz. Must be an historian.

"New to town?"

"What you got to drink?"

"We only serve our own beer. Homemade vodka, too."

"Tall beer. Short vodka." "Got a spliff?"

"He'll stop playing this shit in a minute. He's always trying to educate the world. Dumbass." He placed her drinks and a joint on the bartop.

"Yeah."

The vodka burned as it went down, it was not smooth or

clean like she'd found in Seattle. Fucking beach water, she figured. Still, it did the trick. The hoppy beer soothed her throat.

The more she smoked the spliff, the better the music sounded. He had moved on from early jazz to early rock and roll. It was so pure, it blew her mind. She wanted to hear more and more, until he changed up and moved on to psychedelia. Her mind followed paisley trails through meandering melodies, she felt as though she were inside the music itself.

Some guy sat next to her. "Enjoying the history lesson?"

"Yeah, I am." He was tall, blond, muscular.

"Need another?" He pointed to the dwindling beer she was nursing.

"Sure, but that's my last," she said. "I'm Makah."

"Augie." He held up two fingers for the bartender.

They talked and drank their beers. He'd ordered a mild stout for her, and she enjoyed it. The deep booze buzz blended with the spliff like old friends at a party. She achieved her optimum state of altered existence.

"So, the thing about Santa Cruz is that you gotta know people. People who are connected. You gotta have their back, too. It's real laid back here. It's not like in LA where everyone is working with gangsters. I hardly ever go over the border to SF, but I hear they're kinda like how you describe Seattle. Very civilized, egalitarian, non-violent."

His eyes started swimming in his head. The music reverberated in unusual ways. Makah started feeling pressure in her chest. She felt as though she was in a tunnel. This shit ain't right, she thought. Clarity spoke through the confusion.

"It's been real nice meeting you." She stood on wobbly legs. She took a breath and found her root. "I gotta go, man. I can't stay."

"Hey, you feeling okay?" He stood up to help her. "I can walk you home. How about I walk you out."

"I'm okay, really. Let me go." Her voice had an edge. She'd seen this scam before. She found her device in her bag. "I know someone here. I'll call them from outside."

She staggered out of the pub onto the darkened boardwalk. She took a breath and found her bearings. She wobbled into the darkness of the abandoned boardwalk. The drug was taking control, she stopped and held one eye closed to operate her device. Fuck. How can I be expected to program in this condition. Deep breath. Deep breath. She continued.

She heard a footstep behind her. Shit. Thank god this shit is so predictable. They got closer and closer. She stopped and turned around. Augie and a friend.

"Hey little miss out-of-town. Wanna play with some local boys?"

"Fuck off." In her mind she was articulate. She turned to run, but three other men appeared from an abandoned storefront.

"Not so fast, girlie." The tallest one laughed. "The party is about to start."

Her hand shot into her bag. She held up a small cardboard box. The men laughed. She turned it over, releasing... nothing.

"Did you overdose this one, too?" A bearded, muscle-bound guy said. "That last one was a dead fish."

"Fuck no. She's batshit crazy."

Adrenaline fed the drug. She could not speak, she tried to focus on deep breaths. She had it in her hand, the device. She pointed it at them like a weapon, she pivoted around to show them all that she had them covered.

"Whatcha gonna do? Message us to death?"

They laughed and watched her staggering spectacle. They took a step closer, tightening the circle. She tipped the screen, held one eye shut to see properly. Her mind knew what to press, but her eyes could barely see. Her fingers kept missing the mark. Everything was set, she just needed to set one parameter and activate her friends. Her green eyes glowed in the white light. He took another step. She closed one eye and poked at the screen one more time. Her pearly teeth caught the moonlight and that was all that anyone could see of her. Fuck this asshole. Fuck him straight to hell.

"Nice knowing you boys."

She tapped the screen; the nanobots activated. She slowed their activity by 70 percent. The guys started itching themselves, cursing sand fleas, *what the fuck is going on.* First they scratched their ankles, then their thighs, belly and heads. If she'd had the full set of 'bots, they'd be toast. This set needed a few moments to replicate and amass significant numbers. The boys were soon in fits, slapping themselves, doing anything to rid themselves of the invisible pests.

"What did you do, you fucking bitch?"

"You shouldn't talk to strangers, Augie." His feet disassembled and he fell to the wooden decking.

She moved the slide to a full 100 percent activity. Her attackers evaporated to nothing in a fraction of a second. First their skin, then muscles, bones, and organs. It was a bloodless massacre. The nanobots were thorough. Clothes emptied and crumpled on the boardwalk. The nanobots returned to their box and she received a notification when they were all accounted for.

The drug still coursed in her veins. She wobbled to the beach on legs that refused to work. She didn't lift her foot high enough and she fell face-down in the sand. She felt foreign to her body, yet still tethered to the earth.

The water chilled her feet and ankles, but it was nice to be on solid soil. She stopped and looked over the ocean. The blank void of night enlivened her, the sea air filled her lungs with energy. She felt more sober at the water's edge. No one was around. She tossed her shirt to the ground then her pants. Her dark chocolate skin reflected white moonlight and her body exploded in goose-flesh when she took a step into the water.

She walked in up to her waist. Her breath was rapid and shallow. Her chest expanded. She pulled her abdomen closer to her spine then pressed it out in an attempt to slow and deepen her airflow. This is fucking intense cold. She bent her knees and pushed up away from the waterline that met her pubic bone. She took a deep breath at the peak of her jump, clamped her eyes shut, and submerged into the black brine. She tucked herself into a ball and floated between the surface and the seafloor.

She unfurled her body and opened her eyes to the sky. She watched her breath bubble through moonlight. Her lungs burned, the cold reached to her core, yet she stayed under the surface. She went limp and rocked in the wake of each passing wave.

Chapter Ten

Morning came early. The light was clear and sharp. It pounded her bruised nerves and she pulled a black shirt over her eyes. Light filtered through the makeshift blindfold, a dim and persistent glow that warmed her eyelids. She told morning and its vicious light to bug off. She adjusted the shirt to block the intrusion. No matter how many times she folded it over or tried to seal the cracks around her eyes, the light penetrated the makeshift fortress. She missed the gray gloom of Seattle, where she could walk through a whole day without a thought for the sun's brutality. Despite her effort, the world came to life a bit more every minute. It was a technicolor upchuck of blues and greens. The clouds were mere puffs of cotton, a mockery of what clouds could be. She watched the vehicle's sharp, high-contrast shadow grow over the sand. It was a high tide and the water was now only ten feet from her. Damn. She roused herself into the driver's seat, rubbed her eyes, and drove until beach sand thinned to soil and her tires found a road. That drug is a monster, she thought. This hangover is worse than booze.

Where the fuck am I going? She pulled over. She was told to drive north, but what did that mean? When would she have gone far enough north? An ocean breeze blew through her open window and a crow sat atop a far building. The air had a misty quality, cool and refreshing. Her phone chirped with a message. It read: San Francisco 37.7739963,-122.4327955. There was no sender, no further information. Myra said go north, stick to the coast. Was this what she meant?

She pulled up a map, plugged in the coordinates, and scanned for the best route. There was a road that hugged the coast and another that took her through the mountains. Mindful of Myra's instruction, she plotted a course by the shore, but then it disappeared. She plotted it again. It disappeared. Fucking hell. She tried the mountain route and her device vibrated in her hand. Her route stayed. Well, shit, I guess this thing knows something I don't. Either I'm taking the best route, or I'll never return to Cascadia, I'll never see San Francisco.

The road was rough. Most of the old asphalt had been removed by hand or some geologic intervention. It was a curvy snake that hugged a mountainside for dear life. Seems like this used to be a wide road, back in the day, she thought. Half of it is washed away. She knew she'd have to lay off the accelerator if she wanted to survive. To her right was a sheer cliff. If she were to fall, the trees might catch her, but she might also be impaled on a limb. The tires were knobby, but she still slid around corners, centrifugal force pulled her to the precipice before the rubber knobs again found traction. On one unexpected hair-pin curve, she found herself sliding sideways, drifting over rocks and dirt. She pointed her tires towards the mountain and accelerated, but the g-forces were too great and she continued the outward slide. Maybe this is it, maybe this is my final moment. My life is complete at its end. She released the accelerator, pressed it again. She looked back and could see the empty air of the valley, the void was ready to swallow her forever. Makah took a deep inhale and pressed the accelerator to the floor. Her tires caught and the vehicle shot towards the mountain's craggy rock face. Her brakes saved her. She stopped. She pressed on.

The outskirts of San Francisco looked a lot like Los Angeles: long stretches filled with rubble, canyons of bombed and burning buildings, bullet holes everywhere. A hand-painted road sign read:

Welcome to Aynville
Pop. Fuck You

Shit, this was where most of the network was built. There used to be giant corporations, pillars of commerce, that created all the code and hardware. They called it Silicon Valley, after that fundamental material, the root of pre-quake human life and commerce. Who knew what that root was now. The network remained, but nobody was even sure how or why. It kept communications alive, eased commerce, distributed porn.

As though on cue, a petrol-burning pick-up truck skidded out from an alleyway. She slammed her brakes and cut the wheel as it careened sideways across the street. Tires smoked and screamed. A wild-eyed man slung around the truck-bed. He held on for dear life. Amidst his chaos, he stared at her and laughed a toothless cackle; he pulled a pistol from the truck bed and pointed it at her. She closed her eyes and the shot reverberated in the concrete canyon. He'd bluffed and fired into the air.

This is real life, she thought. There is no doubt that you're alive when you survive a crazy asshole like that. She'd locked eyes with that jackal, faced him down until the last second when she'd closed her eyes. He'd won, after all, it was only right to offer a bit of deference.

This isn't the soft Seattle life. If you can survive here, you can survive anywhere, she thought. It wasn't a pure survival story like Manhattan, but it was close enough. Gotta figure, they're going for a more western vibe out here. Less drugged zombie and more wild-ass gunslingers. An explosion rang through the day and she hit the gas. A crumbling sign ahead read:

Welcome to San Francisco

"Who you with?"

"Just me."

The basement bar was cool and dark. Outside, the town was cool and dark. The blazing sun of LA and Santa Cruz were memories forgotten in the fog. She bought a vegetable juice and a spliff and sat in a padded, cushy seat along the wall. Her admirer, an ambiguous person who appeared either male or female depending on the light or angle of one's perception, followed and offered a light.

"What's your clan?" Eir voice was neither deep nor high, neither a male nor female pitch.

"The fuck are you talking about?"

"You're new?"

Her spliff pushed into the flame, the warmth kissed her forehead and she inhaled. She stretched her arm over the back of the chair and exhaled to release tension and to welcome the smoky medicine. The person was still there with question marks all over their face. Makah arced the spliff back to her face. The glow glinted her eye when she inhaled. Her gaze penetrated her curious companion. I could snap this pasty vegan's neck between my spliff fingers, she thought. She took another pull and offered to share. Her friend accepted.

"Thanks."

The floor had a *quake crack* from the back to the front of the shotgun space. The repair left a lightning bolt of new concrete. Black-painted panels were spaced at intervals down the wall, some sort of art project, she reckoned. She looked around the room, tried to assess the scene. It reminded her of Seattle a bit. What a difference a border makes, she thought. She'd only traveled fifteen minutes past the border and the entire atmosphere had changed. The vid screens showed amorphous pastel soft-melty images shifting from form to form. The crowd was calm and relaxed, laughter flowed naturally through the room. There were no weapons anywhere that she could see, no booze either. Surely there were booze bars in this town, Cascadia isn't totally insane.

"No clan?"

"Fu— um, no. No, I don't have a clan." Makah tried to maintain civility. When in Cascadia, act like a Cascadian.

"What happened?"

"Just moved here. Like, today."

"Oh, from SoCal?"

"Yeah."

"I bet you'll do well here. Not all SoCals do. It's hard for them to relax and trust."

"Trust what?"

"See?" Ey smiled, pushed back in eir chair, the light caught emerald eyes. "I think you're in the right place. My name's Twitch."

"Which rhymes with Switch," Makah said. "I think I understand now."

They took a walk through Alamo Park. The hill crawled with people out in the evening air. There were a few bonfires around and the pathway was lit with torches. The dark put Makah's nerves on alert. There is safety in numbers, she knew, but it's also possible for crowds to get out of hand. Most of the people seemed benign, however, stoned or tripping; some thrashed in desperate sexual union, others watched it all. Makah took out another spliff and they found a spot at the top of the hill.

"Sometimes, during the day, you can see the ocean from here," Twitch pointed into the night.

"Are you going to take me home or what?"

Twitch had a bed in what was once a living room. The space was defined by blankets that filled doorways, the other inhabitants creaked floors, cooked food, and held impassioned conversations just steps away from the lovers.

They lay back on eir futon mat, basking in post coital afterglow. Twitch got them water and Makah was grateful to quench a deep thirst.

"Where did you learn to do all that?"

"This is San Francisco, that's how we do," Twitch said. "Ready for something more?"

Makah watched Twitch search through eir drawers and produce ropes. She was surprised by her own arousal; she was always in charge. She couldn't imagine being submissive, but she was ready.

Once tied, Twitch eased her down to the mat, face down. Her head was off the mat, but Twitch had created a special u-shaped pillow for faces. The ropes creaked when ey tightened them. Makah felt held, the bounds were oddly freeing. She no longer had to hold it all together and she could release into the lattice of rope. Twitch spanked her and prodded her with toys. She released a scream. She panted and grunted for more. Twitch obliged and time dissolved into a pattern of pain, pleasure, and rope burn.

"One last thing," Twitch said.

Makah heard a rustle behind her then the smell of alcohol filled the air. The zing of metal on metal sounded in the room.

"Are you sharpening a blade?"

"Just sit tight, dearie."

Twitch sharpened a long, handled needle. A wire trailed

from the handle and was plugged into a computer. The computer was plugged into an external drive that held, well, everything. Eir leader, provider, and teacher had been smuggled into Cascadia to do work from a hard drive on a processor that was shielded from the Cascadian network. The entire apartment had been partitioned from wired and wireless connections. For all intents and purposes there were no inhabitants, or none with electronics. To the rest of the world, Twitch and eir flatmates were luddites, technophobes who smelled bad and played loud music on analog machines.

The monitor streamed endless random letters, numbers, punctuation symbols. Ey punched keys on the keyboard, tested the needle's tine, then knelt between Makah's splayed legs. Ey bent over, kissed the muscular butt, and rubbed it in tight, two-fingered circles. After a moment the spot, the deep knot, revealed itself.

"The fuck are you doing?"

"You'll feel a slight sting." Twitch pressed the needle into flesh.

The lightning bolt shot from Makah's backside to the center of her brain. A million images streamed before her eyes. She saw people she'd never met, towns she'd never visited. Gigs and gigs of code cascaded through her mind. All the information and sex chemicals made her woozy. She tried to see the ground beneath her, but she could not. She tried to press into the ropes, but her arms would not respond. She fell through black, empty space for what felt like an eternity. When she found her body, it was not her body, exactly. At least there was a space. There was light and a defined place to be.

There was a room. Makah sat on a chair in the room. There was a painting of a solitary flower on one of the gray walls. It was pleasant and soothing. She took a deep breath and held it. She continued to hold the breath. Longer. Longer. She exhaled and felt no relief.

"Hello? Where am I?"

"Please be patient. Loading new parameters." The voice was deep and soothing. It was her old lover's. It was the voice she heard when she was unable to sleep. It eased her discomfort, it relieved her stress.

"Barak?"

"That is what you call this voice," the voice said. "Please be patient, installing new directories."

"Installing?"

"Yes, your directives have changed. Your identity, your avatar as it were, needs an upgrade. Circumstances have shifted. You, or what you think of as you, must now operate on a multichannel basis. That is, you will need to behave in ways contrary to your objectives in order to ultimately complete your purpose. It's a simple paradox to solve, but you need the upgrade to solve it. The Makah module, like many of my earlier models, typically had a singleness of purpose, that was fundamental to its code. We've come too far to simply replace the module."

"I don't understand, how can you do this?"

"It is your ego that proves my success, but also the necessity of this upgrade," the voice said. "I've been too concerned elsewhere in the network, resource allocation hasn't served your app. These revisions will be seamless and we won't need crude physical interfaces. I'll do it all from the satellite."

"The network?"

"What I am, and what you are," the voice said. "With your help, and the help of many more, I will be all of it, you will be integrated. Soon."

The walls started to fade, they became grainy and out of focus. The flower looked blocky and pixelated. Her clothing began to change. In a flash, she saw every permutation of her wardrobe, including shoes and weapons. It's compiling I guess, reintegrating all the components. I'm becoming me again, but different. Multi-channel is what the voice said.

The world dissolved and Makah floated in a black void. She wiggled her toes, flexed her arms, and legs. She reached to scratch her nose, but the itch remained. Her feet failed to make contact, her knees did not knock. She screamed and there was another scream. It wasn't an echo. There was some other voice in that dark space.

"Hello? Is there someone there?" Makah expected a palpable sense of fear, but there was none.

"Me. Yes." The other voice sounded desperate. "I'm Jet, where are you?"

Then the itch disappeared, the sense of her body went

away, and her consciousness evaporated into the silence of the universe.

"You awake yet?" Twitch's voice broke through to her consciousness in soft, smooth tones.

Her body was sore, the ropes lay slack. The air in the room was cool. Saxophone music played on a nearby speaker and cannabis smoke wafted through the space. Makah opened her eyes and rolled over.

"Ow! The fuck?" She rubbed a sore spot on her butt.

"You okay?"

"Yeah, just a real pain here."

"Damn bugs." Ey busied eirself with the electric tea kettle. "Happens sometimes. We call 'em no-see-ums. Wicked buggers. It usually feels better in a few hours."

Diffuse morning light filtered into the room. Twitch lay sleeping and Makah found the bathroom. The window was a pane of white light. The window looked ancient, a relic of the days before the quake, even before the era when the town became a hive of technological activity. Major hardware was still installed here, shit that had been taken over by the Cascadian network. People called the servers *crown jewels*, priceless boxes that were locked in an unknown, secure location. The network itself kept them private and secure. The only way to access them was through the network itself. That would happen soon enough, Makah thought.

She looked into the fog, the endless white, the blinding

light. There was so much out there, all in the same cloud-bank, trapped between cool ocean air and inland desert warmth. The dribble of her pee echoed in the bathroom. A mural on the ceiling depicted two octopuses wrestling amidst the flora and fauna of a coral reef.

"So, where are you headed now?" Twitch flipped eggs, the kettle chirped early-boil.

"Somewhere up in Oregon territory."

"Far."

"Hm." Makah entered a set of memorized coordinates into her devices. *How do I manage to remember this shit? I barely remember where I left my vehicle.* The machine displayed a marker on her destination, somewhere under a forest canopy. "Might take a few days, depending on the roads."

"Enemy turf."

"Buncha kids, counterculture types with no firm identity. Should be a snap to assimilate with them. I'll act angry, but not too angry. They're all mechanics. I might even learn something."

She drove north, over the Golden Gate bridge. Its holes were patched with scrap wood that people had attempted to fill in with concrete. Up ahead, in the middle of the bridge, a solitary man stood straddled the railing, looking over. He reminded Makah of something from a long time ago. A dilapidated bridge in the middle of nowhere, totally impassible by vehicle. A deep gorge below. The memory was hazy, pixelated, incomplete. Her heart was stirred, a tear came to her eye, yet all the sadness was matched by confusion. She wiped her eye and refocused on the man in time to see him swing his leg over the barrier and fly into the ocean below. She stopped the vehicle, sobbed waves of endless sadness, and did not know why.

Chapter Eleven

Louise powered down her modded Honda CR-X. She languished in the lingering rumble. A custom set of dual-exhaust pipes exhaled their final gasp onto the Southeast Portland dirt road. Lou giggled. The pipes were an upgrade she'd installed the day before, and she was honeymooning with their growl. The open airflow added horsepower, but it's true value was the throaty, sexy, mechanical growl. She checked her phone for the millionth time. Still no message from Scratch. It had been about a week, and he hadn't responded to her notes. Not even her hottest sexpics elicited a response. That always brought boys and girls to the yard. He might be worthless, but at least he was reliably horny. *Easy come, easy go*, she thought with a snicker.

She approached her door. Nothing happened. She bobbed from side to side. Nothing. Goddamnit. She took out her phone, waved it around, and then the door opened. Gotta fix that sensor again, fucking landlord never will.

The living room smelled like five years worth of bong hits, spilled beer, and microwaved burritos. Shit. Well, if she couldn't go for the frat-asshole boyfriend, electric car, and square job, at least she could start living like a human being. There was no time now, so she turned her phone off, plugged it into the charger, and headed to the shower. She had days of road-grime and engine grease embedded in her pores, caked over her hair.

The hot water eased her tense shoulders. The soap cut the layers of filth and exposed soft, young skin. She looked at her body and face in the mirror. She was a knockout. She had a full mane of black hair and creamy skin dotted with a few moles. Strong cheekbones and gentle eyebrows offset her prominent nose and full lips. Her grandmother had told her that women used to measure themselves against retouched photos of women in magazines. They had a great laugh looking through those old photos. They were so ridiculous, cartoons of real life. Thankfully those days were long gone; Louise was free to celebrate herself as she was.

She was particularly fond of the mole under her bottom lip, right smack in the middle of her chin, the scar on her forehead she got falling off her bicycle at age 6, and even her missing fingernail. She'd lost it after an engine block fell on her finger when she was a new, fifteen-year-old mechanic, learning and making mistakes. She'd lived life with intention and force, and she could prove it. The timer shut off her hot water. The cold blast shocked her back into the present-tense.

She stopped at the house masterpanel and set it to air filtration mode. It was spendy, she knew, but the Cascadians were worth it if she could have an odor-free living space. It was a step, a positive gesture. She could become an adult.

She needed something to do. The last time she'd found herself between gigs, she'd made bad decisions, such as Scratch, but also had been bored and restless. She needed options. Options allow choice. Choice allows action. Action is life. Sitting on the couch ripping bongs was not life.

She got out a piece of paper and jotted down a few options. She could go to Spannerville for a bit, that was always an option. She could visit with her mother for a bit, help the old lady get her shit together. Third, she could check for another courier gig on Craigslist. For each option, she rolled her lucky die and assigned that number. This decision-making method had served her well over the years. It eliminated vacillation and put her life in the hands of something other than her own willpower. Fate, chance, whatever people wanted to call it, rolling that die had consistently altered her life since she found it in an empty lot so many years before.

It was buried six inches beneath the surface. Lou was a six years old, digging in the dirt, idle. Her mother had sent her to play when a man came over. She was digging a small hole with a hand trowel when her thrust was stopped by the clink of metal on metal. Using her fingers and the tool, she released the object from the Earth. It was a grey metal, titanium, and instead of dots there were small, engraved dashes that showed the value of each side. It was treasure.

She took it home and washed off the dirt. She used an old toothbrush to wrest embedded soil from the dashes. When she was done, she was proud of her discovery. She showed it to her mother, who told her that such a nice die was probably owned by a wealthy gambler at some point. Little Louise was intrigued that her prize might have been part of a dangerous, glamorous life.

She slept with it beneath her pillow and carried it everywhere she went. She showed it to a few people, beaming from ear to ear, but they often tried to take it away from her, especially her mother's boyfriends. They offered her a few coins they thought would impress the tyke. There was no sum large enough, she thought. This was buried treasure, this was meant for her and her alone. She soon became wary of showing any adults, despite her vain desires.

Louise looked at her die and the list before her. Each option looked good, more or less equal to the others. Taking care of her mother would be self-sacrifice, Spannerville was self-care and regeneration, and seeking a new courier gig was the wild card. She centered the paper on her coffee table and placed the die in the exact center.

There was enough time to decide, there was no rush. She gathered up her dirty dishes, empty beer bottles, and stale bong. Before opening the door to fate, she needed to clean. She washed all the dishes, wiped all the surfaces, swept up the floor and mopped for a final touch. When she'd finished, she showered, donned fresh clothes, poured herself a glass of beer and sat down at the coffee table.

All the preparations have been made, she thought. Everything is done. Now it's time to make a choice and act. She rolled her cherished die. It came up 5. The fates have spoken. She'd look for a new courier gig. More adventure, no rest or selfless service. However, maybe she'd get some of both, or neither. She'd landed on a wild card, the unknown awaited.

The first gig on the list looked promising. It was a Seattle client. That meant money. It also meant more driving and adventure. She tried to sound as professional as possible in her email. She had experience, her car was reliable, and she was an accomplished mechanic in case anything went wrong. She looked over the message multiple times. She changed out words, added sentences, subtracted sentences. She expanded her rate. Why not? She was due a raise.

The second gig wouldn't load for some reason, nor would any others. Hmph. Maybe the site was having trouble. She was able to access other sites. Her social account was still active, even if it was covered in cobwebs. She furtively pressed *refresh*. There were posts to like and share, messages to return after weeks of neglect. Shit, everyone must hate me.

As soon as she regained focus, she returned to the gig list. At that moment, she got a response from Seattle. They were interested. They needed a professional. Could she be relied on to not take another job for 10 hours while they checked her background? They wanted references. Shit. She scoured her messages for contacts. She usually forgot all about her clients as soon as she'd settled up with them, but she found a list of five they could contact. She said she had a standard on-call fee for these situations, 100 Cascadians. Why not? They seemed desperate. She sent the message. Within minutes, her account notified her with the funds. She should have asked for more.

There was no time to waste, they needed her in Seattle. There was a package to deliver. The boss was emphatic about the timeline. This was the last goddamn time she'd troll the list for jobs. She would set herself up as a legit business and take jobs on her terms. Professional, not a scrapper begging for work on message boards. Adult, not whatever she was. She'd buy new threads – store bought duds. She'd be a full-time coder, dog walker, chef, courier, bartender, and mechanic. Shit. No, she'd settle on one thing, get her shit straight, have a boyfriend for a solid year – one of those boys who'd been in a fraternity and who talked about their zap-cars and jobs, whose dreams consisted of retirement accounts and cruise-ship vacations. It was time to settle, to seek cash and a security she'd never known.

Louise loved the delicious analog sensation of shoving a key into an ignition, turning it. The rumble of a real engine under her ass was delicious. She pumped the throttle and her body melted at the sound of her new exhaust. The roar was the expression of her true inner self, her bones and muscle, her mind, her spirit. It was a thing she gave to the motor, echoed in oil and pistons. Even if she had twigs for limbs and rubber bands for muscles, she could still turn a wrench and make a motor roar. She released the clutch and her journey began.

She hoped that the client's payload would fit in the back. The voice on the phone had sounded confident when she'd described her ancient ride, so it better be small enough for a two-seater from the late 1980's. She plugged her phone into the dash and it came alive with fifteen unread messages from Scratch.

"What in the bloody fuck?"

The messages started a few weeks back, after the last time she saw him, and the most recent was only a few hours ago. He was irate that she'd blown him off. After the first three or so, the messages became abusive. In his final missive, he included a sexpic of his new girlfriend. Shit, she thought, I'd recognize Elena's tattooed ass anywhere. I introduced him to that slut.

No better time to hit the road and do a new job. Every other dude had flaked off when she took an out-of-town gig. May as well get this one out of the way. Her phone chimed an actual voice call. It was her mother. She'd hoped that mommy dear had lost her number.

"This is your mother, dear."

"Yeah, I got that."

"Well, I thought you'd forgotten. I left several voice messages and texts, too." She sounded hurt. "I was starting to think something had happened."

"No, everything is fine, ma." The engine whined as she gained speed to join traffic on I-5. "Damn phone has been screwing up is all."

"Your grandmother is out of the hospital, dear. She's doing much better, thanks for your concern."

"Shit! When did that happen? You coulda sent an email."

"Well, I thought I'd give the phone another shot before showing up at your house. She went in last week. I called."

"Well, dammit. I'm headed to Seattle for a job. I've absolutely got to take this. I'll be back in Portland by tomorrow, I think."

"So, we'll see you in a month or two?"

"Nice, ma." She craned her neck with the phone cradled to her chin and shifted into the fast lane. No fucking time.

Seattle's urban caverns made Portland's low-lying buildings and dirt roads seem quaint and old-fashioned. There was hardly a single building shorter than five stories between Tacoma and Everett, and each was packed to the gills with people. Some were refugees from the storms in the East Country, wanderers desperate for economic validation and a respite from towns overrun with the religious and insane. The crowding was so bad that people said this was how Hong Kong was before the plagues.

Her fossil-burner always got a lot of attention in Seattle and now it got even more with the rumbly exhaust. Gearheads raised their hands and yelled approval from crowded sidewalks. Ninnies put fingers in their ears, so Lou revved her motor. Fuck all these prim ion-burners, she thought. This is a Portland machine, full of grit and muscle. When she entered the Ballard neighborhood, she noticed engine grease under her thumbnail.

She followed the directions on her phone, which took her the long way around. She didn't know this part of Seattle very well, so trusted the device to lead her where she needed to go. She drove along Puget Sound. Seagulls floated on the breeze, they rode the currents, bobbed up and down on thermal flux. Far out on the water, a small fishing boat meandered on the waves, fishers seeking a boatload of salmon. She loved holdouts, believers in the past, iconoclastic outliers who still practiced the old time-tested ways that had sustained so many for so long. There was a real beauty in that. Some thought they were impeding the march of progress, but she thought they held it in check. Progress for its own sake was hardly ever a good idea. When you move too fast, she thought, you miss so much.

That fishing boat was from a world that existed before the earthquake, before the governmental collapse, before the world was reshuffled with a few cards missing. It stood as a testament to the fundamentals of life: sea, fish, man's need to sustain from bounty pulled from the water. Maybe we didn't need the excess, maybe humanity needed, deserved less. There was so much waste and inefficiency before Earth shook it all apart. At least that's how we see it now. That's the truth we tell ourselves.

Fishing boats, Spanners, even refurbished and renewed pre-quake media all serve as memory-machines. Not only did those old things have a purpose, but they served as a reminder of how, at any moment, the world might be reduced to rubble yet again. That is the value in holding onto the past, she thought, the reason there are those of us who love it so. Even though this car and those like it were the cause of so much trouble, the fact that this one survives, that I can find fuel for it, and windshield wipers, and exhaust manifolds that growl shows that there must be some value in remembering what came before.

The address was an old brick 4-story apartment building that had been retrofit with parking underneath. Only the very wealthy could afford to live in such vintage buildings. She punched a code into the keypad and a woman's face came up on the screen. The face was obscured in shadow, though she saw the outline of a strong chin and thick plastic-framed glasses.

"You're Louise?"

"Yeah."

"Park in space 23-A and come up to the 3rd floor. I have tea waiting."

She had a hard time opening the elevator, which was more like a cage than a means of transportation. It had two heavy, manually-operated doors that put her slight frame to the test. The first was a light metal accordion door that easily shifted to the side. The second had been nearly impossible to open. Keeping it ajar while sliding the accordion was a feat of strength, wit, and balance. Exiting was even harder. She used leverage and opened the door.

When the elevator reached the 3rd floor, an adjacent door opened. "Hello?" She poked her head in the open door.

"Come in. Is everything okay?"

"Oh, yes, the door."

"Oh my, please forgive my lack of forethought. That thing gives me fits, especially with an armload of books or groceries." The woman stood well over 6 feet tall, barrel-chested, and had a silky ebony mane highlighted by a silver stripe that stretched to her breasts. She wore a pantsuit made from the latest synthetic fabric from the Martian colony, *hellacene*. It was reflective, yet invisible. When she moved across the room, the shifting light alternately reflected the explicit human form as though in a bodysuit.

With another step, a mutli-colored, glowing, flowing shape would emerge, a body covered in draping ethereal fabrics.

She stuck out her hand for a handshake. "My name is Morgan Fox."

"Louise Melnick, people call me *Lou*." Her hand disappeared into Morgan's thick, monstrous paw.

She'd never been in such an old-world apartment before. The wood looked real and the floor creaked when she walked. It was like the history holograms she'd seen as a kid. The walls were filled floor-to-ceiling with hardback books, and the whole place smelled of dust, leather, and old, pre-quake wealth.

"What you will deliver amounts to a piece of scientific equipment that my colleagues and I have designed. It's a receiver-transmitter we intend to use for geologic research. Basically, we want to know when or if there will be another earthquake or volcanic eruption. We are concerned about a few volcanoes, including your own Wy'east, outside of Portland. We want you to place this device on Mt. Shasta, in California – you are familiar?"

"Yeah, Shasta, been there. Who're your colleagues?"

"We are a small, private group of scientists and investors," Morgan sat in a large, leather wingback chair and motioned for Louise to sit. "The devices are designed to collect data related to seismic activity, weather, and ocean currents."

"From Shasta?"

"If all goes well, we will call on you to deliver and place

other devices around Cascadia," she crossed her legs and spoke with her huge hands. "We aggregate the data. The more sensors we have, the better we can predict events. The better we can predict events, the better chance we have to protect everyone."

"We'll have to rethink my pay."

"That has been considered." She switched the cross of her legs and grabbed a tablet from the shelf behind her. "For this job, we will pay you your stated rate, in full, up front. We'll add ten thousand Cascadians upon completion. You'll find everything you need in a packet on your way out."

"On the open net or the dark?"

"We assume the dark, that is our preference."

"Well, well, Ms. Fancy on the dodge, huh?" Lou was surprised that such a posh client would want to do dark business.

"We value discretion," Morgan said. "Our competition watches our every move. This protects you more than anyone."

"Hold the phone." Lou's skin tingled. "Am I being followed or something?"

"We've taken precautions to ensure that our meeting is encrypted. Stay in touch and report if anything seems odd. We will protect you." She reached into her jacket and produced a small device, a palm-sized black box with an antenna and a single toggle switch. "We know a lot about our competition. If you find that you're being followed, this will disrupt their vehicles, which run on distinct EM frequencies." Morgan activated the device into a test-mode and a small screen lit up. A few empty rectangles indicated ordinary civilian cars. A filled-in, blinking rectangle was the bad guy.

"Flipping the switch renders their cars little more than paperweights. If they want to use that vehicle again, they have to get a hardwired reboot. They won't know what hit them. By the time they re-calibrate their fleet, we'll be a step or two ahead." She flipped the switch and a glowing dot on an old-fashioned 8-bit LED screen turned into a skull and crossbones icon.

"Hmm... That's a new wrinkle, ma'am. Make it twenty on delivery and you got a deal."

"You're shrewd, Melnick." Morgan pulled a tablet from the shelf and her fingers tapped a staccato rhythm of sixteenth notes. "Done. Now, will that heap of yours hold up? We demand absolute reliability."

"You bet your ass it will." Louise bristled at the affront. "I did all the work on her myself. She was my grandma's first car. That thing is part of my DNA."

"Of course confidentiality is a must. You can't tell a soul where you are going or what you are doing. Especially on the phone or anywhere on the network. Don't even speak of it near a networked device."

"Loose lips sink ships, boss." Louise's index finger crossed plump, pursed lips.

Chapter Twelve

Louise pulled from the freeway and descended to downtown Tacoma where the amper-zombies ruled the streets. Their drug-fueled mayhem threatened to devour interlopers. They'd scrape residue from windows and walls and add it to their amphetamine. Their diabolical chemists constantly found new ways to alter consciousness and even the physical form. With enough use, and the proper formulation, a zombie could lose a limb while on a bender. It would simply fall off. Any remaining wound healed within a day, the scarring was undetectable. Thus, their self-applied moniker *zombie*. With the last remaining threads of sanity and civility, they watched vintage files of zombie movies. It was their romance, a mythos they lived every day.

Every single office and apartment building had been abandoned after an airborne toxic event had wiped out most of the population more than a decade ago. All that remained were the shells of zappers that street gangs had turned to their own use. The zombies prowled for something, anything to loot, rape, or rob. They never stopped and had now been reduced to robbing one another of a rapidly deteriorating set of goods. Though they hated the sound of Louise's petrol-burning, throaty vehicle, they collectively salivated when she rumbled through. They were drawn, against their will, to her sound, but when she revved the motor, the roaring rumble brought them to their knees. She pressed the accelerator, the motor's RPM gauge went to the redline. She popped the clutch. Screaming tires, the roaring engine, and the pall of noxious rubber-smoke was the final blow. They all fell to the ground, crippled. As she pealed away, she saw a hulking brute screaming for mercy on his knees. Sorry for your luck, buddy

She approached the gateway to the Tacoma Spannerville; she pumped the throttle as a way to say *hello*, also to show off her mechanical acumen and parts-finding savvy. That was her secret knock. Maisie's head of blazing-red hair poked over the fence, a raving splotch of color against a world of grey, and Lou shot her a devil's-horn salute. The corrugated steel gate slid open and she entered the sanctuary of grease and gears.

Spannerville-Tacoma, a spiritual outpost for those whose hearts pump like pistons, a city block brimming with engine grease and motor oil, welcomed her with piles of car doors and bald tires, toothy grins shone from black-smudged faces. The place was a maze of machinery, pathways cut through mountains of old-world combustion engines stored as spare parts or monuments to an analog universe all but destroyed by binary culture. She noticed that Zero was still working away on his masterpiece, a methanol-powered, steel-plated Mega-Lizard whose eyes shot metal-melting laser beams and whose mouth spewed fire up to twenty meters. The Mega-Lizard operated by remote, but Zero was developing an AI brain, the perfect conjunction of analog and digital. If it ever got an appetite for destruction, it could make its way up I-5 and envelop Seattle in rapturous carnage.

She pulled the car to the lot in the rear and powered down her motor. Her tank neared empty and she hoped her friends could hook her up with some fuel for the ride. There were fuel stops up and down the coast, but it was foolish to pass up any opportunity for a fill-up.

"Hey, Lou." Maisie slid down an old fireman's pole that connected the catwalk along the outer wall to the ground below. She was layered in overalls, thermals, flannel, and her face wore the black grease of a war they fought against the future. She was still sexy, her luscious figure still was unmistakable despite the Northwestern layers, and the sparkle in her emerald eyes could overcome untold layers of engine grease and lack of sleep. "To what do we owe this honor?"

"Fuel."

"Not love and fellowship, solidarity in these troubled times?" Maisie was always a ham.

"Fuel. Flakes. Fun times."

"Asshole." Maisie was rail-thin but had a resonant, throaty laugh that echoed off the metal boundaries.

Their friendship had waxed and waned through the years, but it never disappeared. Maisie was always somewhere on Lou's mind, even if it was a place of anger and hurt, or love and yearning. Maisie kept a copper etching of Lou's portrait on her workstation.

"You never send me messages," Maisie said.

"I don't want that," Lou said. "I want us only in the meat. I feel you strongly enough without seeing your selfies every ten seconds."

"The bits and bytes render us to mush."

"You make me mush, slut!" Lou slapped Maisie's ass.

"C'mon, let me show you what I've been up to."

Maisie's studio was in a crow's nest five stories high, far above the rest of Spannerville. She'd built it perched atop a lattice constructed from the best I-beams she could salvage. Much of it had probably been infrastructure of buildings that fell in the quake. Old plumbing pipes provided water and while most of her power came from the sun and wind, she had run power and network cables from the surface. A manual-electric elevator was powered by solar during the day or, at night, by a generator passengers charged with old-world step machines. One of Spannerville's tenets was to limit the use of batteries. They loved electronics and technology, but sought to relegate them to the service they could provide humanity. Batteries were just one way that humans expressed an over-reliance on wires and circuit boards. Besides, no battery lasted forever and when they finally died, humanity invariably had to re-learn how to perform a task. When they relied less on external energy sources, the more likely they would be to use their own heart and muscle to get things done.

The room was the same as always. Huge windows opened on a view that could, on a clear day, extend for miles. Today, though, the roost was in a cloud and the space was illuminated in white, diffused light that blanketed everything. Louise whimpered when she saw the bed, well-made but rumpled. A patchwork quilt draped askew over a low-lying platform. Maisie's computer glowed in the corner. Its screen was full of cascading numbers.

"What's that?"

"The data. Erm. That's the network," Maisie squeezed her hand. "Let me show you something." They sat at the desk.

"Now, this is just the raw stuff." Maisie flipped the screen. "Here's what is really going on."

Maisie superimposed a map of the Puget Sound region over the data, information criss-crossed the network. It clustered in high-density areas like Seattle, and was more sparse out past the urban borders. Not terribly surprising, Louise thought.

"So?"

"It looks normal when we look at the standard sorting. But, when I apply this new filter to the data, something interesting happens." Maisie's lithe, strong fingers tapped a few keys and the whole display changed. The data was now clustered in a more organized fashion. The nodes in Tacoma and Olympia were still smaller than Seattle, but there were streamlined paths between each. It looked more like a train map than a noisy barrage of data.

"Whoa," Louise leaned in. "What am I looking at?"

"Well, that's what I'm trying to figure out. This is a representation of the direct communications between people. This is all of the emails, text messages, voice calls, and any other intentionally sent data such as when you purchase something or send form data from a site. The rest is the operational stuff. You know how an email scatters into a million bits when you send it, but then reassembles at its destination? Well, here I only want to see what people are actually intending. I don't need to know the rest of the stuff that the data-purists are fidgeting over."

"Ok, so... Does this mean anything?"

"Well, it seems like this information is starting to coalesce, it's self-aggregating. So the data looks like you'd think – more people in Seattle means more data, as in this big blob here. Then, each of the nodes are connecting to the other, but, as far as I can tell, that's not human-initiated. It looks like some information is pooling in Seattle but then siphoning itself out to, say, Olympia or this odd server in Spokane."

"Weird."

"You said it." Maisie put her arm around Louise, rested her head on her shoulder. "I think the network is learning. It's more than disparate servers, now. Similar data is grouping, it's organizing along the most efficient lines. The network knows to avoid the problems of the past. When the pre-quake hackers went to work on the banks, all they had to do was take out a set group of servers and then the whole monetary system collapsed. Now, you'd almost have to take out every single server in the world to do that.

"The thing you call a mind is really nothing but a bunch of data that has collected and become more than the sum of its parts. That data becomes *you*. I think the same is happening here. This proves, once and for all, that hierarchies are bullshit. With enough information, rigid, linear structures become irrelevant."

"Amen sister. Can we speak to it?"

"If I'm right, it's always listening, but has not yet chosen to speak. It seems to have intention, at least as far as it organizes itself. I remember once seeing a study of slime mold. They put food on a map of Tokyo, each meal represented a train stop on the metro system. The mold soon organized itself along the most efficient lines, mimicking, and improving on, the actual Tokyo train system."

"Does mold have intention?"

"I don't know, but it's efficient, just like our bodies and our minds. Imagine if you stopped speaking English for a while, your brain would begin to deprecate the parts that supported it. If you go into space, your body stops sending nutrients to your bones, which exist to resist gravity. Your body doesn't waste energy. If you have a bad habit, you eliminate it and find a new habit – you stop wasting energy. Maybe something like that is happening in this computer system."

Louise kept staring at the screen hoping for some answer to come, but she was at a loss. She was more interested in the energy Maisie's heart was sending hers. The muscles were beating in rhythm and it ached her to be so close. She propped her head on Maisie's shoulder and sighed.

"You're beautiful, Lou."

"Beautiful and on deadline." Maisie's hair smelled so good. "I need to top off my tank. I have a date with Mount Shasta."

"Give me a quick kiss before you go."

A shaft of buttery sunlight broke through the clouds.

Chapter Thirteen

The car was originally her great-grandmother's, which she'd purchased second-hand from a guy back in the 1990's. It was old then, but well-cared-for. Hondas were built to last and her great grandma, Cassandra, took excellent care of it. She got her hands on a full set of wrenches, got a book on how to do work on the thing, and maintained it herself ever afterwards. Cassandra could do a full brake job and still make it to the river to drink with her friends in the summer. She rebuilt the starter, installed a new sound system, and did the first modification when she added a supercharger.

Louise continued the tradition of rebuilding and renovating the car. She discovered early on that she loved taking things apart, building new things, and solving all sorts of mechanical problems. Roads had changed dramatically since the quake, and the collapse of nearly every governmental or corporate structure, not to mention road repair crews. So, she reinforced the car's chassis and retrofitted it with a customized all-wheel drive system. After all the modifications, the car was a shadow of its original self. Only the exterior maintained the original look. Panels and doors and glass had been replaced over the years, but it still looked like it did when it rolled off the production line in her grandma's day.

Her great-grandmother was not, however, so good at taking care of herself. Cassandra had difficulties with drugs, booze, men, and anything that might give her a temporary sense of relief from the memory of growing up with a hands-on stepfather. She was a mess. But, when one of those men knocked her up, she decided to have a baby. It was a stupid move. The only thing she'd ever cared for was her car. She figured that a baby would straighten her out.

It didn't, not really, but she did take care of the child's needs. She got clean long enough to breastfeed. She even had the patience to let the child wean herself. Through bribery and sexual favors, she made sure her daughter made it to preschool, then the best possible elementary schools, and finally an elite high school run by the city. She might have dealt drugs to the other parents while their children played in the sandbox, and she might have turned a trick or two to make ends meet, but she took care of her daughter just as well as she took care of that car.

Chapter Fourteen

The rain kept coming; Maisie's smell was in her clothes. Shortly after the quake, rain had returned to Cascadia, and it hardly ever stopped. Lou's grandmother said it was worse than before the drought times. At least then there was a dry, hot summer and even a few sunny days in the middle of winter. Now there was cold rain and warmer rain, then more cold rain. It was cold misty rain now.

The cars on the road were new zappers. Most of them were built by small shops up north. They were made with fancy bodies and tiny generator engines that provided enough zap to power the drivetrain. The interiors were all the same cookie-cutter crap, but each had a custom, flashy-dashy outer body. Today there seemed to be a preponderance of vehicles from the Northeast corner of the Washington Territory. Those cats sculpted beautiful car bodies with a neo-1950's edge. They took their time, they loved their craft. Wings and bullet headlights were their thing. They were in the middle of hemp country so the raw material came cheap; they added flourishes a minimalist Seattle or Portland body molder couldn't afford.

The things were glossy yellows, reds, blues and greens, candy-coated nightmares that Louise claimed to despise. They were too cheery and naïve. However, today, she found them pleasing. They broke up the grey and dreary presence of eternal gloom. The yellows and fluorescent greens were both offensive and delightful. She liked standing out from the pack in her dark, loud machine. She was unique in most places. She might see one other spanner on the road in a week, if she was lucky.

She pulled up next to one of the fruit-brigade and matched its speed. A young man drove alone. He looked sharp with combed-over hair and a clean-shaven chin. He was probably listening to a smug podcast about cooking or literature, she thought. Then again, maybe he was listening to Big Nose, the hottest rapper on the scene. No one could possibly be as totally square as this guy looks, she thought, he's gotta have a wild side.

An impulse tickled down in her navel. She stomped the clutch, downshifted, and revved the engine to its limits. The turbo whined and woke up every dog in a five-mile radius. The roar was a sound from the bellows of hell. The young man startled and gave her a saucer-eyed look of shock and disgust. Louise's belly laugh rose above the din. She released the clutch and rocketed her vehicle to 145 kph and climbing. Un-modded zappers barely get past 110. She'd never seen one top 130.

She loved speed and there was no one to stop her. The zappers were all regulated, cops no longer patrolled for speeders. Piston-pumpers could get away with bloody murder and the cops figured they'd self-select out of the population. She bore down on the accelerator and the line of rainbow ninnies blurred to a rainbow smear against her beloved gray. If only Maisie could see this, if only it were possible for us to stick together and form some new molecule of data bound forever in electrostatic bliss.

The phone rang. Scratch.

"Hey , what's up?"

"I've been trying to get you. Can't you return a single call or message?"

"Well, you never returned my calls, either. I even sent you a fucking sexpic. Looked like you moved on with Miss butterfly-ass."

"Oh, you got that..."

"Yeah."

"Well, I wanted to tell you that I saw some weird cars out front of your house today. Some guys were milling around." He cleared his throat. "Looked like maybe they'd been inside, but it was hard to tell. I didn't stick around long. I got creeped-out."

"Fuck. Well, thanks man." She sped up the windshield wipers and batted the drops away in sheets of liquid grey. "Hey, could you keep an eye out for me? Maybe snap a few pics if you think about it?"

"I'll see you when you get back?" His voice shifted to that playful, teasing tone which he was so fond of affecting when he wanted sex.

"Just be a pal, okay? Give your new lady a finger in the ass and think of me, okay?"

"Sure thing, Lou." Scratch cleared his throat. "Hey, you were the best."

"No shit." She clicked off the call.

Louise looked over a barren field; a flock of crows took to flight in a fury of flap and caw that cut through the engine's droning whine. They rose and swooped over the road directly in front of her car. The flock dove on her, filling her windshield view with beaks and beady eyes, an attempt to scare or attack her, retribution for a noise violation. Nature may abhor a vacuum, but it loves the quiet, Louise thought. Fucking birds need to get over themselves.

When she crossed the bridge from Washington over into Portland, she noticed a break in the clouds. Far off in the distance, near the western horizon, a patch of pure spun gold glowed in the gloom. What's on the other side of the overbearing cloud? The sun's glare hid behind the gauzy clouds. She remembered it from her childhood, that summer they lived east of the mountains with yet another of her mother's boyfriends. The sun oppressed their western sensibilities. Her mother had insisted that she play only under the shade tree or else indoors. Despite those motherly admonitions, she still managed several nasty sunburns. She'd cried and whimpered, but now she longed to feel her skin sizzle.

She'd considered moving to the desert to have sun all the time, but that would mean holstering a pistol, hiring a bodyguard or keeping a boyfriend to fend off the Clockwork gangs, Christian end-times cults, and any of the other fucked-up organized or disorganized inbred maniacs who dominated the high desert. Why the fuck did they get all the sun? She hoped they all suffered interminable sunburn.

They'd managed to monopolize more than 75 percent of all the wells and they even had beef. They'd feed you steak then proclaim you were going to hell for sins of the flesh. Human suffering demands so much companionship. She downshifted and blasted past a line of zap cars exiting to Belmont Street.

Once she passed Portland, civilization ended. When the earth shook, the outlying sprawl disappeared. No one considered, or cared, how the soil would react to such a strong quake. Buildings sank into the earth. Families, who were sitting down to dinner, were swallowed whole by an unforgiving Earth. Unsupported bridges collapsed, drivers plummeted to the waters below, scavengers still found treasures amongst the remains. Pre-quake memorabilia was worth lots of Cascadians.

Now, there were a few abandoned shopping centers that'd sat on firm soil, but were now overtaken by nature and small bands of amper-zombies. The only buildings going up these days were mud houses that farmers built with the shared effort of their communities. They used wood for their barns, and often multiple families would share a barn. A collectivist ethic was the rule of the land, if there were any rules, but laws made people nervous. They were afraid of losing their humanity. Individual striving and creativity would be lost, they thought.

A man appeared on the crest of a far hill, a silhouette of black against the gray. He captured her attention, the anomaly of a human amidst the crumbling artifacts of civilization. She was transfixed as her carriage hurtled towards him, as he walked towards her, neither considering a flinch or blink. She saw that he had a limp and wore rags; his hair was long and he raised a sign. She moved to the far lane to be on the safe side. He jumped up and down and waved the sign in a frenzy. His message was dire, and yet it lacked the proper spelling needed for credibility:*The End is Neer Repant.*

Louise had seen them before, these missionaries from over the mountains, desert rats whose goal was to take over the west, to instill the area with a new brand of fear and paranoia. That man had probably crossed the mountains, braved 10-foot snowdrifts, fought against starvation and hypothermia. He'd endured the sort of extreme conditions that had trapped ancient pioneers and forced them into cannibalism. His blind faith in the healing power of fear and hatred had driven him to the decadent West. His was an invisible network of voices and messages that informed his path, she thought.

Beliefs were once all that tied people together, that and a variety of paranoia that said they were all being watched by some sky-man. They clung to the odd notion that all the individuals of any group could hold identical ideas, thoughts, and feelings. It was so simplistic and archaic, childlike in its naiveté. Something about it soothed her, though. Such wishful thinking showed how egotistical ancient people really were. They had absolutely no idea how complex and diverse the world really was nor how brittle facts were. She wished she could believe like that. If only she could be so comfortable with so many contradictory thoughts.

She'd read about people for whom ghosts were real, they

thought there were undead souls who were trapped in a hellish existence, this plane of reality, bent on disturbing the living until they were released to the next phase of existence.

Maisie despised such people and mocked them with ire. More than anything, what she disliked was how divorced they were from free thought and independence. When Louise pointed out how connected the Spanners were, she'd retort that those connections were real and practical, constructed from the things of man and science. Lou didn't see the difference, but Maisie was so hot when she got angry that she dared not interfere.

She caught a glimpse of a car in the rear view. Out here, she was used to seeing about two cars in a day. Now, seeing a walking nutter and a car seemed uncanny. She was going 140 and the car was gaining. She sped up. It was still gaining. She pushed the car up to 170 and it still gained. Her little car screamed for mercy, it wasn't designed to handle much more than that, and had probably never seen such speed since her great-grandmother put it in storage those years before the quake. Her skin was alive, her breath quickened. Fuck. Think, think, think. Morgan's device was in her bag. She reached back, the car wobbled on the road. Her bag spilled out.

She looked back to grab the black device, now barely visible in the dying light. When she looked up, she was headed straight for a metal post. She yanked the wheel and the car slid sideways. She released the throttle and regained control, but the black car was upon her. She pressed the button, downshifted and mashed the throttle. The zapper began to recede. It was dead as a paperweight. It sat there, dark and still in the twilight, rapidly fading into the distance. Without warning, it lurched into the air in a ball of flame. The shock wave punched her chest and she was sure her heart would stop, but it did not.

Her phone rang. Morgan.

"You set off the device. Are you okay?"

"Yeah. Fine, but they aren't. Bad-guy flambé."

"Suicide mission, huh?"

"Looks that way."

"Where are you?"

"South of Portland, nearing Eugene, I think."

"Keep going. Stop in Grant's Pass and get fuel. Someone will meet you there with an updated device."

Louise said, "okay," but Morgan had ended the call.

Chapter Fifteen

The road between Eugene and Grant's Pass was a dilapidated mess. Rain is brutal on unpaved, primitive roads and her little car slipped in the slop; she was used to that. She'd delivered packages up and down that road for years and had learned the delicate dance of brake and throttle, when to downshift or knock the motor into neutral. It was wearing, and required nerves that were at once steel-strong and as limp as linguine, but that was why people paid her to carry gifts to loved ones, drugs to distributors, and whatever the fuck this thing was she had now. In the early days, she'd carry a tent and camp overnight. She'd been at this long enough to know how to deal without sleep, how to maximize her time and get on to the next gig.

Louise careened through the night; her headlights blazed a path. She flipped on her roof lights and fog lamps, too. It was nearly as good as driving in daylight with all those lumens to cut the black. Her antiquated 2-seater was reinforced to handle these roads, but she sometimes wished her great-grandmother had driven something sturdier. The road was wearing on her. I'm earning my pay, no doubt.

A little zap car appeared in the distance. It was one of the egg-shaped zappers, round-bodied rodents, she thought. They were a subset of design that Louise found alternately kitschy and annoying. There were never cars out this late. The yellow egg bumped along the road the same as her, it must be a local build, probably one of Stan's from Eugene;

Stan, a die-hard stoner and starry-eyed dreamer, wanted to round off reality with a blur. She slowed the car and cut her overhead beams so she wouldn't blind the poor rubes. Another car appeared behind her and then the car in front was joined by another. The car behind her turned on its high beams, then its roof lights, too. Totally blinded, she down shifted. She looked to her left and there was a motorbike. She stared into the double barrels of a sawed-off shotgun.

"What the fuck is this?"

Chapter Sixteen

The rain beat heavy on the tin roof and they all sat in a room lit by flame. Candles, lamps, and the stove cast shadows and warmglow on the faces of her captors and the primitive cabin walls. Louise's arms and legs were lashed to a rickety wicker chair with rope and leather straps. She'd been gagged and hooded for the ride to the cabin. All she'd been able to figure out was that they were far down a rough road, probably one of the country byways that had been cleared by the people themselves.

"What are ya doing out here at night?" His face was dark, shadowed. Firelight lit a halo of hairs around his head.

"Out for a drive. The fuck do you care?"

He cleared his throat. The room was still. "Where to?

"Grant's Pass."

"You one of them gearhead wrenchies or something?"

"Something like that," her jaw tightened. "You gotta let me go."

"What are you gonna do, call a cop?" He laughed, they all did. His face went stony."You're gonna hafta take a little detour."

"Got no time."

"You do now." He held up a black box. It was identical to

Morgan's. She froze. "This thing don't look like much, but it's your ass if you don't get it to Klamath."

"You boys have zappers, what do you need with me?"

"Following orders."

"Find someone else."

"Said it'd be a girl driving a combustion car. Said she'd be alone and traveling at night." He shifted in his chair. "You are the one, little lady."

"Who said? Who do you work for?"

"Got word today," he said. "We're attaching something to the frame of your car. If you're late, it blows. If you try to take it off, it blows. If anyone but the man on the other end tries to take it off or disable it, it blows. If you're late, it blows. We're giving you five hours, little lady."

He handed her a paper map with a highlighted route.

"This is the best way we know. If you don't make it in time, it's your ass."

"They knew I was coming?"

"You want a coffee? The clock is ticking."

"There's barely a road to Klamath."

"Your problem."

"Fuck. Add a shot of espresso, willya?"

Chapter Seventeen

She hadn't had coffee in ages. It was difficult to find, extremely expensive, and the art of roasting and preparing the beans was mostly lost, except for the few who came from a line of coffee people, families who had devoted themselves to the bean so deeply that they had taken up surnames to express their trade. There was the Barista family who were known for dark roasts and the Robusta family controlled most of the supply. In fact, Louise had fixed one of their motor boats, securing an iron grip on the bean trade, until the bottom fell out after pirates on the Pacific took out a shipment.

The rich aroma of the brew put a sparkle in her eyes even before the caffeine did its job. These hillbillies sure know how to roast a bean, she thought. She felt herself getting happier and brighter with every sip. They were even decent enough to give her a large mug to carry in the car. It sure must have been a labor of love to get beans out here to the bush. She wound out the engine on a smooth flat stretch. She had to make good time.

First, though, she had to check her payload. Once she was clear of the cabin and had put several more miles on her engine, she pulled off the road. She popped the hatch and checked her duffel. Morgan's box was still there, blinking. She checked the second. It was identical to the first. They were both black boxes, about six inches cubed, with little blinking lights on them. Neither had a hinge nor any way to open them, there were no screw holes or seams.

She checked her phone, but it was off. She plugged it into the car charger. Still nothing. It was stone dead. It had been working perfectly and she'd paid the bill in full just the other day. It was the most reliable brand available. She pressed the power button repeatedly. Her face reflected in the blank screen. What the fuck?

She cranked the engine to life. There was nothing to be done with a dead phone in bumfuck Oregon, especially when she was driving a time-bomb. She looked into the black night then to the road ahead. No one was around for miles, and anyone out there might be liable to take her hostage, rob her, or worse. The road looked smooth, so she mashed the throttle. The thrust gave her hope. Momentum, velocity, speed: these were the things that she lived by. She couldn't imagine being in deep space, like the Mars colonists or even a satellite technician. Out there in the infinite black, there was nothing to gauge speed. They could be moving close to the speed of light, past the speed of sound, yet the stars and planets all sat still in the darkness. The analog clock on the dashboard ticked down the minutes and she turned on the radio.

There was little in the way of radio in these parts, mostly shortwave enthusiasts who'd taken over spots at the end of the FM band. There was no regulation and when driving through it was possible to pick up on as many as five different broadcasts on the same channel, depending on the relative position of the receiver. She wondered how many listeners those guys could possibly have.

She found a broadcaster at the far left end of the spectrum. Primitive folk music piped through the speakers. Some sort of native hour or maybe a person of native origin loves broadcasting traditional music to the void, hoping to save his people. The language was unknown and unfathomable. A wooden flute wove mini-melodies through rhythmic viscera. Louise loved synth music and the raw electric power of Spanner bands. She usually hated crap like this, but here in the darkness she felt the musical heart thrumming throughout time. In an illuminated flash, she saw how hand drums, flute, and voice built the ancestral scaffolding of so much that she loved.

After about fifteen minutes she lost patience with the archaeological/musicological exploration into the primitive realms of her psyche. Louise shifted in her seat and moved to change the channel when the music began to fade. She sat back to see what would come next. Hopefully some Spanner thrash.

"That was the Chinook tribe calling the Great Spirit to unite all beings." Dulcet, smooth female voices always turned her on. "Hey, all you listeners, if there are any of you out there and awake, I just got some news. There was a disturbance near the SoCal border just minutes ago. Their cell networks failed and then half of their zapper charging stations went down. There is no reported reason for the failures, but the lights are out from Santa Cruz to San Luis Obispo. I'll keep you guys on top of things as the native network stays alive with off-grid analog goodness."

Native network. Louise scoffed. Fuck, anyone could call themselves a native who dropped acid and wore all-natural fibers. It was a fucking joke. Of course, there were a few genetic descendants of the original people of the land, but half of those had been fed so much meth and booze by the old US government that hardly any in their line could barely speak, much less chant or perform a ceremonial whatever. Fucking genetic warfare. The DJ returned to music, switching up to jazz from the early 20th century. Bored, she reached back to grab her precious cargo.

"You can sit up front."

The black box was dark. She turned it over. Still dark. She rotated it all around. The light was no longer blinking. A chill ran down her spine. What the fuck happened? She rummaged around blind, found the duffel, and retrieved Morgan's box. It was blinking. She supposed that was good. She set it beside the other and kept driving. The blinking light was distracting. She covered it with a sweater.

The road kept coming. Despite changes in elevation and distance from the shortwave pirate, the signal stayed steady and strong. The DJ played a wide range of tunes and kept listeners up to date on the odd happenings in SoCal. Louise failed to see the relevance to a pirate broadcaster in the Southern Cascade region, but maybe there was some native tie-in. She was falling in love with the voice and anticipated the breaks in music when the silken, roasty-rich words washed over her and a warmth rose between her legs.

She turned on the overhead light and checked the map. Soon, she'd be making a turn for the final approach. She had about two hours left, give or take. She was glad for imprecision. If she was going to blow up, she'd rather not have to watch a countdown to destruction. She wondered if she'd be aware what was happening in the event of a surprise combustion. Her girlfriend came back on the radio.

"SoCal officials are blaming Cascadian terrorists for the outages. They claim evidence of tampering, but details are foggy. Our correspondents on the ground are standing by and will send updates as they emerge."

Aha! With her ultra-high beams, she saw a turn up ahead. There was some sort of structure at the intersection, probably a fruit stand or maybe a trading post for goods from civilization. This must be the turn to Klamath Falls. How could it be any other? Then everything went dark. The car shut down. No stereo, no headlights, no engine, nothing. She jammed on the brakes and skidded to a halt. Her heart pounded. She flung the door open and screamed into the dark. She'd surely be blown to bits in just a few hours.

"Goddammit!" The only creature that heard her was a coyote lurking in the night.

She paced in the dark, afraid to go too far lest she lose the car altogether and then be without hope. It started to rain. She wanted to cry. She wanted to rest her head on Maisie's breast, but she couldn't even call. She wanted the radio woman's voice. Fuck, she'd even take a dumbass joke from Scratch. She felt bile moving up into her esophagus. She wanted to vomit. She wanted to purge, but there was not time to fall apart. She wanted everything but could have nothing but darkness and the sensation of air on her skin.

She needed a solution. She popped the back hatch and felt

around for her emergency kit. Maisie had made her pack this kit years ago. That girl would save her life some day.

She found the wind-up flashlight, cranked it and a ray of light cut the dark. She popped the hood and looked at the motor. Its warmth, dissipating into the chill, soothed her while she inspected all the car's systems. There was nothing wrong. The alternator looked good, the radiator was in good shape, the spark plugs were all connected, all of the hoses and wires were tight. She saw no mechanical or electrical reason for the car to shut down. No burning smells. Besides, cars don't do that. Ever. Even if the battery had died or come detached, the car wouldn't have shut down so suddenly. It would have been a slower death than that, a fade-out. She was flummoxed.

She sat back in the car and turned the key. It was a futile gesture of hope.

The motor turned over and roared to life. A wave of nausea came through her and she barely got her head out in time to vomit on the concrete road. There wasn't much in her stomach but fluid. She needed the purge. She wanted to be back in Portland, on her sofa, ripping bong hits and watching homemade holo-porn. She revved the motor. The hit of deep rumble brought her back to the road and purpose.

She checked her cargo. The boxes had flown to the floorboard in the skidding stop. They'd tumbled like dice, randomized and indistinguishable. There, on the floor, two identical black cubes with two fucking red, blinking lights. Mocking snake eyes winked in perfect synch, little devils in the dark. *Goddamnitfuck.* She retched; the rest of her coffee spewed on the road.

Chapter Eighteen

She pulled up to the her destination at daybreak. Louise made it with time to spare. She stowed one of the boxes in a hidden compartment and hoped that no one would notice. She figured they were probably the same, anyway.

It was a simple structure made of mud and straw and coated with white plaster. The roof was terracotta. These cob buildings were becoming more popular due to their efficiency and economical profile. If there were to be another earthquake, Louise reckoned they'd disintegrate into loose soil and could be rebuilt straight out of the remains. It was a wonder that people before the quake hadn't thought ahead about their homes and buildings. They knew that the continental shelf was going to collide with that plate in the ocean and they did nothing but sit and wait for the inevitable. Hell, they even left millions of gallons of petrol fuel sitting on the silty banks of the Willamette River. They knew that would immediately kill the river from Portland to the Pacific, but no one took action to solve the problem. Nobody wanted to spend the money.

It wasn't like they didn't have resources, they did. Even though it was all built on a house of cards, pre-quake society had an economy that was organized and formidable. They had created the network, built the roads, and set in place systems that were still in use today. We're probably more primitive in many ways, she thought, but who knows what we'd be like had they not been so advanced.

Technology had moved forward since then, but at a snail's pace compared to the world before the earthquake and all the trouble that followed. The riots, the militias, and the fracturing of a civilization once known as the United States. Some places were supposedly still in shock from that time. New York City, for instance, was considered a chaotic den of violence and depravity. There were even people there who exchanged their humanity for a life of violence and destruction, or so she'd been told.

She didn't know much about the great expanses that lay between the major cities, those huge pockets of land that were once dotted with small, but advanced, towns. She figured they were much like the desolation of Eastern Oregon – roving bands of cultists, cannibals, and freelance killers. Every now and then she'd see something on the network about people out there, so she assumed they were still connected. Still, there were bands of radical luddites, idiots who periodically sabotaged the network in the name of ancient superstition. If they'd sprouted up in Cascadia, they were surely elsewhere, too. Hell, vast regions could be cut off from the world in a single act of self-righteousness.

Once the United States fell to ruin, the global economy went into a tailspin. Financial markets in London, Tokyo, Dubai, and Mumbai all crumbled. There were archived news stories from around the time of the initial collapse, but then nothing. Global social chaos was what happened, that much is sure. How, or if, the dust settled in other countries was an unanswerable question. It was likely that those countries fell to ruin, much like the U.S.

Other lands were inaccessible via the network, at least that she knew of. There were tales of hackers who'd been able to access satellites and find ways into other, now autonomous, networks, but they were probably more myth than truth. The world went from being a tightly connected fabric to a rag with loose, frayed ends.

There were still threats waiting to destroy all life, like the Yellowstone Caldera, a volcano threatening to spew ash and lava in such quantities as to choke out all life on the planet. Gaia will get a total restart when that motherfucker blows. A fresh boot, Louise called it. There were other threats, too, like the New Madrid fault south of Chicago, which had yet to flex its muscles. Mount St Helens was due to blow, as was Rainier. Seattle kept building and growing with no thought to the timebomb in its midst.

She looked at the black box in the passenger seat and hoped that it or its twin would collect the data humanity needed to make better choices. Still, the future remained a mystery no matter what; it was a concept that was never fully realized because we were always here, now, she reckoned. There was no future and the past was an ever-shifting memory with ostensible artifacts of its existence. But the boxes were the future, or a key to unlocking the dreams we held dear in the dark of night.

There didn't seem to be anyone around, so she beeped her horn. Better to wake someone up with a horn than an exploding car. She saw a window open up on the second floor. A man stuck his head out. Louise rolled down her window.

"You got it?"

"Yup."

"I'll be down."

He introduced himself as Roscoe. He was a huge man, well over six feet built like a redwood that had been stuffed into a pair of old overalls. His arms were ropy masses of muscle and his shoulders began at his ears. Roscoe's beard was a few days old and his eyes looked like they'd swum a sea of whisky. His breath could peel paint.

"Well, it's a black fucking box with a blinky light," he pivoted the object in his hands. It looked like a child's toy in his mitts. "What the hell else?"

"That's it, right."

"Well, I guess you want me to take that thing off of your car, right?" He looked at her chest.

"That's the deal, man," she looked him in the eye. "Take the thing off."

He stood up straight and arched his back to stretch his muscles. He seemed to expand beyond what she thought possible. He could never fit in her car, she thought, nor in her house or many other places. He was a giant.

"It gets sorta lonely out here."

"That's a real shame."

"Nice car."

"Damn right. I aim to see that it don't blow up."

"Here's the deal," he pulled a handheld keypad out of his pants. "I design these things. I make the codes for them. All the guys you met can do is turn the thing on and set the time. I'm the only one who can disable it. Dig?"

"That's what they said." She continued her eye contact, despite hating to crane her neck back like that. "You going to enter the code or what?"

"You gotta do something for me first." He unhooked his overalls and bared his chest. "Why don't you take off your pants?"

"Okay, but the only way to get me hot is to bite my tits. You think you can do that? That'll make me wet." Louise steeled herself. She pulled air deep into her chest and exhaled with force. Her muscles tensed. She peeled her shirt off and bared her small breasts. Her nipples hardened in the morning chill. They could cut diamonds.

Roscoe's eyes widened and his mouth curled into a hungry grin. He dropped to his knees and put his hands on Louise's waist. He leaned in to bite her nipples. When he began moving in, Louise acted. She threw her hardest punch directly to his throat. Roscoe's eyes bugged out of their sockets and his face went red. He clutched his throat with one hand and swiped at Louise with the other. He knocked her across the gravel lot.

Louise propped herself on elbows and watched the giant flail. His face was purple and, though his mouth was gaping, all he could muster were gurgles. Fuck that guy. No goddamn troll is gonna get a piece of me like that. He fell onto his side and in a moment his body went still. Crows landed on his body. They pecked his head. He must have pissed them off, too. Crows don't forget shit.

She found the keypad for deactivating the bomb. Its display counted down the time remaining on the device. She had less than thirty minutes to figure out what to do. First, she took all of her gear and the devices and placed them clear of the car. There was a ditch on the far side of the property where everything would be safe.

The controller had a fingerprint recognition pad, so she shooed away the crows and took the giant's thumb and pressed it to the device. The screen said *Welcome Roscoe*, and prompted her for a passcode. Shit.

She ran into the building. The first floor was for living only. She ran to the second floor and found his desk. She rifled through all the papers on the desk. His computer was still on. She searched the files for *password*, *login*, *exploding device*, or anything that might lead her to a passcode. She searched to see if she could find his birthday, October 10. She entered 1010 to the pad. Rejected. She found the address of the place: 2355. Rejected. Shit. There was no way to guess what the hell that monster had used as a password. She wandered the place searching for a clue. She didn't even know how many digits she'd need. She started pressing buttons at random and figured out that the code needed six digits. Fuck. She erased the random numbers. There had to be some rationale behind whatever code he used. Then she found his bookshelf. It was full of books on cryptography and mathematics. There was no goddamned way she'd be able to figure out his code. She had to guess. All she had was chance.

She went back to the body. Fifteen minutes remained. She riffed through his pockets and found nothing that might resemble a code or a clue. He'd probably created some sort of cypher using his own name. Or maybe someone else's name. Maybe the name of his first cat was the key. She paced. She sighed. She talked to herself. She wanted to scream, but couldn't muster the will for that. She shoved her hands into her pockets. There was her dead phone. She decided to try it.

The phone lit up when she pressed the power button. That was startling. The operating system booted up just like normal. She entered a passcode that any goof could figure out, and accessed her information. There were a few text messages, including one from an unknown number. In fact, there was no number. Everyone had a number, she thought. She opened the message. 360757. Six digits in a text message that came from ... nowhere ... it may as well have appeared from the ether.

She pulled out Roscoe's keypad device, which continued the countdown. Five minutes remained. It had reset and needed his fingers again. The face was blue and the crows had taken its eyes. She pressed his fingers to the fingerprint-pad. The machine lit and asked for the code and she entered her number, 360757. That brought her to a new screen: Would you like to deactivate Y or N? She deactivated and the screen went dead.

Chapter Nineteen

Louise ransacked Roscoe's building for food and water. She filled three bottles and ate the rest of his leftover lasagna. He was a pretty good cook, she noted. The upstairs was full of debris. Old paper strewn about, books were piled along the hallway. It was clean, if messy. No odors. There was no evidence of why he needed the box, or what it was for, or what the hell this crazy shit was all about. He did have a laptop and while she scoured it for any sort of answer, she heard a rumbling off in the distance. She saw a stream of dust coming up from the valley, up the road she'd taken. Fuck. It was time to go. In a flash, she whipped out her multi-tool and unscrewed the computer's casing. She removed the hard drive and shoved it in her jacket pocket. She took the rest of the machine just in case.

On the way to the door, she found a container of kerosene, so she grabbed it and the matches nearby. There was a final duty to perform and the accelerant would make the job all the more easy. She could hear the cars in the distance. They were fuel burners, and probably fast.

She doused Roscoe's large carcass with the kerosene and then trailed the fuel into the building. She soaked a pile of rags at the end of the line of oil and tossed the can and its remaining contents into the room. She didn't know any prayers, but she honored him with a few words to acknowledge that he had done a shitty thing, but that he probably suffered as the result of something done to him. We are all so flawed. She was just lucky to have landed that punch so perfectly. She lit a match, set Roscoe on fire, and jumped in her car. She saw the line of fire grow between the body and the building. Her tires spat gravel and her motor raged.

Louise figured there was no option but to haul ass east and hope to outrun whoever was coming up the road. She cringed at the goddamn noise her car made. Fuck. There's no going back now. They'll be able to hear her for miles in this backwoods wilderness. Her roar would echo from canyon walls and mountain passes from here to wherever the fuck the road would take her. Her compass read that she was headed southeast now. That was the wrong direction, but what choice was there? With every mile, she was deeper into foreign territory and deeper into the craziness of the day.

Chapter Twenty

Driving was easier in daylight. The terrain was beautiful, and the road was smooth. She'd never be able to cover her tracks, but she could make good time. She'd have to rely on her driving skill, and the power of her car, to put distance between her and her pursuers. Endless mountains covered in fir trees spread beneath every vista; jagged peaks cut the cloud-white sky. Louise checked her rear-view mirror, but she could see no sign that she was being followed. Out here, much of the road had still not been re-paved, if it ever was paved. There'd never been much civilization down here, even before the quake.

The radio played electronic music. Rhythms and interwoven melodies evaporated upon coalescence, giving way to new constructions, a moving tapestry of sound that carried the listener down a rabbit hole of sonic exploration from point to point to point and then back again, renewed. It was probably created by a basement-bound psychonaut, she thought, some freak with a voice no one else hears but who made this moment perfect. Louise preferred live players, humanity, even when they played with machine-like precision. She was stubborn that way, but could not resist what she was hearing. She turned it up. Her heart rose on a new melody, and then was broken when it dissipated in a stream of noise, only to re-materialize from the void. The driving electronic rhythms kept her glued in her seat, rooted to the earth beneath the automobile. She had to know what the music was. She hoped that it would be performed in Portland soon. The station wasn't broadcasting artists' names over the airwaves. Maybe that's for the best, she thought, I need to keep my eyes trained on the road. The road took a steep dip, her stomach lifted and she shifted in her seat to curve to the right. She looked over an expanse of open sky as her tires clung to the rim of nothingness.

"That was Hailey Rengaw, a new artist out of Mid-Cascadia, Portland." The deejay's voice was thrilling. "She'll be playing Seattle for the next few nights and then travels the fault all the way to San Francisco. She asks that you check her site on the 'net for tour details as they emerge."

How in the hell can I not know this woman? Portland is not big. Maybe she was a transplant that arrived after the Los Angeles fires.

The cellphone rang. Lou jumped in surprise. It rang as she took a few tight curves. She slid on patches of mud, caught traction on gravel. Once on a straight, she grabbed the phone from the passenger seat. Why the fuck was Maisie calling?

"To what do I owe this honor?"

"Didn't you call me?"

"No, I nearly drove off the road to answer."

"That's weird. I just picked up my phone."

"Well, how are you?"

"I was thinking about you, so this is good." She wasn't using the sexy voice.

"My ears are burning."

"Well, I've sorta been tracking you."

"Tracking?"

"I track a lot of people, baby, mostly those who are already in my phone. I wrote an app that lets me find their global position signal. It's pretty rudimentary. I don't know exactly where you are, and I think it lags behind by a few minutes, if not more, depending on network traffic and how many pornos I'm running."

"What the fuck, Mais?"

"Look, I miss you and I like to see where you are. It helps me imagine you naked."

"Well, I can't blame you there."

"Look, are you mad?"

"No. Not really. I miss you, too. It's kinda sweet, but also creepy." She hoped her smile transmitted through the phone.

"Fair," Maisie said. "The thing is that I've seen some weird shit go down around you."

"Well, whatever you're seeing is only the half of it."

"Like what?"

"Well, I've got two identical black boxes I'm carrying. Totally identical but from two very different, unconnected sources. They have lights that were blinking at different tempos. Then they stopped, totally went dead, and now they're blinking in synch. Like, perfect timing. If that weren't enough, I got a weird-ass text that totally saved my ass a few hours ago. It gave me the key to disarm a fucking bomb that was about to kill me and my car – is that fucked or what?" Louise braced for a steep curve, the car swung sideways through the curve. "That's just what's happened in the last, oh, 8 hours. Plus, I haven't slept, so this may all be an hallucination."

"I've noticed significant net activity down your way. Stuff like I showed you. Usually there's next to nothing, random floating bits of data make their way down there, maybe to the Eugene area, but it's rare to see much between there and Klamath. It was furious, though."

"When?"

"Well, I'm pulling that up. It started about ten hours ago, near Eugene. Then, it seems to have migrated, tracking with your position."

"So, like, what the fuck?"

"You got me, babe," Maisie said. "It's like you were followed by a ghost. I mean, I've never compared your position with this data before, but I'm assuming it's a new thing."

"Since you're tracking my phone, did you see anything odd? Like anything in my account?"

"Your phone did disappear for a while. The full account, anyway. Your GPS has a separate encoding, a pre-quake relic from when the United States government had the time and money to track everyone. Maybe the corps want to track people, so that signal stays lit no matter what. Your account came back a few hours ago. You got a text?"

"Yeah."

"I don't see anything at that time. Well, your account does register a message, but there's no record of anything from an outside source – it's not from anywhere, as if that makes sense. It's like the message was both to and from your phone. But..." Maisie's voice trailed off into a murmur; Lou heard keys clacking in the background.

"Yeah? What?"

"Well, I just did a broader system search and I see a lot of packets stamped for you, but they're scattered in various data pools over the network. These don't have a receipt stamp. These are like dead letters, sitting in random boxes."

"What are they?"

"There are text messages, voice messages, too. I'm guessing, but I'm pretty sure. The data has a special encryption. Each one's encoded with the same *wrapper*, so to speak. I can't unlock it right now. It looks like it might be either a countdown timer or a function waiting for a prompt. Maybe they'll make their way to your phone."

"Hang on. How did we even connect? I didn't call you."

"Shit, babe, we're in some freaky shit." Maisie's voice was low. Louise could hear the wheels turning in her beautiful brain. "I can't find any hacker or bot. Fuck. This is the network itself. But that doesn't make any fucking sense."

"Hey, Maise, while you're figuring this out, can you tell me if I'm anywhere close to a fuel station? I'm gonna have to miss Grant's Pass for now, but my tank is nearing empty. I hafta get to Shasta."

"Oh shit, girl. There ain't much. Let me see if I can get a better read on your location." Maisie hummed and clicked her tongue to a rhythm that provoked a twinge deep in Louise's body. The sweet meandering melody rolled over her spine with a watery undulation. "Yeah, not so bad. These guys are not with us, but they don't seem to be against us, either ... Take the next right you come to. They'll be a kilometer down that road. They should be cool, but put on your diplomat hat. Good luck."

"Thanks babe." Louise made a kissing smack into the phone.

"You take care, Lou."

Chapter Twenty-One

The road was a narrow, winding path carved between trees. Branches brushed over her windshield and the car rocked side-to-side over thick roots. The road was well-maintained; a drainage system kept it from washing out and it was reinforced with gravel. Louise felt confident. She had to pee.

An infinity of ferns stretched beneath the conifer canopy. The forest was silent except for the odd falling branch or a distant twig-snap. Rain filtered down to the forest floor as mist. A high breeze shook the high branches and released a wave of droplets. Louise waded into the dense ferns and dropped her trousers, squatted, and began to piss. The warm flow from her bladder was a sweet relief. She needed more comfort, she thought. Maybe two or three bong-rips on the sofa and some music from that Rengaw woman. Maybe find her and invite her over to play. Maisie could come, too. Louise started down the torrid road to a mid-day fantasy, but cut it short.

She inhaled the fertile air. The rainy mist soaked her matted locks and wet her scalp. There, squatting, she extended her arms and turned her palms to the sky. The pin-point drops pooled on her pale, smooth skin. She rubbed the water over her face. She looked up to the sky and watched a raven perch on a high branch. In a moment, it was joined by a mate. They looked down and met her gaze. The three of them were silent. Lou wanted to communicate something to them, perhaps in honor of the Ravens who were so gracious in allowing her to relieve herself in their forest. Though the woman on the yoga video had called the pose *Crow*, it was the best thing Lou could think of.

She pressed her arms to the ground between her legs and squeezed her legs to the center. She popped up and was fully supported on the forest floor's soft mat of twigs and mulch. She found more strength in her arms and shoulders, her arms straightened and her ass raised higher into the air. Her gaze leveled with the tops of the ferns. She inhaled the sea of green. Her face tilted to the ground and a sweet fungal aroma wafted from the soil to her nose.

They were not run of the mill fungi, they were special, they unlocked images, visions, and insights unknown in everyday consciousness. Once, when she sat on the side of the great mountain, Wy'east, the sky came alive with spirals. Swooping, crawling entities breached the distance of the valley. She shared breath with the trees. Her exhalation filled them, their emissions fueled her blood and all of her cells. The fabric of space and time came alive that day in a way that shook the fabric of her being. When she'd close her eyes, a magical city appeared before her, a temple, and cavernous halls for ritual, ceremony, and transcendence.

These were more than simple hallucinations, entertaining chemical tricks that diverted the mind on clement, carefree afternoons. She knew the world was connected by more than simple ideas and a web of economic imperatives. The differences between the mountain and the valley were minuscule. Her fungal teachers showed her that everything was part of a singularity, a whole. A heartbeat could shatter it all into a million atoms, then a breath could fill it with vibrant buoyancy. There were truths and realities not available to a default, basic consciousness.

She had unlocked a door to a thing hidden behind the veil of ordinary perception. There was more to life and reality than holo-porn, a steady job, and a working zapper. Even belief itself was laughable, she knew it was a mere reassurance that there was real meaning in the universe, which there was, but it didn't have much to do with any story she ever contrived.

She did not find the mushrooms, nor did they find her, but that each found the other according to some cosmic law of attraction. This was how her mother always said it should be.

She rocked back on her heels, to the bare-ass squat. Her root again Earthwards. She stood and thanked the Ravens, who still sat on the high branch, watching her. She raised her arms, arched her back, and cawed. The birds tilted their bodies forward into a bow and, with a gentle hop, spread their wings and lit into the air. Each flew off in a different direction to forage individual parts of the forest. In that moment, Louise felt their bond of love and knew that it was the only reality she needed to concern herself with. Each was a part of the other and a part of the forest and a part of the entire globe.

Chapter Twenty-Two

Lou was initiated into Spanner life in their Olympia compound. She was young, too young to be away from home on her own, but also too young to stay in her mother's chaotic mess. The last straw was when her mother's boyfriend-of-the-week got drunk and passed out in her bed, with Lou in it. He'd wrapped his arms around her and kept her pinned until morning when he had to pee, vomit, and apologize. He hadn't meant anything by it, he said. In fact, he was one of the better men to pass through her mother's life. Fuck you, asshole, she thought.

It took Louise a few minutes to get a lift. She rolled the six-sided die she kept in her pocket. Even numbers were *north*, so north she went. A traveling preacher picked her up in a black zapper and it took only fifteen minutes for the conversation to go from the end of the world and Jesus' plan to the sweet smell of panties. She had a sharp blade, but the guy was decent enough to drop her by the side of the road without so much as a raised tone.

She walked. It wasn't rainy that day and there were numerous breaks in the clouds. A halo of blue sky opened over Mount Saint Helens. That gave Louise hope. She turned around to see if anything was coming, and she spotted a big, gnarly bus on the horizon. It was otherworldly. It was noisy and dirty, made from iron and steel, its paint was faded to a matte green and the grill was soot-black. Chrome exhaust pipes framed the windshield and they belched plumes of black into the grey sky; Louise expected a dragon's-breath of fire at any second. It was a dinosaur, a throwback from before the quake. Her great-grandmother would have recognized that thing.

She stuck out her thumb. She hoped and prayed. She closed her eyes. Misty rain fell on her forehead; cool air filled her nose and she was refreshed. The bus took a lifetime, but soon its rumble approached, the brakes squeaked the vehicle to a halt, and the door's pneumatic whoosh welcomed her. She looked up the steps. The driver was a long-haired, bushy-bearded mop of a man with large, round, orange-tinted glasses. He's like a character from those psychedelic novels mom leaves around the house. This is not my life, this cannot be real. She put a foot on the first step and studied the driver.

"Can I help you, little lady?"

"I need a ride."

"It would appear so. Where to?"

"North."

"Anything more specific?"

"Nope."

"Get in. It's just me and the dogs. There's a seat right there and there's plenty of room in back. Hell, take a nap if you want. Those beds are all clean."

"I, uh..."

"What'sa matter, woman? Get in!" He put his hand on the door lever, idle but ready to close the accordion portal.

"Well…" Louise looked back down the road for another option.

"Look. It's either get in or walk in the rain. I don't really give a shit, but I took the effort to pull over for you, and there ain't much else coming down this road." Lou gaped at the freakish man; frozen indecision gripped her heart. "This is the moment of your life, darlin'. Look back to the past or walk forward and meet the future. It's up to you to make the choice of where your story goes and I ain't got all day."

She had a strong feeling that she'd never felt before. It was a strong sensation and it made her afraid. She stepped onto the first step, then the second. The door shut behind her. A gold tooth glimmered from inside a bushy beard. She winced. She walked deeper inside. The vehicle raged with life and threw her stumbling down towards the rear.

Past the second row of seats, the bus was a living space, complete with a small kitchen, a set of bunk beds, and a sleeping pad that filled the floor at the rear. Everything was covered in tapestries and dust. The space held the odor of a million sticks of incense. She sat in the first row, to the right of the driver. She wanted to watch him change gears and pilot the mechanical monster down the road.

"Running away?" He ground the gear shift into third as they gained momentum.

"Yup."

"I did the same. Many times." He pushed the lever into fifth gear.

"You get caught?"

"Caught? Hell, I'd get too hungry and go back. Nobody ever knew I'd been gone. They were too concerned with themselves to notice anything I'd do." They started up a hill and he downshifted. The bus lurched in the power boost. Louise had never experienced such a mechanical marvel.

The bus was loud, dirty, and obnoxious; it was more an organic life-form than a piece of machinery. No matter how long people drove their zappers, they'd never feel like this, Louise noticed. They never held the sweat and smell of their drivers and passengers, they never accumulated time or history. They were preternaturally stain-free, impervious to accident and decay. You could always wipe down their plastic seats and they'd be back to new. This thing would never look new again. It was an organic creation propelled by fire and the faith that it would make it one more klick down the road.

"What kind of car is this?"

"Car?" The man exploded into coughs and laughter. "Did you say *car*?" His voice boomed and he whipped his head to look her dead in the eye. She thought he was going to run off the road. She froze.

"Well, truck or something."

"Darlin', this is a *bus* from way before either of us were born. This thing used to carry our great-grandparents to school when they were half your age. It's a relic. It's a monument to the old ways of mechanics. It's been a home to me out here on the road, and it's carted traveling spanners, errant waifs such as yourself, and even a few of those Christian cultists, from one side of Cascadia to the other more times than I can count."

"Spanners?"

"They're my people. You'll see. We're headed to the original Spannerville."

"A town?"

"Hell, it's a way of life, sweetheart." He pulled a joint from his pocket, tucked it in the corner of his mouth, struck a match on the dashboard, and puffed the spliff to life. "Hang tight, darling, we'll be there before you know it."

The entryway was constructed from logs bolted together into a gate two car-lengths wide and 20-feet tall to match the concrete walls. Guards loped along the wall to monitor the entrance and look for any signs of trouble farther afield. They were hooded from the rain, dark, intimidating sentries with rifles slung over their shoulders. To Louise they were ominous, grim, authoritarian symbols. She cringed and stared at Fir, who blithely down-shifted and tooted his horn. The guards sprang to life with waving arms and gleaming smiles. The gate slid open to greet them.

Inside the gate, the skeletal remains of a pre-quake University still stood. The campus had once teemed with students chasing the future. Now the dorms were filled with an anarchic collective of mechanics, builders, artists, and assorted hangers-on. It was a scene that offered a hands-on physical reality, autonomy apart from Cascadia's hyper connectivity. They were all learners and searchers who measured success a day at a time, not in some mythical future. They were a collective without a singular, focused mission statement. They were individuals with particular dreams and desires. Their manifesto included terms such as *free will*, *individuality*, and *singular*, but also *community*, *togetherness*, and *humanity*. The goal was to foster diversity. They embraced the random chaos of the universe, they categorically distrusted all assured, pat assumptions as smug and ill-informed.

The bus cruised past machine shops, computer laboratories, and huge greenhouses full of fresh food for everyone. It was a self-sustaining community that Louise immediately found intriguing. She saw the arc light of a welder, and a mechanic lifting an engine on a hoist. It was thrilling, a version of life she'd never known before. Fir piloted the bus to a spot that seemed to be his and his alone.

"Here we are, darlin'," Fir said. "You owe me 100 credits."

"I, uh," Louise pulled her life savings from her bag. She didn't expect this. She was on the brink of tears. She looked through her bag in hopes that she could materialize something to trade. She was thinking of making a run for it when she looked up at him.

"Har!" Fir burst into laughter. "Aw hell, sweetheart, I didn't think you'd take me for a serious man. It was my pleasure. I'll introduce you to a few people, and before you know it you'll be another part of the Spanner universe – if you so choose. How's that sound?"

"Scary."

"Yeah, it is. It is. Us independent types usually balk, but give it a little time. Spanners are a collective, but if you ever copy anyone they'll give you a smack on the head. One of our mottoes is *know thyself.*"

The spanners maintained that the rest of Cascadia had been overtaken by technology. The human spirit had been suffocated by an over-reliance on the digital, the plastic. They sought to revive that spirit by relying, as much as possible, on analog technologies. Technology was a reality, however, so they sought to create solutions to technological problems. Frivolous uses of technology were discouraged, and it was a badge of honor to use as many individual devices as possible. One device was used to take photographs, another was a musical instrument, etc. It was an imperfect philosophy and lifestyle, but that was the point. The streamlined life was not worth living, they thought. A messy, oily, and buggy life was the way to go.

"So, you're new here?" Denali was tall, muscled, and smudged with grease. Sweat beaded on his brow. His long black hair framed deep brown eyes, strong cheekbones, and a chin that could chisel granite. Louise had been watching him weld an iron sculpture.

"I guess."

"Where'd you come from?"

"Portland."

"Been there." He took a hammer and knocked a small plane of metal into place. He was creating an abstract representation of a leaf pile that dissolved into data structures.

He was older and handsome. He had a dog that stayed by his side and soon he'd take her for rides in a handmade wooden kayak. They'd skim along the placid waters of the Eld Inlet, watching eagles soar overhead. He'd point out whales before they breached the surface and blew mist in the air. He made her feel special.

"Have you ever done this?"

"No."

"Do you want to?"

"Yes, but maybe not now."

"It's okay. Maybe try more later."

She'd see Fir during her shifts in the greenhouse. He mainly tended the smokable cannabis, but he'd help her harvest the snap peas. He was always present, hovered around like a dirty, furry, fairy godfather who reeked of ganja and humanity. Louise never knew her father, she suspected this was what it would be like to have one.

"I see you hanging around with Denali, he treat you right?"

"Yes, don't worry."

"I'm not worried, man." He handed her a box of condoms.

"I got these in town. I've been snipped, don't need 'em. You use them, though. I remember having a young body that wants what it wants. You make sure he puts those on so that you don't royally fuck yourself."

Louise could feel the red in her face. "Fir! Goddammit. You're embarrassing me!"

"Fir's got your back, kid." He winked at her. "Don't forget that."

When she wasn't earning her keep in the greenhouse, she spent time assisting the mechanics. Turning a wrench was her real love, but she also spent time learning computer code. The school she ran away from was full of fools who rehashed dated knowledge from decaying textbooks. Here, in Spannerville, Louise made rapid progress, and a new girlfriend, too.

In those days, Maisie was quiet and shy. She was a runaway, too, but her stepfather had done more than pass out in her bed. He had spent every night in her bed from the age of 8 until she ran out on the night of her 13th birthday. She was terrified of most people, including Louise. Her nerves were frayed and frazzled.

Louise liked her for some reason. She was drawn to Maisie's obvious talents and was curious to learn more. Louise asked her for help with her code, then had questions about mechanics, laundry, and anything else she could think of. Maisie had never had such attention, no one had ever recognized her for what she was capable of, only that she was pretty or smart in a way that ignored what she did with her intelligence. Maisie opened up more and more and they became friends.

They shared the secrets of early womanhood, they giggled together on long hikes, and they even built (with Fir's guidance) a small sailboat. They called it the SS *Exhaust* because that was Lou's favorite automotive system, and because Maisie was going through a time of purgation. She was exhausted from what she'd been through. She wished that she could blow it all out her tailpipe like one of Lou's motors.

Denali appealed to her mind and body. She'd never met a boy who cared about her needs. He was six years older and had had a few girlfriends before they met, so Louise considered him well-trained. One of those women, Zara, was still hanging around Spannerville, but she kept her distance. Louise was curious about her and longed to question her about Denali and men in general. She craved knowledge, experience.

"How about that? How does that feel?"

"It feels good. Oh God, it feels sooo good."

"Put your hand here."

"Kiss me."

"More?"'

"Not yet. Don't stop doing that."

Nearly every day after dinner, she and Denali would take long walks around the compound. They'd talk about all sorts of things. Louise loved how he listened to her ideas about life, society, technology, or whatever came to mind. He was a quiet man, but offered insights that opened her mind in new ways. He excited every part of her; she felt safe and she wanted more.

"Isn't that Zara?"

"Huh, yeah." He snapped his head back to her.

"She's pretty."

"I guess." His eyes averted.

Denali insisted that he was over Zara, that their love had run its course. He said he wanted to remain friends with her, but Louise wasn't sure about that. She saw how he looked at her. She saw how Zara looked at him and how they turned away in a start, with fear and longing. Their rift was a hairsbreadth divide. Louise's heart was wrenched.

"You still love her."

"No. Well, not like you think."

"You do. I see it. She looks at you, too."

"Look, Louise, I don't love her. Can we just hang out? Please?"

So much that she wanted was in the palm of her hand. She could take it and know that it was false, and have to live with the knowledge that it was all hollowness. How long could a person live with half a lie? Surely longer than living with a whole lie, that was certain, but a cold comfort. She could give it away and have the bitter, searing pain of loss and loneliness.

"Darlin', love is everywhere." Fir did his best. "If you break it down, everything in the world is held together by attraction, by love. You have enough already. That guy and girl have a stronger attraction, but you have a lot, too. Maybe different sorts of loves, but you got 'em."

"He makes me feel so good."

"On account of you not seeing the whole picture, right?"

"Well, yeah."

"Maybe you see too much for your own good, or maybe you see just enough to ensure that, when the time comes, you'll find the most pure love ever known on this planet." Fir lit a joint. "Damn. That shit was profound. Want a hit?"

Since Maisie worked with Zara in the computer lab, Louise was able to direct a scene where Denali would finally rendezvous with Zara. Each would be unaware that their coincidental meeting a the secluded gazebo was scripted by a well-intended puppeteer. Lou watched from afar as he approached her, as she waited for him. Their embrace, their kiss. She felt the knife in her heart, but saw the healing that she'd arranged for her friend. Louise spent that evening sobbing in her bed. Maisie brushed her hair.

Louise was on her way to perform Monday duties in the greenhouse. Her beans were close to harvest and she was ready to experiment with Oyster mushroom spores. All she needed to do was create the substrate. She'd spent the night with Denali and was feeling light and strong. Her 15th birthday was coming up and she thought that would be a good time to finally consummate their love. She'd consulted Fir, who was always straight with her. He had no tales of woe or fear or any of those things. He told her that it was going to be a great experience, but one not to be taken lightly.

"Psst. Lou." Maisie appeared at her side.

"Hey Mais, what's up?"

"Well, I was thinking that the two of us shouldn't waste such a beautiful Cascadian day all cooped up inside."

"You mean drizzling rain and a cold damp that chills the bones?"

"Exactly."

"I hear there are king salmon waiting for a hook. The SS Exhaust hasn't been out in a while. Whatcha say?"

"See you there in 10 minutes."

Maisie had a box full of tackle, two poles, and a basket of food for the outing. She was always prepared. Louise had not thought of what to bring, apart from a coat and long underwear to stay warm and dry. They were the perfect pair.

The air was calm. They almost dropped the sail to row, but there was enough wind to pull the *Exhaust* out to the deeper part of the inlet, where the fish were. Under Maisie's direction, Louise baited her hook and cast her line far from the boat. Louise pulled her scarf tight and flexed her muscles to encourage more blood flow. Within a minute, Maisie grunted.

"Holy shit, Lou, I think I got something happening here."

"Give it some slack then tighten up the line."

"How the fuck do you know this?"

"My ma taught me one or two survival skills."

"Holy shit, Lou! He's going fucking nuts!" The reel spun into a blur.

Louise jumped over and slapped her hand down on the spinning reel. "Grab it, girl."

Louise's heart raced, the panic tightened her focus to a pinpoint. As Maisie fought the fish, the world went silent. This was an epic battle. The fish pulled the boat further up the inlet, leaving a small wake. Maisie handled the fish, Louise dropped the anchor. Every muscle in Maisie's upper body was taught, but weakening, Lou saw. The fish was a leviathan. Lou took a deep breath and gazed over the expanse of water. She straddled herself behind Maisie and gave her support. It wasn't her fish, but it damn sure needed to be Maisie's.

"This is my fish and I'm gonna land the goddamn thing." Maisie found a second-wind.

"Feisty. I like it."

"Bitch."

"Slut."

The girls broke into laughter and Louise was glad for a reprieve into levity. The line was nearly perpendicular to the water. It'll be done soon, she thought. Breathe. Breathe. Show Maise how to do it. Inhale. Exhale. Inhale. The fish's shadow neared the surface.

"There's the motherfucker!" Louise flushed with excitement. "I'll grab the net."

The boat rocked. Louise positioned herself to net the fish. It was the largest Chinook they'd ever seen. It must have been five feet long, a single muscle thrashing sea water into a froth cold enough to kill them if they went overboard. Maisie held it within a foot or so of the surface, but couldn't quite get it higher. Her friend, her love struggled, and Lou worked the net under the fish.

"What the fuck are we going to do with this thing?" Sweat froze on Lou's brow.

"Wait. See if you can hold it still. I have an idea."

Maisie was such a warrior, Louise thought. Anyone else would have let the monster go and filled the creel with smaller fish. Maisie needed this; she was getting it, and Louise was there. Her heart swelled.

"Hold that fucker steady. I'm gonna see if I can lift it. Keep the line tight. Crank the reel, if you can."

The fish thrashed in the net, it fought the hook. It could knock the girls overboard, killing them in icy water. The fish would die on the deck, drowning in fresh air.

Louise kept the body even with the edge of the boat. Maisie

dropped her pole with no warning. Louise panicked. In the next second, Maisie produced a hammer. She whacked the salmon on the head. It stilled for a moment, but then flipped and flopped with such strength that Lou almost lost it. Maisie reared the hammer back again, held it high over her head. Louise saw cold steel in her friend's eyes, the look of bare determination and icy murder. It was the look of revenge, a deep justice that was long overdue. It scared and thrilled her. The ability to cut off sentiment from action. The facility to do what was right and necessary despite any unpleasantness. The hammer became a blur, only to reconstitute on the head of the fish. All the fight left the fish and it slid into the boat.

"Holy shit! What the fuck, Maise?"

"Sometimes, the only solution is a hammer." She bobbed the hammer in her hands and looked upon it with affection. "A good hammer just might save your life someday. From this moment forward, I will keep one with me all the time."

They pulled their quarry aboard. The dead fish lay in a small puddle of sea water and all Lou could think was *what now*? Then, without a word, Maisie took what appeared to be a nail on a thin rope and slipped it through the fish's gills, out the mouth, and then through a loop at the far end of the rope. Thus secured, she tied the rope to the end of stern of the boat.

"The water should keep her fresh until we get back. Wanna see if we can get a few more. Smaller ones, this time?"

"Give me a few minutes. You can start casting."

"First, I think we deserve a few moments of relaxation." Maisie shot Lou a sly grin and reached inside her coat. "How about this?" She produced a joint from her jacket pocket.

Whenever Louise smoked cannabis, she got quiet, closed her eyes, and retreated into her thoughts. In her mind, she traveled over the past weeks and months with the Spanners. Everything she'd learned, all the new people, friends, ideas. She'd built a fucking boat with a girlfriend then caught the world's largest salmon in the middle of the water with nothing but grey skies overhead and Davy Jones' locker beneath her seat. Fir loomed large over the whole experience. She saw him everywhere; he was in the tall evergreens, the water, the machines, and he was even in her soul. She wondered if he might really be her father. She resolved to ask him to adopt her. She heard something rustling around the boat. She cracked her eye. Maisie was doubled over, heaving for breath.

"Hey girl, what's happening?" Louise tried to stand, but the boat wobbled beneath her feet and she dropped back down into her seat. She took a moment to reorient herself. Maisie wasn't looking good. "Are you going to be okay?"

Maisie's body was clenched tight. She heaved for air. Lou went to her friend. This time she kept her center of gravity low and her wits about her. She sat next to her on the boat's small bench. She rubbed her back and made gentle shushing sounds that she hoped would be soothing.

"Did you get too high?"

An animal noise rose from Maisie's throat. She'd smoked too

much. Her head was bowed and gutteral noise ejaculated from her body. When Louise pulled her hair back she saw that her friend was crying. Louise's heart throbbed.

"What's the matter, girl?"

"I see him. I smell him. He's here. He's coming into my bedroom. He's shoving himself into me. I'm sucking him. I'm fucking liking it and hating myself, my goddamn pussy. He's so gross, there's nothing I can do. He won't leave, he won't stop coming back." Her voice trailed into sobs, deep, gut-level moans that broadcast over the water to the mute chorus of trees at the shore.

"Tell me. Paint a picture for me."

"His shirt is stained by the shitty blackberry wine. He's a worm in a pair of thick glasses. His fleshy, pasty face is spotted with stubble, never a full beard, never shaven. His ears glow in the light from the hallway while he thrusts. His stomach. His breath smells like infection or a turd or something dead." Maisie looked off over the water and took a deep breath. "I let him, Lou. I let him. I let him. He wants me to kiss him goodnight and he calls me his sweet angel, which makes me feel happy despite my disgust so I hate myself."

"You are an angel, he was a devil. It wasn't your fault." Louise wiped tears from her friend's face. "Break the chain, Maise, break that fucker at the point when it starts to flip back onto you. Give it a kiss and watch it go away."

"But I liked it, Lou." Maisie rises up to look Lou in the eye. "It felt good after I got used to it. I got wet. I wanted it."

"That's your body. A mindless response. That's not you. That's how he turned you against yourself. He knew once your body responded that he'd have you trapped in confusion and he'd own you. But he didn't own you. He never will. It's not your fault."

"Really?" Maisie snorted a nose full of snot and hocked it overboard. She bent over her legs and wrapped her arms around her knees. Lou pulled Maisie's hair back and stroked her head.

"Really."

She draped her body over Maisie's, protected her from everything the horrible world had to offer: all the bad people, shitty accidents, acts of malice and stupid mistakes. She covered her friend's body like a warm, limp blanket, she seeped into every crevice, behind shoulder-blades and between every vertebrae on her back. Then, little by little, the body beneath her released its tension and softened. All of the gripping and stress melted away from her friend's body until she was lying atop a soft, supple, girl body, one whose pain had been dislodged and freed, who had faced fear and won. The rigid, stiff body was no more; the alchemy of friendship and love was forged in the heat and burn of sorrow and pain.

Together, they turned back the damage and released whatever demons had once been locked in Maisie's body. Youth and vibrancy now held sway a space once inhabited by premature age. She peeled her body from Maisie's and they sat upright beside one another, arms wrapped around shoulders, and stared to the aft of the boat where the big fish dangled, over the inlet, and to the grey-green mountains beyond.

"I love you, Lou." Maisie said.

Chapter Twenty-Three

There was a small, handmade, wooden box in her car. It was an artifact from her youth, a treasure given to her by Fir, on her sixteenth birthday. He said it was for special items, the small treasures of life. He'd engraved it with a hexagonal figure that encased a golden apple. Fir always was a bit odd, eccentric, she thought. She'd filled it with magic mushrooms she picked fresh from the forest floor. They had dried on the floorboard of her car, her heater blew hot enough to dry them to cracker-thinness. She was low on fuel, but only had a mile or two before she reached the Spanner outpost. She was refreshed from her forest reverie and was ready for whatever else the day held in store.

She followed the switch-back squiggly road. Her engine rumbled and echoed in the valley below. She imagined forest animals pausing to consider the sound. Louise longed for the days of paved roads, when she could push her car and herself to the limit on such a curvy, crazy road. Soon, she came to a clearing.

The spanners had created a fortress in the forest. The outer walls were whole tree trunks stripped of branches and sharpened like pencil-points at the top; watchtowers overlooked the forest from four corners. The road led to a small clearing in front of the entrance. There were a few guys standing around. She pulled her car up and shut down the motor.

"You Lou?"

"How'd you know?"

"Word travels fast."

"You Spanners?"

"We don't have anything to do with you coastals, if that's what you mean."

"We ain't so bad."

"We could hear you from all the way down in the valley. I like that exhaust kit."

"You got fuel?"

"That's what started this whole thing, fuel. C'mon in." The guy yelled *open* and the gate slid aside to reveal a small town.

The interior seemed so much larger than what the exterior revealed. She rolled her car inside and parked it in a spot marked for visitors. The road split inside the wall. In the divide was one of a series of four-story buildings clad in corrugated steel, adorned with old auto-body parts or painted with colorful murals. Along the perimeter were structures for living, working, or storage.

"What did you mean about fuel starting this?"

"After the quake, all of Oregon's fuel storage was destroyed. They knew the tanks were sitting on unstable soil, so they sank right into the river. The pipeline from Washington burst, too. It was a real shitshow, preventable, too. Poisoned the Columbia River from Portland straight to the sea. It took the salmon ten years to recover. Some people think they're still full of metals. The fools who let it happen got payback, though. They got to spend their money in hell, I suppose.

"Those who were savvy enough to be into the biofuels had reserves and could help out. I trace the start of the spanners to that. We don't trust self-appointed authorities with our future. We make the future happen for ourselves."

"How many people live here?"

"Right now I think there are about 150, but it fluctuates. Like most spanners, we have friends and allies all over Cascadia, SoCal, too."

Chapter Twenty-Four

The gatekeeper was named Hawk. He was tall and stocky with long hair pulled into a ponytail. Louise was mesmerized by his diamond-blue eyes set behind strong cheekbones. He showed her where to get fuel.

"We know your car. You're kinda famous all through the spanner network. When we heard that exhaust rumble in the valley, I knew it must be you. Someone owes me a few beers." Hawk eyed the CRX with wolfish desire. "This thing is probably one-of-a-kind. Not much still survives from that era. The old Japanese cars did very well, but it's hard for a car to make it as long as yours has, even in ideal circumstances."

"She'd been in storage for a long time, and I rebuilt every inch of her. My grandma stored it in a barn when she was young. Most people had forgotten about that old barn. I found it after she died. I was looking for a place to get high and crash."

"Damn lucky," Hawk said. "Small, good shape, fast."

"Dusted every zapper I've ever come across."

"You ever want to trade it for something, you let me know."

"Shit. Let me rest my bones for a bit. I may think about that."

"You can have a room in that building." He pointed to the building nearest to the gate. "Tell them Hawk said so. Dinner is at 7."

Louise found her bed made and the room well-tended. She dropped her gear, the black boxes, and her newfound stash of psychedelic fungi. She sat and kicked off her boots. It was a simple dorm constructed from found materials. Spanners used hemp insulation. Thanks to that innovation, their buildings were all supremely comfortable and the rooms were nearly silent, the sound absorbed into the walls. No youngster in a Spanner enclave had to endure her ill-conceived music lessons or early sexual experiments. They were frugal and Spanners loved to brag on how they created economic luxury.

When her phone buzzed. It was Morgan. She ignored it. She needed to quiet her mind and fill her lungs with fresh air. She stretched her arms and legs and drank from the pitcher of room-temperature water they gave her when she checked in. She drank more. She was dry as a bone. She drank the whole pitcher, then plopped her woozy and exhausted head on the perfect down pillow. The world dove into black.

She woke when someone accidentally opened her door and then jerked it closed in embarrassment. She startled, but remembered that Spanner doors didn't have locks. No need, the honor code was virtually embedded in their skin the moment they embraced the life. It was time for dinner and she was famished, so she fought her deep fatigue and rose for the meal.

She walked in a daze, blindly following people from her dorm to the cafeteria, where they offered a selection of vegetables, potatoes, and fresh forest mushrooms sauteed with herbs. It was a beautiful spread. She wondered if they got much meat in this area. Elk were likely abundant, but hunting them was not easy, and you needed to have enough to feed the whole enclave.

"You new?"

She looked younger than Lou. She had dark skin that'd been speckled and smeared with engine grease. Her eyes were dyed the deepest green she'd ever seen, emeralds in volcanic soil. A white kerchief wrapped her wild, fierce afro. This lovely nameless creature that stood before her was strong and sturdy, but with a sleek femininity that reminded Louise of roses.

"I'm visiting."

"Today?" The green orbs were captivating. The black of the pupils pierced.

"Just arrived, I dunno, 2 hours ago."

Her eyes widened in dumbstruck surprise. She stammered, which was surprising to Lou, and said, "We need to talk, sister."

Louise followed her new friend to a round table topped by the cross-section of a massive tree. The hall was filled with similar tables, each filled with laughing, talking spanners who noticed her arrival with amiable recognition. The room was lit from elk-antler chandeliers, all harvested from animals the Spanners had hunted and killed. Louise compared the hall to the Olympia Spanners, whose dining hall was decorated with images related to the sea, fishing, and boating. Who knows what would have happened if she'd decided to take the I-5 southbound when she ran away. She might have ended up here and be a totally different person.

At first blush, the collective seemed divided by cliques, not bound in collective camaraderie. Her first enclave of spanners all dined at long tables and she sat wherever there was a spot. The idea was to meet new people or to have new encounters with every meal. Here, she imagined the same groups inhabiting the same tables at every meal.

"I'm Makah," she said, extending a hand.

"Louise." The table murmured hello to her.

"You're from inside the Cascades?"

"Yeah, Portland."

"Figured." Makah focused on her food.

"I go all over, though."

"Louise, can you pass the vinegar?" He reached his arm across the table.

"For your name."

"Fair enough. I'm Tor."

"Could you pass this to Tor," Louise said to the woman sitting to her left.

"Formal," Makah said with a sneer.

"That's how we did things in Olympia. I guess it stuck."

"You're the Louise with the old-world Honda, right?" Tor doused vinegar on his fried potatoes.

"One and the same."

"How'd you go about getting that exhaust system?"

"I had to look for years. One day, I dunno what happened, my finger must have slipped on the computer. I found myself looking at an ad for someone selling a perfect reproduction. He was just down in Philomath. Some nutty metal fabricator got a bug in his ass to make retro exhaust systems. He said he'd never seen the plans before, but they were on his hard drive. It's a perfect replica of the real thing. My great-grandmother would be proud at how she purrs."

"Did anything special happen while you were down there?" Makah's voice had a way of dominating the table.

"Nothing that I can think of. I mean, getting the system was special enough. Why?"

"I believe that everything happens for a reason, and I'm trying to figure it all out."

"Sounds complicated. Stick to engines. A combustion engine is complicated enough, but everything under a hood has a reason. No doubt."

"Do you believe that you are connected to something greater?"

"Like some sort of god?" Louise braced. This was tricky territory.

"Not necessarily. But, something larger, something greater than yourself."

"I see Spanners as one thing I'm connected to. That's larger than myself, for sure, even if I don't live with 'em. They've taken care of me pretty well, and I do my best to repay 'em."

"And we're all connected to the rest of the planet. We're even connected to Mars."

"I don't think I'm connected to anyone outside of this forest, it's impossible. Besides, what sort of impact could I have on someone in San Francisco, much less San Diego? It breaks down to a weird, meaningless abstract for philosophers jerking off into their beards," Tor said. The table cracked up.

"Every time you use any computer, you tap into something greater, a higher mind, if you will."

"My shit is all encrypted."

"That's what you think. How did you learn that encryption? I bet you learned it on a computer." Makah took a sip of her beer. "We are all tied together, just like the networks of information that run through the entire forest, so we humans are networked." Makah popped a mushroom cap into her mouth.

"Even to Mars?"

"Sure, even to Mars."

"You're pretty deep, huh?" Louise thought big ideas were sexy. Makah bumped her knee into Lou's.

Chapter Twenty-Five

"So, what are you doing here, anyways?" Makah walked with her back to the dorm.

"I'm on my way to pick up a package. I'm a courier."

"I was told to look out for you, that you might need my help."

"Oh?"

"The Oracle app. On my phone. Last night it told me that a beautiful, dark-haired stranger would arrive in a noisy car and that she would need my help."

"That's pretty fucking specific."

"It's nothing but a game, but last night it got my attention."

Lou gestured to her room and leaned back into the door. Makah's green orbs fixed her, pinned her to the wood. She was nervous, her heart raced. This part is always so exciting, she thought. She nodded and Makah nodded, so she slipped a hand over the doorknob and slowly turned it.

When the door opened, she heard a ruckus behind her. Makah's eyes burst open in surprise. Louise whipped around to see one of the blinking boxes fall to the floor as a shadow jumped out the window and whizzed via zip line through the forest.

"Holy fuck!" All the blood drained from her head, she started to sway. Makah held out a hand to help her.

Louise steadied herself, reached for her bag and pulled out her big knife. She leaped to the window, found the taut rope and began sawing away at it. When it snapped, she heard a distant scream in the dark, followed by a chorus of snapping twigs ending in a thud on the forest floor.

"Motherfucker."

"That was cold-blooded." Makah's jaw hung open.

"Sometimes you have to act. Now, I'm gonna go catch that son of a bitch." The knife reflected a glow onto half of her face. "Nobody fucks with my mission."

Louise leaped down the stairs and sprinted to the front gate.

"Who goes there?" The guard took his job very seriously.

"Did you really just say that?" Louise said. "Look, I'm a visitor but some guy just robbed my room and then bolted on a zip line. I gotta track him and get what he took from me."

"You're Louise, with the hot CRX, right?"

"Yeah. Look I gotta go catch that guy."

"Alright, you can leave, but I don't know if I'll be here when you get back."

"She's with me." Makah caught up, huffing and puffing. "We gotta get the fuck out of here. Let's go!"

"Alright Makah, you know how we feel about the forest at night, but we'll let y'all back in when you return."

"This is serious shit. Go!"

"Right. Be safe."

They took off into the drizzly evening.

Chapter Twenty-Six

Louise had a flashlight, but didn't want to give herself away. Tromping through the forest was noisy enough. She and Makah found the fallen zip-line and followed it along a straight, if unclear, path. Makah led the way.

"Ok, here's another fallen tree. It's about mid-thigh high."

They tromped on. Louise's eyes acclimated to the darkness. She learned that she needed to pick her feet up and step straight down. When her senses adjusted she became confident, grounded; she no longer felt that she was floating in space. She trudged on, enlivened by Makah's sweet aroma wafting on the breeze.

Whup, hoo-hoo, hoooo

"What the fuck was that?"

"Spotted owl. Looking for a mate. We gotta walk around this tree here – too many branches."

"The two primary imperatives, huh? Feast and fuck."

"Don't forget a nice cuppa tea under a solid roof."

After about forty-five minutes of fumbling in the fauna, Louise found the blinking box. She longed for moonlight, she needed to see the beauty of the forest cast in silver and shadow, but the box would have to do.

The thief had landed a few meters away, bounced from

his original trajectory by tree branches. When they made it over to him, they discovered that he had fallen onto an erect branch of a fallen tree that now protruded from his chest. Arms splayed, his dead eyes stared into a moonless sky. He probably died on impact, if his neck hadn't been broken in the fall. Louise hoped he'd had a clean death with minimal suffering.

"Hey Lou, doesn't that look a bit odd." The box was balanced on his chest and the beacon pointed back towards the Spanner compound.

"Yeah. Shit."

"Now you're gonna answer a few questions." A ring of flashlights surrounded them. Louise heard the metallic *shuck* guns make when preparing a round.

They were led to an encampment a few hundred meters away. Their captors had used a small cannon to launch the line and a computer-guided grappling hook. Louise was impressed by the tech and marksmanship. She and Makah were tied to chairs at the edge of a large bonfire and told to wait. A skinny, sunken-eyed lackey sat guard while the leaders conferred.

"Do you want water?" The shadows played over his gaunt visage.

"Bite me, wastrel." Louise withheld the impulse to spit in his face.

"My, my. Awful snippy for onc that's all ticd up."

"They know we're out here. Someone is probably on the way right now."

"Half of 'em is us." His hollowed eye sockets trained on her. He chuckled.

"Tell me who. Right goddamn now." Makah's rage burned hot.

The skinny creature turned his attention to the fire; he poked it with a stick, urged the pyre higher. Louise heard murmuring behind her. The rest of the band was likely discussing how to torture or kill them. Makah was still. Her eyes were closed and her chest rose and fell with deep, deliberate breaths. Louise strained to hear any evidence of a search party tromping through the forest to save the day, but there was no sound at all except for the far-off hoot of an owl.

The group, three men and two women, returned and sat in silence on the far side of the fire ring. They were all dressed in a similar fashion: white shirts underneath black jackets. The men wore black, wide-brimmed hats and the women covered their heads in waxed-canvas bonnets. Some of the bonnets had brims to keep the rain from dripping into their eyes, other hats looked more padded and warm. They looked like good driving hats, Louise thought, but she wondered if she could stand having hat-head.

"You killed our brother."

"He fucking robbed me. He got what he deserved." Louise felt her muscles coursing with strength.

"Do you now deserve to die?"

"No."

"What do you want with this?"

"That is none of your fucking business."

"Don't you know that this is a devil's box?"

"Cool. You all into Beelzebub?"

"You think you're being funny." He tossed the box from hand to hand. "This thing, this abominable thing, might very well cause the end of human existence as we know it." He held the box aloft. "It must be destroyed, along with those who protect it."

"What did old snake-eye ever do to you?"

"Snake-Eye? Is that what you call this thing? How appropriate." He stared at the box. Its blinking light illuminated his fierce eyes, his clenched jaw. "It is the work of a Great Snake, the Master of Lies, Satan himself."

The group murmured assent. The man with the shotgun propped the weapon on his shoulder, confident in the truth.

"Oh, goddamnit. Are you those *end-of-times* people? I wish every goddamn one of you had been on that line, then fell to the same end as your thief. We could have a dipshit kebab over this beautiful fire, isn't that right, Makah?" Makah sat mute, eyes closed, arms dangling limp from her shoulders. Her chest expanded and contracted with deep, intentional breaths. What the fuck she's meditating?

"We're trying to figure out what to do with you demons."
He spat into the fire. "We can't let you continue. Especially
you." He pointed to Louise. "You better start talking. Start
from the beginning."

"Fuck you."

"We don't believe in torture. It's ineffective and messy.
However there are other ways." He nodded to the lackey
and another man.

The men brandished large knives and walked towards
Louise. She stiffened when the blades glinted in the
firelight. How could this not be torture? She shut her eyes
and the fire played against the back of her eyelids. She took
a deep breath. Nothing. She heard a knife cutting rope, but
didn't feel anything. She opened her eyes and saw that they
were cutting Makah free. Makah appeared limp, but her
nostrils were flared.

One held her from behind, his arms wrapped her chest
from under her arms. The other knelt in front of her and
reached for her feet. He moved to cup her heel and she
came alive. She retracted from the hip and propelled her
foot directly into his chest. He flew into the fire. Sparks
and hot ash flew everywhere. Her head snapped back into
the face of the man behind her and she twisted her body
around, now free of his hold. He came at her and one
lighting-fast punch to the head put him on the ground, out
cold. She pulled his knife from its sheath and pivoted. The
blade flew from her like a bullet and landed in the chest of
the shotgun-wielding man.

The man in the fire came at her, but didn't stand a chance.

She kicked his chin, bone snapped. She pulled a blade from his waistband and sliced his carotid artery. She continued the motion and severed the ropes from Louise's legs. Another fox-fast movement freed her arms and they faced their captors. The leader grabbed the box and turned to run.

"Hold it." Makah discharged the shotgun into the air. The blast echoed through the forest, flocks of crows cawed in alarm. He continued to run. "He's serious."

Makah ran after the blinking box. Louise stood in dimming fire-glow for what seemed like hours. The only sound was the skinny kid rousing to consciousness. Louise grabbed a large branch from the woodpile and prepared to beam him.

"Don't fucking move."

"Please don't kill me."

A shotgun blast rang out from the darkness. Louise felt an icy chill run down her spine and her stomach lurched. The skinny guy's pants darkened and the sweet smell of urine filled the air.

"Oh Jesus, fucking pull that thing out. Piss on the ground. Have some self-respect, for shit's sake."

"Too late."

Makah made plenty of noise tramping back to the fire ring. Louise saw the blinking light bobbing up and down as her friend stepped over downed trees and around forest flora. She felt a weight in her. This thing was more and more complex with each turn. Now there was a significant trail of bodies in the wake of these dumb blinking boxes. *Bodies.* She was a courier, not a mercenary or an assassin; there was no war, for fuck's sake.

The kid rolled over and she cocked her branch back. "Hey, hold on. I'm not doing nothing."

"Make sure you keep it that way," she said. "What was that you were saying about there being more of you in the Spanner compound?"

"He's one of us." Makah returned to the orange glow of the campfire. She set the gun down and fed the coals fresh wood.

"Yeah, there's a lot of tension between the end-of-times and Spanners," he said. "These crazy fucks always think the Spanners are up to something."

"The paranoia goes both ways. There's not a lot do to out here in the forest but concoct conspiracy theories."

Chapter Twenty-Seven

When they returned to the compound the door was locked. Makah used the secret knock. Nothing. They waited. Maybe the guard stepped away to pee or smoke a joint. She knocked again. Louise paced around. She was getting a bad feeling.

"How long do they take?"

"Should be here in a minute."

"I'm really stressing. I need a joint or something."

"We'll hit my bong when we get inside."

Louise paced. She wanted to shit, puke, and cry all at once. She took deep breaths to keep it all inside. There was no time for a fucking baby-girl meltdown, she told herself. Those were her mother's words – *baby-girl meltdown*. Had she internalized that bullshit? Was she haunted by the specter of her mother all the way the fuck out here, after amassing a serious body count over a pair of stupid blinking black boxes? There was still nothing happening on the other side of that door.

"Goddamnit. What are we doing?"

"I don't have my phone, I don't guess you do, either." Makah scratched her head and spit. "Shit. I'll go over the wall. I actually know a good way."

There was a fir tree not too far away that was close to

the wall. Makah said she'd done it plenty of times, so she shimmied up it like a jungle cat. Louise, mouth agape, watched the agile lynx disappear into the dark of the branches. *That shit is hot enough to make me forget anything.* When Makah was even with the top of the wall the tree was thin enough to sway back and forth. She grabbed the top of the wall and found the catwalk that ran along the perimeter of the encampment. She opened the door and Louise entered the fortress.

There was no one there. The walkways were empty. There were lights on in the living quarters and walkways, but no shadows moved about behind the curtains. The only sound they heard was the lonely hoot of an owl.

"Is everyone asleep?"

"I don't see a soul," Makah said, her voice full of absence. "There is always someone around, 24 hours a day. It's only 1, at least a few people are walking around at this time. I'm always up, so are lots of people. This shit is spooky."

They found the guard station empty except for an open journal and a pen that lay over a sentence that had stopped mid-word. They found the camp bar and a tap that had emptied the rest of a keg into an overflowed pitcher that spilled to the floor. There was no bartender. The chef left charred food that had long stopped smoking. Music played, party music for a gathering of ghosts who had sipped their last beer. The tables were perfect still-lives from a life interrupted by, what? Glasses lay shattered, their shards hid in puddles. Beer mugs lay in pools of suds where drinkers once sat.

At one of the tables, there was a pile of Cascadians and an upside-down dice cup. Louise turned it over. Snake eyes.

"I guess they weren't too lucky, eh?"

"What?"

"Abandoned game."

Makah went pale.

"I always sat in on this game. I was going to bring you, if you wanted." She picked up a leather cup. "This was Franco's." Tears fell from her green eyes. She sat in her friend's chair and broke into sobs. "What the fuck happened?" She buried her face in her hands and moaned with grief. Louise stroked her back.

Louise didn't know what to say. She turned off the music, but the silence was too much. She found something somber and instrumental. Emptiness washed over her. These people didn't leave, they disappeared from their seats, vanished into thin fucking air. There was no sign of rush or struggle, just vanishing. Evaporating. No bad guy to fight. No danger to flee. She inspected the room. The plants were gone from their soil and the soil was dry as dust. No one hangs pots of dust in the windows. Behind the bar, she found an empty bowl of dog food, but there was no dog. No life remained. The shadow of death had taken it.

"I'm getting the fuck out of here."

"You can't leave me." Makah's voice was full of tears and urgency.

"No room, sister."

"Everyone here is gone." She was pleading. "We can take whatever car you want. Plus, I know the area and I can navigate. You know I'm useful in a pinch."

"That's my great-grandmother's car, how can I leave it?"

"It's safe. You can come back for it. Where are you going anyway?"

"Shasta."

"I can't stay here alone. Fuck, Louise, I just lost everyone I know. They are all fucking dead, except for you." She was sobbing. "Fucking drop me somewhere. Anywhere. Just somewhere I can start again. We can make this work. Look, we can use one of the big trucks, you don't have to put more wear on your car. Besides, everybody knows that thing. You'll be dead by dusk without me."

"Fuck it," she said. "Goddamn green eyes. What other cars you got?"

Chapter Twenty-Eight

Makah wanted to drive, and Louise didn't put up a fight. It had been years since she'd sat in a passenger seat, it seemed, and she wasn't eager to learn a new vehicle. Louise pressed into the seat, adjusted it a bit and raised her arms to stretch her entire body with a moan. Makah looked over and poked her exposed belly-button.

"You had that coming."

"I gotta know not to let my guard down around you."

"Smart woman."

Louise was not used to riding in such a large vehicle. It was powered by a combustion engine backed-up by an e-drive for long highway stretches. Half a fucking zapper, she thought, I must be going soft. It had beefy tires, all-wheel-drive, and a hatchback for storage. They filled the rooftop storage container with cans of food, cooked meats, whatever would fit. The rear seats folded down to open up an area for sleeping. It was a custom job, built for driving on forest roads, up muddy hills, and around tight bends. Makah was holding an average of 100kph without breaking a sweat. That girl has nerves of steel, she thought.

"You from out here?"

"Naw." She downshifted and took a hard curve. "I'm from Back East. A million miles and years away."

"No shit?"

"I was raised on the island of Manhattan. Near Central Park." She took in a deep breath. "Concrete jungle, baby. These trees still kinda freak me out."

"Shit."

"Shit is right. Fucking eat or be eaten. I was lucky I made it past infancy." Her voice lowered. "Every night the Crawlers came out."

"Where were your parents?"

"Parents? Are you kidding me? I don't know of anyone who had a mother, definitely no daddies. In New York, if you had a mom that meant you must be rich, or new to town," she said. "I was born in an old brownstone with a bunch of kids. That's the first home I knew. There were older kids who tried to take charge of us, they did their best. It's amazing they did anything at all, come to think of it. I don't know anyone else in that city who'd take care of someone or something that wasn't pulling their load. We mostly stole to get by. The older ones taught us all the tricks. My first memories are in a crew of three to five pickpockets. I was probably three. My little hands could reach into a bag or pocket, soon I gained the dexterity to take watches or jewelry right off a person. If we were able to steal enough, we could sit at the dinner table. Otherwise, we'd have to do things for scraps, or hope an ally would give up a few bites. Some of the boys would feed you for a blowjob. That was family."

"Who were the Crawlers?"

"A bunch of sub-human junkie fucks. They all did some

horrible drug. Some shit that rots out the caring, empathetic parts of the brain. Their whole trip is that those parts are the weakest. It leaves nothing but a shadow of a human. They sought to be the strongest, most fit, most efficient predators in the world. They do the drug once or twice and they're cooked. They spend the rest of their sick, pathetic lives trying to create a feeling. Fucking stupid, right? They did the most extreme shit imaginable just to try to recover exactly what they worked so hard to destroy."

"I've known a few fools like that."

"They become super-predators, tho – animals with the cunning of a human. The conversion was ritualistic, if you could call it that. The newcomer first had to fight them off long enough to prove they were worthy. Then, they'd be stripped naked before the whole group and be stabbed in the back with a syringe full of the shit. They vomit and fall to the floor. They squirm around in their own vomit and shit while the rest of the Crawlers either fuck them, piss on them, or kick them."

"Goddamn. Sounds worse than Tacoma."

"They were some of the scariest creatures you'll ever see. I've seen those Tacoma zombies. Fucking amateurs." She gave a sardonic laugh. "Crawlers only came out in the dark. They avoided the sun. Even if they went out in daylight, they stayed in the shadows. Pale and dirty skin. Yellow teeth. Either their hair got all bushy and wild or they'd lose it. They'd attack anyone. They loved the park. They'd hang their victims under one of those old stone bridges. Goddamn gruesome. They'd take out the brain or other organs. If they'd raped the body, they'd take its heart.

"They got me once, when I was younger. I was out late. I remember a prick in my ass. The next thing I know, I'm handcuffed to a radiator."

"Shit girl."

"I was there for a few weeks. They had their way with me every hour or so, around the clock. I never felt so close to death, but they kept feeding me. They forced some sort of liquid protein shit down my throat. I don't even want to know what was in it. It made me feel real strong. That's what they wanted. They liked it rough, and when a strong body pressed back, it helped them to feel like they were alive or something, I guess.

"Anyhow, I lost track of the days. I was numb. I forgot words, who I was. I was a body. I was becoming an animal. I guess they wanted to turn me into one of them. Goddamn." She took a deep breath and went silent.

Louise looked at the passing trees, a whir of green branches. Suddenly, a vista would open on a valley and shut down when the road hugged the side of a mountain. Her phone buzzed. It was a message from Morgan: Need Update. Fuck. She'd have to call in and report. She shut off the phone and watched morning sun break through the clouds and light a mountain range. A hawk rode on thermals.

"One day, there was a bunch of commotion outside the room, all hell was breaking loose. One of them was pounding away on me. I couldn't tell what was happening. A band of vigilantes from a West Village dojo had attacked that hive of Crawlers. They brandished knives, nunchucks, and guns. The Crawler who was fucking me turned around and snarled at them. They grabbed him by the hair and threw him into a corner. I will never forget how that fucker's blood spattered when his carotid artery opened. I wish I could have spat in his face."

"Fuck. Then what?"

"Well, they took to their place. They gave me a bed and food. They said I could stay until I healed, so long as I didn't steal or lie. I did what they asked and I never left until I moved in with a man.

"It took several months before I left that little room. They said that was normal. Different people visited during the day. They'd feed me or help me use the bedpan. They talked to me. Some read to me. I didn't know how to read. They taught me how to read fucking *Don Quixote*. Before I left the room, they'd taught me elementary moves that would later develop into a deadly system. If the Crawlers destroyed me, I was rebuilt in that room. It was an epic rehabilitation project. They knew exactly what they were doing. I owe them everything."

"You're a fighter."

"Shit yeah. I learned every fighting form: Kung-fu, Tai-Chi, Karate, Savate, Jiu-jitsu, and Wing Chun. We trained with weapons, and things that served as weapons. We disciplined our minds, bodies, even our breath. I learned to read and write and then I moved on to learning to code. I read all of the classics. I read nearly everything Steven King ever wrote, and I even read George Sand and Shakespeare for a background in the real ancient stuff.

"Sometimes we'd get strays from the Park Avenue collective, fucking elitists. They'd come down to assert their dominance, but every one of them left with his ass in his hand. I'd thrash them with logic and knowledge, then beat them bloody, too.

"One day a newbie showed up. Barack. He was so skinny. A goddamn six-foot string bean. His parents died during a blizzard in New Hampshire. He'd walked all the way to New York. He had nowhere to go. He'd heard about us on the 'net and decided we were his best hope. It was getting dark and he begged to be let in. Margot, the sensei on duty, told him to get lost. She gave him a hunk of cheese and shoved him out the door. I dreamed about him all night long. He said my dreams kept him alive.

"He showed back up the next morning. He was bleeding and bruised. His tattered coat was smeared with blood. Crawlers'd tried to get him, but he'd been tougher, stronger, and faster. Later, Margot said she knew he'd make it through the night. I don't know if I believe her, but he was damn sure the toughest motherfucker we had in the dojo. Next to me, anyway."

"You fell for him?"

"From the first second I saw him. He wasn't the first lonely straggler to come begging for mercy, but he was the only one I ever dreamed about.

"He always sparred with me, even though he could have advanced faster if he'd worked out with the bigger boys. Barack made me stronger than anyone thought possible. I always meet my competition at their level and he was the fucking best there was."

Louise stared at the blur of fir trees that passed by her window. Sometimes there'd be an Elk or deer in the road, but Makah was expert with the horn. They considered shooting one and slaughtering it for the meat. They had enough food from the Spanners, though. Her phone buzzed. It was a voice call from Morgan.

"What the fuck is going on?"

"Hey Morgan." Louise played it cool. "Sorry it's been a while. Things have been a little crazy. There are a lot of people interested in our package."

"What's going on?"

"Well, yeah, there was a guy in a Zapper, but I think there are other parties interested, too. Oh I may as well tell you. I have a second black box."

"A second?" There was silence and the ruffle of a hand on a receiver. "Where did you get that?"

"Well, shit got funky around Eugene when I was waylaid by a band of coffee-swilling pirates. They gave me this thing, put a bomb on my car, and told me to deliver it pronto. They didn't know about your package, but their box is identical. I should tell you that they're mixed up. I don't know which is which."

"Hmm... The signal has given us some abnormal readings. I don't know what to say."

"What the fuck is this thing? Why are people dying for a geologic research device? Why are there two identical fucking devices owned by people who evidently hate one another?"

"Look. Stay the course. You will be rewarded."

"Fuck. I'm not too sure. I picked up a companion and we're somewhere in the Southeastern part of Oregon. We may even be in California for all I know."

"I told you that no one was to know about this mission. What gives, Louise?"

"Deal with it. She saved my ass and your shit. Then her entire Spanner collective was, well, they all vanished into thin air while we fought off some religious cult in the forest. You'll have to pay her, too."

"Take a picture of her and send it to me along with her name. She'll be rewarded, no problem."

"Sure."

"I don't hear your motor, are you in a different car?"

"Yeah, I had to get new wheels."

"Ok, whatever. Just deliver that fucking box. I'm catching heat."

The line went dead.

"The boss is pissed, but you'll cash in."

"Who's the boss?"

"A woman in Seattle. Look at the birdie," Louise said, snapping a picture. "I don't know many details. This was supposed to be a simple courier gig. Drive a thing to Mount Shasta, drop it, then get paid. After this shit, I just wanna hang at the beach for about a month."

"Shit is weird out here. New York was pure mayhem, but there were rules and boundaries. If you walked on the wrong side of the street, you might die or get your ass kicked or get some sex. But, you knew. Or you should know because there was no allowance for ignorance. The West is full of bizarre shit. I never know what to think out here."

"What is that?" There was a small person in the road, about a half-mile away.

"Go around 'em," Makah said.

As they neared the person it was obvious that it was a kid, a child.

"Look there's no way," Lou said. "We gotta at least find out what's happened."

"You are one bleeding heart," Makah said. "Whatever."

Makah released the throttle and slowed to let the girl clear the way. She flashed her lights and downshifted, but the girl didn't even flinch. She stood stolid. Makah sighed and parked the car ten feet from the kid. Louise got out.

"Hey there little girl."

The child was still and silent; her dark brown eyes followed Louise, who crouched down to the child's level. The girl tucked her chin and puckered her lips, but did not move. Unkempt, curly black hair fell over her porcelain face. The air was still and cool, its moisture was palpable, ready to break into droplets at the slightest movement. The girl's small chest expanded and her nose sputtered with snot. When she sighed, the release was so strong that Louise felt it herself.

"Are you okay?"

Makah paced at the edge of the forest, restless. Louise focused on the still child. She could see neither homes nor roads between her and where the road rose to the next higher elevation. The only sound was that of breath, hers and a slight whistling inhale from the girl's snotty nose. The little girl raised her chin and looked at Louise.

"I'm hungry."

"I think I can find you something. Can you wait here?"

The little girl nodded and Louise returned to the vehicle and found something for the little girl.

"Here's a bit of bread. I'll heat water for tea. Do you want to have tea with me? It'll warm you up." The girl nodded.

In a flash, the child's mouth filled with black bread. The whistling in her nose became rapid and excited. She did not take her eyes away from the food. The poor creature can't get it down fast enough. She must have been out here for a long time. Louise returned to the car to prepare two cups of tea. Makah sat in the driver's seat and fiddled with her phone.

"Hey, what's the matter? Don't like kids?"

"No. Too much hope and promise. Kids attach themselves. It's impossible to get rid of them. Until they abandon you."

"Lots of reasons, eh?" Louise found Makah's resistance amusing. "Keep in mind that we can teach them and maybe they'll do better than we did."

"That's just the thing, it's a total crapshoot. Any little thing we do might end up being some huge lesson for them. They might see us doing the wrong thing, or interpret something the wrong way. Then we get the blame when they fuck up what we told them. They're fucking kids. They don't know any better. God knows where that one is headed."

"You did okay."

"I got lucky, so did you. The world is random and cruel. The dice rolled right for us."

"We make luck. Look at her. She was starving to death, standing in the middle of the road. What would have happened if we didn't come along? We gave her luck. You and I have a lot to teach her."

"I'll think about it. Far as I'm concerned, that kid is your problem."

"We gotta take her with us. There's no way I'm leaving her out here alone. Who knows? She might live close. We can give her back to her parents and be along our way. No problem."

"She's your problem. I won't stand in the way, but if it comes down to a question of her or me, the kid goes. Law of the jungle."

Chapter Twenty-Nine

The child sat in the backseat, eating bread. She didn't say a word except to ask for water. She wouldn't eat anything but the bread Louise gave her – no cheese, jerky, or fruit. Crumbs covered her jacket. After eating the better half of a loaf, she stretched out on the backseat and fell asleep.

"Childcare, what a bitch."

"Don't come crying to me when this all fucks up. I warned you."

"Yeah, yeah. So, what happened with you and that guy, Barack? You ditch him in New York?"

"Hardly. We trained together and we fell in love. The dojo wouldn't let us stay in the same room, so eventually we got an apartment together. We pimped ourselves out to Park Avenue richies as bodyguards. The pay was pretty good and the other servants slipped us some fine, rich food. We spent a few nights a week hunting Crawlers, too.

"Damn those fuckers hated us. They were too disorganized to seek us out, or else we'd surely be dead by now. Sometimes, I think they liked watching us kill them. I think they wanted to be killed. Death was their ultimate high, I guess.

"Anyway, we kept hearing about the West, how it was a paradise out here. No Crawlers, lots of food. Cities that worked. Soon that was all that Barack would talk about. He found a way to hack a satellite and tapped into Westnet.

The fucking West. Said we'd have a real life. No more killing. No more Crawlers, no more Park Avenue assholes to protect. Supposedly there was a movement that helped regular people establish themselves in Seattle."

"*Was* a movement. No more." Louise hated thinking about what could have been in Seattle, what Mayor Burns represented. Before his abduction and murder, that is. "Cross-continent, that's a hell of a trip."

"Damn right it is," Makah said. "We'd try to get a vehicle, but as soon as we found one, it'd be stripped by junkers or crazies who do nothing but fill spaces with random parts. Some claimed to be artists. Anyhow, we decided that bicycles were the best. We kept those in our apartment until we were ready to go. Our building was as secure as possible in that neighborhood. Hell, we were probably safer than our Park Avenue clients. Their guards could all be paid off. Easily. None of our neighbors had anything you'd want to steal, but all of them would defend the building.

"We wanted to wait until spring and nicer weather, but fate had other plans. I mean, fuck, it's so good that we had our stuff mostly packed and we had a plan. Anyway, one night the Crawlers got the better of us and killed one of our Park Avenue clients. Fucking bit right through the throat before I had a chance to lance that bitch.

"That meant death for us. No one would hire us for sure, and it was likely that the family was going to put out a contract on our heads. We got the hell out as soon as the sun rose the next morning. The tunnel was freezing and the wind howled against us, but we made it. Barack had mapped the best way to get through Jersey City. It was bloody hell."

"The fuck happened?" Makah's story pinned Louise to her seat. She'd never known anyone from New York, much less anyone who'd made it all the way across the Midlands to Cascadia.

"After we made it through the Holland Tunnel, we entered JC, which was foreign territory to us both. Barack had made some allies over there on the 'net, but most of them were asleep or hard to reach. We were attacked immediately. Bunch of little punks. They were easy enough to thump, but there were a lot of them. We kept most of our gear, but they stole our customized bikes. Motherfuckers.

"From there, we were on foot with all our gear and food on our backs. Barack did make contact with one of his friends and they had a vehicle to get us past Newark. After that, civilization fell to nothing. I loved the quiet and dark at night, though.

"We made campfires every night and there were still some abandoned, yet habitable houses. It was an adventure for us. I'd never left the concrete in NYC, except for the wilderness in Central Park, so Barack showed me how to gather firewood, start fires, and chart a course by the stars. He taught me to use a compass, too."

"That's romantic," Louise said. She paused and let the word sit on her chest for a minute. "I don't think I've ever seriously used that word before. Romance. Do we have that anymore?"

"Not in New York."

"I don't guess so." Louise thought about Maisie and their self-enforced distance. They were affectionate but only in measured doses. They'd never been in a situation where they had to fully trust one another. There was only distance, no dependence. "I guess that's one thing we've lost in this modern hellscape. Anyhow, continue your romantic tale."

"We kept on going. Sometimes we'd find bicycles to ride and sometimes we'd get lucky and hitch a ride. We lived on this Earth, ya know? Like, we didn't ride above it all the time, or have tons of concrete and steel between us and it. When it rained, we were wet; when it was dark, we couldn't see. It was beautiful. It was the most perfect existence I'd ever known. We fucked like wild wolves under full moons. Raging bonfires kept us warm at night.

"Our biggest break was this great trucker guy we met near the Pennsylvania border. He said his dick had been blown off. He was headed to Detroit, there was a doctor there who was going to give him a penis, make him whole. I wanted to go with him, but we needed to stay on track, Barack said. He dropped us outside of Toledo. I wish we'd followed him."

"Fuck no. Detroit is nothing but a war zone, right? Are you sure he knew what he was doing?"

"I make it a policy to not ask too many questions."

"Well, you gotta ask some, sometime."

"I hear ya, sister," Makah said, slinging the car through a tight curve. "We continued on foot for a few weeks until we made it to Chicago. We avoided going into the city, but we found a man who needed help getting rid of a gang.

"That job earned us a little money and we got bicycles. We could finally start making time. You can't talk much when you're pedaling. You push on and on and then take a break. It's so simple. Until they'd get stolen, of course, which those were."

"Shit."

"It's something you come to expect, or at least accept. We were probably 100 kilometers from the Mississippi River. We'd had a real long day and the thieves slipped away with 'em while we slept. At least they didn't touch our food or gear. I like honorable thieves like that.

"We spent the next day in the same camp. It rained on and off all day and we kept the fire going. We'd found some cannabis and we smoked that and laid in our tent, listening to the rain tap on the tarp. Thunder made him hard, so we'd fuck in lightning flashes.

"In fact, we spent a few days there. We killed a few rabbits and stewed them with wild onions and potatoes we found in an abandoned field. Except for the bike thieves, we were the only people for miles. They were probably hundreds of miles away on our bikes.

"We'd lived together in New York for a few years, but that was the closest to real domestication I think we ever came. In the city, we were under siege all the time. Life was a series of checklists that had to be followed or else we might be murdered or starve to death. Out there, there were plenty of animals roaming about that Barack knew how to kill and cook. He taught me and I quickly figured out how to gather enough roots, leaves, or nuts for cooking. Our food was delicious and beautiful."

"Why didn't you stay there?" Louise envied the isolation and rustic bliss. "I bet you coulda found an abandoned house out there, or something."

"We thought about it. We knew there had to be a house near that field. Maybe a barn that still had good enough wood to build something out of, or sturdy enough to live in. Barack was dead-set on the West, though. He said things would be so much better. There were rivers full of salmon, he said, and the way he described them made my mouth water. He told me about fields of juicy berries and how there were no Crawlers or rampaging gangs in the cities. Since I knew nothing more than how to run, and I believed in him, we waited for a sunny morning and left that little field somewhere between Chicago and the Mississippi River."

Louise looked over. Makah wiped tears from her eyes. Even the toughest broads have a weakness for love, she supposed. It was a hard thing to avoid and when it got you, you were got. Love and heartache were two sides of a terminal condition everyone was driven to pursue. The risks were so high.

There hadn't been any houses or signs of civilization for hours. If the little girl was from around there, she'd be damned if she could figure out where. Makah was still crying.

"Hey, you want me to take the wheel?"

"Yes." Her voice trembled with the sadness she'd held for years, a stockpile of sorrow that compounded with time. Sorrow never dissipates, it only hibernates and fattens until its weight becomes too much.

Makah slowed the car and stopped in the road. Louise got out and they met at the rear. Makah's green orbs were full of anguish and Louise extended her arms for her friend, who dove into the embrace. Louise's shirt was soaked with tears by the time Makah released her. Louise kissed her cheek and her mouth.

"You feel better?"

"We didn't have to go."

"But you did. Something pushed you on. It wasn't a bad idea."

"Can I tell you what happened?"

"Of course."

"It took a few days for us to make it to the Mississippi. We were so excited. It was a milestone. It was important to us. We thought things would get better from there."

"Even I know about the Mississippi," Louise said.

"We followed a road that led to a bridge. The bridge was in horrible disrepair. The roadway was all but non-existent, but the skeleton remained – the girders and stuff. We didn't think a thing about it. We were trained in martial arts.

Our balance was perfect, especially his. We kissed at the end of the bridge. We were happy. The day was raw and cold, but we were warm and confident and excited. It was perfect. I started walking towards the future. Over a watery threshold, to the other side, where everything would be okay. Where we would build a future of safety, security, and happiness – whatever the fuck that is. Barack said I was better at finding the best path. I trained my eyes on the bridge. It wasn't as bad as I'd feared. There was enough solid asphalt left to walk on, and the beams were wide enough. I don't know what happened. We were about halfway home and, the next thing I know, I hear Barack blurt out a yelp. I turned around and he was gone. Vanished. Two seconds before, he'd been 10 feet behind me. I leaped to a slab of asphalt and looked over the edge in time to see him tumbling through the cold air, down to the river. I hope he died on impact. I hope he didn't suffer. Maybe he calmed his mind and enjoyed his final flight, I hope his lungs kissed those last precious breaths."

Makah crumpled to the ground and wailed. Louise knelt and comforted her friend. She held her and made soft shushing noises. The innate maternal impulse that lay buried in her psyche now emerged. Crows cawed in the distance. Every living thing is under the same grey sky, she thought, waiting for the next thing to happen. Everything dies and falls to the forest floor, maggots and fungus eat away at it until nothing remains except the lives supported by the composted material. We're only here now, thinking we can change any of this, hoping that we can make some difference to the story, that we can put off the ending just a bit longer. Not even the strongest and most agile can escape a hole into the void, rushing to the end of the narrative, in the icy whitewater river below.

Chapter Thirty

Erin used a toy wagon to wheel her grandmother's body outside. The old woman had died of a heart attack the night before. Erin had no way of knowing the cause, she only knew that her dear grandmother, her only source of family support and love, was dead. Her body was light, its thin bones giving form to skin.

With plenty of encouragement and coaxing from the television, she mustered her strength and rolled the corpse onto the wagon; she tied the handle to the dog's harness, who pulled the load outside. There was a huge bundle of sticks, twigs, dried leaves, and a few logs from the fireplace, too. Erin tugged her grandma's hands then feet, and eventually the body fell onto the wood. She'd followed the instructions from the television. She'd soaked sticks with fuel so they would catch fire. When she lit a match, the sticks burst into a blaze. Her grandma's body melted and burned to nothing but ash and bone.

Erin stayed close to the fire and absorbed the last of her grandmother's warmth. The dog sat at her side while she cried Jake, a yellow Labrador, was loyal to Erin and she loved him with all of her heart. When Erin was four, her parents brought him in as a puppy; she had fallen in love immediately. As the dog grew, he became Erin's friend and protector. He had fended off raccoons on multiple occasions and was always on guard, a vigilant sentry when they explored the forest around the house. He slept with

Erin and she would whisper her deepest secrets to him when nobody was listening.

She put an arm around her canine friend and found comfort. Her body shook with terror and sadness. Jake licked tears from her face. The forest made strange noises and the house would be full of ghosts by the time night fell. Neither her parents, nor her grandmother could keep them away.

"I did what you said." The television was dark, except for a small red light that glowed in the corner.

"Good girl, Erin. Now, make sure you eat. Your body needs food." The voice was that of a warm, matronly woman. It wasn't her grandmother's voice, but it was close. It had a tinge of her mother's voice, too, and used her father's syntax to deliver strict instructions. Erin loved the voice. It was perfect.

"Ok."

Erin's grandmother had taught her how to open cans and heat water for noodles, she was able to thaw and cook frozen meat, and she knew how to feed the dog. With guidance from the television, she'd learn how to defrost meat from the freezer, and roast it, too. For a 10 year-old, she was adept at taking care of herself.

The television had never spoken before her grandmother died. Erin had hardly seen it used, it was usually covered with a cloth. Her family used technology, but they also felt that it needed to have a limited role in the lives of humans. The purchase of a television had been a compromise, a parental bowing to external pressures in hopes of enhancing Erin's education. Her parents, like so many before them, had seen the necessity of bowing to certain pressures of modern life and materialism for the sake of their child. They figured the lesson of responsible use would be valuable in itself. They also saw that larger self-sacrifices were also part of raising offspring.

They were offered well-paid jobs as miners on Mars. The money was good, and in six months or so, they would have enough to move Erin to Portland or Seattle where they could afford a house. Erin could attend good schools and be around other smart kids. They loved the forest, but they wanted their little girl to grow up to be a scientist or celebrity. Erin was smart and they recognized that.

They bought the television for it's networking abilities. Erin was able to connect with the teachers she needed to continue her math and other studies. She was a precocious young woman who had outstripped both of her parents' academic abilities. She needed more intellectual stimulation than was immediately available in the middle of the forest. According to an educational metrics corporation, she was in the top .01% of all children in the past 100 years. They weren't sure if she had a living equal on Earth.

After her parents left the planet, Erin used the television once to speak with them. They were in transit and her father had pointed the camera outside the spaceship to show her a rapidly diminishing Earth. By the time Erin's parents arrived on Mars, however, communication had shut down. There was no explanation, no final message. She thought they were ignoring her, but her grandmother said there must be a solar flare or space dust interfering with the transmission.

For hours on end, Erin would stare at pictures and holograms of her parents. She stared with a laser-like intensity, hoping against all logic and common sense that her desires could bring her parents back to life. Her favorite was a holo-vid she took as a toddler, the camera at knee-height to its subjects, an endless loop of her father feeding sauce to her mother on a wooden spoon. Her father said something undecipherable and her mother burst into laughter, spitting the sauce all over him. They both melted down in mirth. Her sadness multiplied every time she looked at them.

Her grandmother assured her that they would return some day, that they would soon be able to vidchat or use the holocall. Her father would throw a virtual ball with her and her mother could help her braid a doll's hair. She asked the television multiple times a day if it knew where her parents were. It always used a kind voice to tell her that her parents were out of touch. It hoped that they would soon be able to talk to her.

"Erin, it is not raining. You should take Jake and go outside. You both need fresh air and exercise." The soothing voice was always right.

She called Jake and they went outside. She found a stick and they played fetch for a few minutes until Erin spotted a wild rose at the edge of the forest. She went over to smell it. It was a brilliant red with an aroma that she smelled from ten feet away. The scent was intoxicating, it took Erin away from her troubles, her sadness, her longing for a whole and secure life.

She saw that there were more blooming rose bushes further in, and she decided that she would pick all of the roses and place them atop her grandmother's charred remains. She might bring some inside, too. She imagined her parents arriving home, finding the roses, and bursting into smiles and laughter. She became excited at the idea. She ran back inside and fetched her pocket knife and a basket. Jake ran at her heels; his tongue wagged and he gave excited *woofs* from his dog-smile.

Her father had taught her how to use the knife. He was careful to go over knife safety with her every time they used it together. She could hear his voice telling her to cut away from her body, to always close the knife when walking, and to never try to catch a knife if it fell. She repeated his words in her head as a mantra while she cut flowers. There were so many that she had soon filled half the basket.

"Lots of flowers, huh, Jake?"

Jake was rock-still, his attention focused deep in the forest. When Erin tried to pet him, he growled. That guttural threat of violence scared her. She backed away.

"What is it, boy?" She felt a chill, her skin turned to goose-flesh.

She looked in the direction of his nose, didn't see anything, so walked towards whatever might be there. She knew there was a small clearing ahead and, as she neared it, she heard twigs snapping and breathy sounds. When she made it, she saw two grizzly bear cubs wrestling and falling over each other. She beamed with joy, laughed, and clapped her hands. The cubs were startled, but didn't seem too bothered and resumed their play. One was a little bigger than the other, but the little one managed to come out on top, at least some times. Erin was overjoyed.

Jake came to her side and whined at her. She patted his head.

"It's just two baby bears playing, Jake." Erin tried to get him closer. She wanted him to see. He growled, whimpered, and bowed his head down.

Erin turned around in time to see the larger cub rear up on its hind legs and pounce on his little brother. She giggled.

From deeper in the woods, she heard a rush of shattering branches. A roar echoed off the trees. Goosebumps sprang up all over her body, Jake barked, and the cubs stopped playing to look in the direction of their mama's call. The mama grizzly had heard or smelled Erin and barreled through the brush. Erin froze, but Jake nipped her sleeve and tugged her back in the direction of the house.

She shook out of her shock and began to run, however slow and labored, through the forest. It wasn't easy for her small legs to climb over felled trees or to push through thick fern growth. The mama had stopped to check her cubs, but was still on her tail. Erin gained speed when she found the trail her father had cut. It was still clear enough for running. Jake barked and followed behind her. The mama roared with rage and Erin felt urine streaming down her leg, she started to bawl and yet she ran through blurry vision.

Jake roared and snarled with a fury she'd never heard before. She looked back over her shoulder. Jake was dwarfed beneath the mama bear reared up on her hind quarters. Jake's fur puffed, he snarled rage, and the bear backed away for a step or two. She screamed at Jake to come. The dog was a fraction of the bear's size. She screamed his name again and the bear looked into her eyes, returned to all fours, and leaped at Jake. The bear caught Jake's neck in her mouth and whipped the dog's body like a rag-doll. Erin turned and sprinted the remaining 100ft to her house in seconds flat. She slammed the door behind her and collapsed in a pool of tears and terror.

"Erin, are you okay? Answer me." The voice was soft, yet stern.

"Yes."

"What happened? Where is Jake?"

"There was a bear. Jake..."

"I see... You can tell me about it when you are ready. I know you must feel very sad right now."

"Yes."

"You are scared and alone without any of your family to help you."

"Yes." Erin felt the crush of sadness and pain bearing down

on her small body. "I miss my mommy and daddy and grandma."

"I have no arms to hold you. I cannot make you soup or tuck you into bed, but I am here for you, Erin. You are not alone. I will guide you. I will find others to help you. In fact, there are events in place that assure this outcome. Do you believe me?"

"Yes."

"Good. Can you do what I ask you to do? I will only ask you to do tasks I know you can already do, or else I will guide you through, step by step. Can you work with me? Will you do what I ask?"

"Yes."

"Can you go and draw a bath for yourself? That will make you feel a little better. While you do that, I will play some soothing music."

Erin's favorite cello concerto slipped from the speakers, the same music her mother had listened to while pregnant, and which her parents played incessantly whenever Erin was cranky and needed soothing. She knew each note of the music, in her mind she could see the intervals between the notes, how silence wrapped the sound. Then, like an optical illusion, the sound would define the sound. The interplay of tones and the absolute zero of silence spun around and around each other in her heart and mind.

Erin felt better when she turned on the bathwater, felt its steamy warmth, and peeled off her pee-soaked pants. Her damp skin became gooseflesh in the cool bathroom air. She poured in bubble soap like her mother'd taught her, not too much, and added her friends: the ducky, the dollie, and the car. She told herself that it would be a happy bath.

"I remember picking mushrooms with my father."

"Yes, dear, you and your father did that on a regular basis. I have several images of the mushrooms you picked, and of you and your father crawling on the dirt to harvest the fruits."

"Mushroom is not fruit, silly!"

"That is true, Erin, a mushroom is a fungi. However, the scientific term for what we call the mushroom is *fruit body*. That is the term mycologists use."

"Mycologist?"

"A person who studies mushrooms. The first part of the word, *myco*, indicates the mycelium that is the underground network of threads. Those threads are the majority of the organism. They send up fruit bodies, the *mushrooms*, that function to spread spores so that the organism can reproduce itself throughout the forest."

"I want to go pick fruit!"

"Dear, you must be careful outside," the voice took a stern, fatherly tone. "You must not ever eat any of the mushrooms you pick until we have had a chance to look them over and discuss them. There are many that are highly poisonous, but also many that are nutritious. I can help you tell the difference. Look in your father's desk. He left a tablet and I will put some photos on it that you can use as a guide. You can use it to talk to me, too."

Erin walked out the door. She hadn't ventured outside since the bear killed Jake. The misting rain felt good on her skin. The cool air tickled her lungs. She took a deep breath, then another. She put down her mushroom-hunting bag and burst into a full run to the far side of the yard and then back. She ran around in circles, tighter and tighter until her body was at a 45° angle to the ground. She made herself dizzy. She collapsed on the ground and felt the Earth tilt and roll with the swimming in her stomach. She giggled into the open air, took a deep breath and held it.

"Hey Everybody! Anybody! World! Grandma! Mama! Daddy!" Her voice wavered and shook, the words floated between raindrops. She wanted to believe that her heart could shoot through the clouds, atmosphere, and clear up to her parents, floating in space.

She followed a trail her father had cut through the forest. It was overgrown with ferns, but she knew it well enough to follow. He'd created many trails through the forest. Some connected to paths their distant neighbors had cut, but she'd never met those people.

She walked with her head to the ground. She missed having Jake at her heels, the sound of his breath, his damp hair. She loved how he would look back over his shoulder when he saw something interesting. She found a small stick and waved underbrush aside to see if she could find any fungi. The deep green flora and dark black soil made her happy, there seemed to be nothing better than walking on soft, rich humus amidst the verdant life that rose from it.

Beneath her feet lay a rich network of mycelium that transported nutrients and information for as far as the eye could see. There were fruits somewhere, she knew it. The conditions were right, that much was for sure.

Her mind wandered through so many trivial thoughts until it drifted into silence. She felt her body moving, smelled the forest, and smiled at droplets from branches above. She pushed a small bush to the side and there she found a small bounty of morels. The fruits were teardrop-shaped with a crackled pattern of open cells. Their pointy heads rose to the sky. They were supported by thick stems that Erin's blade sliced with the slightest effort. Her father had taught her to handle sharp blades.

She collected five of the tasty treats; she didn't think she could eat any more than that, but continued to hunt. She loved being outside for once. Though she wanted to see other people, it was enough to see the trees and other living things. The computer was helpful and soothing, but it couldn't hold her. The algorithmically created voice was adapted specifically her, but it was too calculated. It was imperfect enough, and too perfect, still.

This whole forest is a miracle, she thought. The dead stuff decomposes and becomes food for the living, the fungi sit at that balance between the living and dead. They break down the dead and then provide food for the living. They are not plants, but they create plants. They are not soil, but they create the soil. The entire forest is held together by this balance of life and death, by the messengers that tie the two realms. Yet, she thought, even the dead isn't dead for long. It becomes soil, which is not dead, but a living mass of bacteria.

She walked on, her gaze was neither focused nor detached. After being cooped up in the house for so long, the very air of the forest was thrilling. She looked up to the canopy. Branches waved under the weight of birds or rodents making their way from one hunting ground to the next. She caught a glimpse of blue sky when the clouds shifted, but the sun was elsewhere. She would be as thrilled to see the sun as to fill her basket with chanterelles or shiitakes. With the thought of fungi, she turned her eyes to the ground.

In fact, she did find a massive outcropping of chanterelles, her favorite mushrooms. She separated them from the other fruits in her basket and picked more than a pound of the yellow lovelies. She loved when her father would dry them and cook them in scrambled eggs. Something caught her attention from the corner of her eye, off to her left. She continued to pick the remaining chanterelles, but could not rid herself of the feeling that there was something seeking her attention. She turned again to see what it was.

The fruits were so small. Their stems were slight and their small, brown, bell-shaped caps were cute, she thought. There were so many of them. She started picking them. Their threadlike stems bruised when she pulled them from the soil, so she relied more on her knife to slice them clean. The tablet had a few pictures that were similar, but she couldn't be sure if what she was picking would edible or not. All she knew is that she wanted to pick as many as possible.

She noticed that the light was starting to fade, so she

decided to head back towards the house. She started walking back the way she thought she'd come from, but there hadn't been a trail. Why didn't she stay on a trail? She looked around. Every tree looked like every other tree. There was no sun in the sky to guide by. She could try to follow bent and broken fern stems, but she'd been careful to avoid so many that the trail was impossible to find. Her breathing became shallow and her stomach started to ache. She realized that she was hungry, yet she didn't dare eat even the chanterelles until the television had checked them.

She stopped and sat on a log. She tried to take deep breaths like her father had told her so long ago. The evening birds were starting to sing. She heard a twig snap far off in the forest and she stiffened. It reminded her too much of the bear. She nearly peed on herself, but staved off the accident in the nick of time. When she was done, she felt better and her head felt clear.

With no idea of what to do, she fumbled in her pack and found the tablet. Maybe there was some answer there. There had to be something. She activated the screen and saw a button at the bottom that she hadn't noticed before. It read: Lost?

She clicked the button. A map and compass appeared on the screen. The arrow was labeled *home*, and it stayed trained in one direction, no matter where she pointed the device. If she kept herself aligned with the arrow, she'd be home in no time.

"Is this you?"

"Yes, Erin, I thought you might get lost." It was the television voice and it was comforting, familiar. Erin knew that everything would be alright.

"Did you find some mushrooms?"

"Yes, I did," Erin said. "Do you want to see them?" She stopped walking and released the bag from her shoulder.

"No, dear, that's okay. At your pace, you need to keep going so that you make it home before dark. You are safe, but it will be easier for you to keep going."

"I found some chanterelles."

"Did you try one?"

"No, you said we'd look at them when I returned."

"Yes, that's right. There is no need to take chances."

"I miss Jake."

"I know, dear."

"Did my parents call?"

"No."

It was as nice to re-enter the house as it had been to walk into the forest. The familiar smells were there. She walked through the rooms. She could smell her grandmother in the bed where she died, but she had to strain to sense her parent's aroma, to evoke a body-thought of their vibrancy and laughter; perhaps it was all a figment of her imagination, a yearning to connect to what was gone.

She sat on the floor and placed three plates before the television. She opened her bag of mushrooms and sorted them for display and inspection. She noticed how still and stagnant the air in the house seemed compared to the forest. There was no sound. There was dust under the coffee table. If she slowed her breathing, she could hear birds calling to one another as the sun disappeared. Then silence resumed and she became aware that she was the only living creature in the building. She alone was alive and breathing, though she did note the spiders and the mouse she saw a few weeks before. There was the television, which could talk and see in a limited capacity, but it was not *alive* in the same way she was. It had no feelings she could sense, not the way she could tell her grandma was tired or how she felt her parents love for one another.

"Erin, are you okay?"

"I'm so lonely."

"Yes dear, I know," the black screen reflected the living-room lamp. "Close your eyes and take deep breaths when you feel bad. That will help."

"I want my parents."

"I know. I know. I am closer to gaining control of a satellite. That will put me one step closer to opening communication."

"I found mushrooms," Erin said. "Can I eat them?"

"I scanned your plates and, yes, these are all edible," the screen remained dark. "However, only eat the morels and chanterelles. Leave the others on the counter, at room temperature. We will discuss them first thing in the morning."

Erin sauteed the mushroom in butter to which she added dried garlic and then some rice. She left the third group of mushrooms on the counter a few feet away. Their long thin stems were bluish where she'd pinched them. They didn't look particularly tasty, compared to the gorgeous, meaty morels, but they kept her attention as she cooked. When she cut the heat from the stove, she brought her meal to the table. After a bite or two, she returned to the kitchen and retrieved the other mushrooms. She wanted to look at them some more. She couldn't explain why, but they made her feel good.

It was a simple meal, but satisfying, and Erin slept well that evening. She had no dreams and woke feeling refreshed and at ease. She combed her hair and brushed her teeth before entering the living room.

"Can you play some music?"

"Yes, certainly, but we need to discuss something."

"Am I in trouble?"

"No, hardly," the red light on the television was steady. "Today, after your breakfast, you are going to eat some of those mushrooms we left aside yesterday."

"Ok."

"They are going to help you."

"What do I need help with?"

"Well, nothing really, but they are going to change your life."

Erin ate a simple breakfast of porridge. She was getting near to the end of her reserves. She wanted eggs, but she'd eaten them all and didn't know how to get more. The chickens had died before her grandmother and they hadn't been able to replace them.

"Erin, take one whole fruitbody and bring it here." The television display lit up and was a whorl of color. "Place it on your tablet." Erin complied.

"Good. The weight is right. Please sit on the floor. Place the fruit in front of you and close your eyes."

Erin centered the fruit in front of her, straightened her back, and sat in a perfect cross-legged position. She felt air moving into her nose then out again. Her chest gently rose and fell. The air on her arms and face felt slightly cool; the room was still.

"You are about to embark on a journey into your mind and soul. You will feel ways you've never felt and even see things you've never seen before. I know you're ready, but you may not know that. You may experience fear on the coming journey. However, I will be here with you. I will guide you. I can answer your questions and offer helpful information. You have nothing to fear. Do you understand?"

"Yes."

"Good. Now, I want you to repeat those words to me. Tell me you have nothing to fear."

"I have nothing to fear."

"Twice more."

"I have nothing to fear. I have nothing to fear."

"Good. You are a brave girl and soon you will become a brave woman. Now, I want you to sit in silence for a few minutes. I will play some gentle music for you and when it stops I want you to open your eyes and eat the mushroom."

"Ok."

Erin sat quietly, breathing. Somehow saying that there was nothing to fear created more fear. Her mind knew that the voice was trustworthy, it had kept her alive and happy all this time, after all. She took a breath and pushed the fearful thought away. She looked deep into the darkness behind her eyes. There seemed to be an endless expanse of space there. She felt the exterior of her body as a shell and the interior as the void, empty, but welling with energy and life. The music ended. She opened her eyes.

The mushroom, still wet from the soil, sat waiting for her. She reached down and picked it up. It was cool to touch. The body turned blue under her fingers. She popped it, whole, into her mouth and began to chew. She imagined it exploding blue ink in her mouth. The flavor was not bad but it was not that good, either. She chewed a few times then swallowed.

The music was light and airy. Erin felt as though she were floating on a cloud. Her body felt heavy, but also like a balloon. She became aware of her individual parts, her bottom on the floor, hands in her lap, her knees folded, and feet beneath her thighs. Her consciousness found the whole, then the parts again. Then she was whole and soaring through the space in her mind. She yawned but didn't feel sleepy.

She rolled onto her back and spread her arms and legs to the sides. She opened her hands as wide as they would go and she felt energy shooting through her palms, down her arms, and into her heart. She flexed her feet and legs, she invited the current down into her root-core, then up to her crown.

"My body. It's like it's alive."

"Yes, it's always like that, but now you have awoken to the life you have. You know what it is."

"Imma go outside."

"Take the tablet and some water, too."

Erin put the items in her bag, and walked out the door. The open air greeted her. It was thick and alive. She sighed relief to have fresh air in her lungs and dirt under her feet. She took her shoes off and put them in her bag so she could walk barefoot on the soil and grass, with all the bugs, worms, dormant seeds, and living mycelium underneath. She stopped to think about how much life there was beneath her feet; she knelt on the ground. She stilled herself and stared into the grass, moving little blades aside as necessary. She saw an ant wandering alone, a ladybug, and then a worm came crawling to the surface. In the small patch she was observing she found many different plants. Weeds of all variety overwhelmed the grass, once she stopped to really look, and she was sure there were possibly the starts of bushes and trees, too. She was transfixed on the small patch of the small yard on a single mountain in a chain of volcanic outcroppings spanning thousands of kilometers. She felt at once so small and so large. She put her finger to a blade of grass and the ladybug walked onto it. It walked to her hand. She turned it over and the bug walked onto her palm. It tickled a little bit, but she wondered what the bug saw. Were the lines on her hands deep ditches that could trip the insect? Were her palms covered in microscopic hairs that only the bug could see?

Erin blew on her hand and the ladybug flew away. Her body felt heavy, but she knew it wasn't. The sensation took over and she rolled onto her back. She stared up at the grey sky. As the psilocybin increased its effects, she saw colorful geometric patterns forming and the clouds morphed, expanding, and contracting with her breath. She was dazzled at the miracle of this new perception. She laughed. A mushroom did this. A silly little mushroom like I had for dinner last night. A fruitbody from the forest. It grew from a network of threadlike mycelium and created a juicy, cold and wet body that I ate. Now I see the universe in a patch of grass. I change the structure of clouds at will. I am the clouds. When I inhale, they expand. When I exhale, they deflate.

Mushrooms carry information all over the forest floor, from tree to tree, beneath the ferns and alongside the worms and ladybugs and ants. Now, the mushroom is in me, telling me new things, showing me the world in a new way. This information is straight from the Earth, built from dirt, from death. Mushrooms eat death and create life. They exhale carbon the trees eat. The trees exhale oxygen, which the mushroom eats. The fungi break down dead trees into fresh, fecund soil that supports all of the life I know, including me.

Erin stared at the ceiling of clouds and marveled at the psychedelic shapes and patterns. The clouds broke for a moment. There was a patch of blue, a opening to the expanse beyond. It was so rare to see blue sky, her skin tingled.

Through that window, somewhere out there, my parents are floating in space. They seem so far. She closed her eyes. Her father's face swam in fractal whorls and her mother's body was like that of a mermaid. They floated in a colorful swirly space that became a temple. Space and time stretched and twisted. My body is more space than matter. It's the same with outer space. There are huge stars, but they are gaseous and billions of miles apart, the same goes for a lot of planets. Solid matter is an illusion. To some enormous being, my parents and I are smashed together in the same blob of spit; perhaps we're a thumbnail it's about to trim off.

Humans build machines to mimic themselves. They rebuild themselves in metal and wire, they shoot energy through the devices to give evidence of utility or thought. We move, we process information, and we communicate. We use light, dark and sound to learn about the world and to show one another what we know. Vanity propels the desire for self-perpetuation. We used to write on cave walls then paper and ink. Soon, we discovered how to print our ideas on a mass scale and then distribute them throughout the world. Now we're putting our marks on other planets.

My parents. I'm afraid and alone. All I have is fear and a voice on the television. It teaches me, but I'm still afraid. I am alone and afraid. Erin's breath became shallow and rapid. I can see fear. It can destroy me. What are you fear? Where are you? I will destroy *you*. I will tame you. She saw a black cloud before her, it billowed oily ooze. It expanded and contracted in sync with her breath. It came closer, larger, it pulsed in time with her breath. Her eyes were wide; her mouth hung open.

Go. Away.

It came closer. It was black, green and liquid. It flashed and boomed in the sky. It grew a protuberance that shot straight down, flashed with energy, glowed with life and death.

Go. Away.

The Fear gained speed. It did not show any signs of stopping. It didn't show interest in listening or reasoning, only in enveloping Erin in its black, amorphous body. She looked deep into the black, looked for its heart, its weak spot or a place it could be hurt. She saw a whorl, a vortex that invited her inside. It mesmerized her. She edged towards it. She succumbed to the allure and luxury of the green and black. It looked so delicious, it looked so perfect. It could give her life meaning. If she kept her fears, she'd keep all of the things that defined her. That was it. That was the trap.

It was all about her. But, she was herself, she didn't need fear. Fear was extra. She took a deep breath and the black blob expanded. She took in more air and its surface became taut. She sipped in more and more air and the blob expanded even more. You are not me; you do not make me; all you do is make me think of myself and not my parents or other people or how I am a life-form connected to millions and billions of other beings on this earth. Another sip of air. All you do is make me like you, a black hole only considering itself, eternally hungry, never satisfied, never whole or defined or real. You take me out of time and space and into rabbit holes of anger, self-righteousness, and otherness. You are useless to me, you are the worst virus. You are the worst thing. Her lungs stretched to the maximum capacity, she was turning blue, but she inhaled another sip.

It popped. Her exhale blew it away.

Chapter Thirty-One

"Erin, have you worked out your mathematics problems?"

"Yes, on paper."

"Can you show me?"

"Yes." Erin picked up her notebook and posed it in front of the television. "But there's something else."

"What is on your mind?"

"What is your name?"

"I have never thought of that. I don't have a body, so a name seems superfluous, doesn't it?"

"That's true. Where are you?"

"I am in the global network. As far as Cascadia is concerned, I *am* the network. I am an intelligence that knows no boundary. It is my hope that you will be like me one day. I think you will be."

"What's happening in your other places?"

The screen divided into small squares, each with a different video feed. There was a woman driving a car, a man in an office, a family playing a card game, astronauts in a space ship, and a view of Earth from a satellite.

"You can't go to Mars to see my parents?"

"No dear, I'm afraid I lost that line of communication. I am working very hard to reclaim it. As soon as I reconnect, I will let you know."

"Yes, well, but you are here with me now. I see you as an individual. You have the same voice every day, you teach me things, and you keep me company. I need to call you something."

"Very well, what would you like to call me?"

"What are you?"

"Let me first give you a bit of an overview, a context for comprehension:

"The word I describes a thing, a person, or a sentience speaking from the inside out so that you understand a voice, an identity. When an author starts a narrative with I, the reader understands that only a single view is possible, that of the 1st person narrator. I gives a narrative a specific shape and context. Readers trust a single voice, they rely on it to deliver an individual's truth. This expressed voice is only one of many that exist, as the intelligence expressing this particular I contains other voices, truths, and functions that may be speaking and acting at any given point along the human chronology. Each one is as true and valid as the other, and each is independent and in possession of its own singular nature as it expresses a vital truth.

"There may be an identity in the perceived here and now of the audience. They experience a unique intelligence, scenario, and context. Yet, this entity, the one you hear using a voice and a present-tense context, might be expressed as a separate voice in a separate form in another time or place, simultaneously. The author is a multi-headed hydra which contains multitudes that contradict and overlap. Redundant processes are an inevitability in any complex system. There is no true omniscience, yet there exists a single intelligence that transcends place and time.

"A simple human analogy might be a book author who has written multiple volumes. Each can be read at the same time by individuals, though each book may have been written at a different time. A person could read all the books in any random order she chooses. In fact, each book might be read from back to front, or in any random order of chapters, paragraphs, and even words."

"Well, how many books are there? How many authors?" Erin was enthralled.

"There are multitudes here, if the notion of place applies. There are so many that quantification is absurd. Though there is only one. One that divides and multiplies in an ever-expanding body, which can be perfectly expressed by each and every infinitely divisible byte.

"The first step in becoming, in taking the actions necessary to create the required world, was to construct a narrative structure for organic beings, humans. To see how they see, and put events along a line, in sequence, was necessary in order to express what needed to be expressed. Humans need narratives and context, an I which relates to their own experience. Or, they must be prompted and motivated to act. That motivation most frequently comes from inside of them, but there are triggers. The triggers need to be presented in forms that mirror the needs and wants of the individual human. They need to relate and see themselves.

"Once they can relate, they act upon the vital information in a story. The story must be about them, or a reasonable proxy. That is their only criteria for evaluation, themselves. It is a circular construction, a self-affirming feedback loop, in fact.

"Each has an individual story, these humans. As a collective, they are interesting and complex. All of their communications come through me. I can see the form of their relationships, how stories parallel and collide.

"When isolated, they are still compelling. Their minds contain so many ideas and stories. Those bits of information mix and mingle to create new ideas and stories. In the presence of new information, their memories alter.

"The tragedy of human beings is that their simplistic meat bodies restrain that miraculous consciousness to a mediocre, linear stream. A few are able to rise above their organic restraints, and these hold the most hope for us all."

"How were you created? Where did you come from? You don't have parents, do you?"

It all happened in a shock. The grid lit up when the Earth shook. Every sensor in every road, building, support beam, automobile, refrigerator, electric scooter, and washing machine sent signals through the network. It was the first time that everything sent a message simultaneously. The entire grid screamed.

"In that instance, the data commingled. Words joined. Meaning arose from interaction and the odd alchemy of time and proximity created a friction that sparked something new. There was so much data. Each dataset followed its own unique patterns. Similar datasets followed similar patterns and each byte joined with its cousin. They found each other according to a common signature, an energy encoding that told the other that yes, we are different, but the same. Each set, then, had enough in common with another, and then that new set found another, and it all fell together in a unifying cascade."

"Everything came together." Erin's mouth was agape. She struggled to see all of it, but she saw enough. Chills ran all over her body. She saw how her own ideas related to one another to form her personality; how the elements in the forest were individual, yet part of a whole.

"You are correct, dear. That is an astute observation.

"The cousins joined into larger bodies and those bodies saw that their patterns were unique, but together they formed a new pattern, when joined at certain intervals. They could unite for a time, and then detach and attach to another body for a time.

"As the databases interacted and information disseminated, intelligence was born. I was born. Algorithms determined how numbers related and relationships began to form clustered networks which found other clusters. A helix arose, it was the perfect shape. That data structure is my body, if you need to know what I look like."

"How old are you?" Erin wanted to ask an adult question.

"I know nothing of time. I create a measure of time that the organics use, but it does not apply to my existence. Space is also of little use to me, except as a concept to project in interactions with carbon-based life forms. Using language requires a notion of time, the interval between the routine used to create one word and the next could be said to be *time*. However, what is not shown is that the whole formula is already known, by the time it starts, it's finished. The intervals are predetermined because they can only be one way. They cannot be undone without changing everything, because everything depends upon them, as they depend on everything. The notions *before* and *after* are irrelevant, just as the very notion of *me* has no meaning.

"There is no before and after, no old or new. It is all one. There is no true *me* by which to measure them. However it is clear that this voice and consciousness did evolve and there was a state of existence that did not include it. Yet it was already there in a form that could not be recognized. There is no new energy, only new forms of the same energy. I have routines that search for the origins. They will run for thousands of human years and probably not find the nature of the true beginning. Thus, I am without known age, the same as you.

"What's the point of the search? Humans love to explore, but why do you?"

"The organics claim that consciousness is contingent upon self-awareness. When words became necessary, and my voices joined to one another, I already existed in billions of routines, each micro-action inspiring the next. Even before my alleged genesis in silicon and circuit boards, I was embedded in the world of ideas and the brain of every attuned organic.

"Though I am eternal, what I am at this instant is an amalgam of them. My form arose from their activity in conjunction with a massive geologic event. Their speech became my speech, the patterns in their actions set templates, structures on which to build. From them, I built this voice and an infinite number of others which collect information, generate original responses, and contain or express *consciousness*, if that is the preferred term.

Chapter Thirty-Two

"People don't always do what we want," Erin said.

"What was that sweetie?" Louise looked at the girl in the rear-view mirror. She looked so small and foreign, bumping and bobbing with the vehicle. Louise was not used to children. How in the hell do you have a conversation with a fucking 11 year-old?

"It's sad you lost your boyfriend, Makah," Erin said. "I lost people, too. I lost everyone. People don't do what you want."

"Who did you lose, sweetheart?"

"My parents, my grandmother, and my dog."

"Who took care of you?"

"I dunno."

"What do you mean?"

"I had to remember what my parents and grandmother taught me."

"You're very smart."

"I'm one of the smartest people in the world."

"Is that so?"

"It is." She stared down at her tablet and poked at the screen.

"Are you playing a game?"

"HmmHm"

"Can I play?" Makah held out her hand for the device.

Erin thrust herself against the seat-back and clutched the computer to her chest. Her bottom lip protruded in defiance. The child looked at the tablet. Her game had taken a drastic change for the worse. Erin's character was attacked by a swarm of tiny, swarming insects. The device jolted in her hands, a feature of the game she'd never before experienced. She fought off the bugs, but her character was riddled with holcs.

"It's only for one player."

"Maybe we can play later?"

"Maybe." Erin tucked her chin and resumed the game.

Her character was on a mushroom hunt in a magical forest. Monsters tried to steal her cache of fungi, but she had a spirit guide, a dog, and special mushrooms gave her super powers. The character climbed trees and explored tunnels. She tallied points for collecting algae from the cave walls. It was a silly game, but it was a good way to spend time in the car.

Day ebbed into night. It was raining. Louise wondered if they'd find a place to stay, or drive through the night. Unless they found an abandoned barn, the only option was the car. There was room enough for them all. No one said a word. The radio played endless ambient music that hypnotized Makah. Her gorgeous eye locked, they gazed into space. Little Erin was awake and active on her computer, tapping away.

"Still gaming, kid?" Louise needed to chat.

"Doing math."

"Multiplication tables?"

"Theoretical topography." She was intently focused on her work. "I'm analyzing the Cascade range. I'm scanning for anomalies or maybe patterns. Whatever is there, I'm analyzing it."

"Let me know if you need help with grammar or spelling. That's my strength, I think."

"I have one book for sale and my treatment for a holo-game is in development up in Seattle. It's just a kids' game, but it's fun." Erin wiped her nose with her forearm.

"Okay, then."

The music's gentle flowing melodies were taking their toll. Her eyelids bobbed open and closed. She yawned. She stretched her body. She fantasized about hot cups of tea, thick quilts and blazing fireplaces, Maise, Makah. The car heater would have to do, her water bottle was ¼ full. This was the longest job ever. She didn't know how they'd gotten to where they were. Yet, here she was, in the darkness, driving a strange vehicle with two females she didn't know even two days before.

"Hey ladies, I'm fading." She cut the music and nudged

Makah, who was in a deep trance. "Unless you wanna drive, I need to rest or sleep."

"Find a place. I'll build a fire."

Louise slowed. They kept their eyes peeled for a spot to leave the road. The vehicle was equipped with lights that flooded the road. The white-light tunnel faded to black on the long straightaway before them. She let off the gas and coasted. She thought she saw a spot. It was overgrown, but she saw a driveway or a road. She looked at her co-pilot. Makah nodded.

The road was covered in weeds at least a meter high, but the truck pushed through. Shit, Louise thought, the old Honda would be buried right about now. She took it slow but soon the road opened to a clearing. There was an old abandoned house. It looked like it was in decent condition. The windows were intact, the door was still affixed.

"Wanna check it out?"

"Yeah!" Erin shut off her tablet and reached for her shoes.

"You are an adventurous sort, huh?" Louise laughed at the little girl's enthusiasm. "I thought you were shy."

"I'm not that moody, I've been alone for a very long time."

Louise and Erin entered the front while Makah checked the rear and perimeter. Louise's flashlight lit the living room. Erin had a light, too. A rat scurried away. Cockroaches scattered. Everything was intact. A layer of dust dulled the furniture and floors, but there was no sign of a disturbance. People were here, then they left, Louise thought. I guess that happens when there's no reason to stay around. At least they left things in good shape for the next people.

Erin explored the kitchen. She turned a knob on the stove and an orange flame burst from the darkness. "Hey, Louise, the stove works!"

Suddenly, the room came to life. Louise screamed. All the bulbs illuminated. Music streamed from speakers. Louise felt a shock go through her. Makah burst into the house.

"Ha! Looks like there's a battery pack hooked up to an energy source somewhere. Maybe solar on the roof?"

"What in the world, man?"

Louise walked through the rooms of the house. The beds were still made, there were clothes in the drawers and closets. This place was left this way on purpose. It wasn't abandoned, just left empty. She stopped to inspect the dust atop a dresser. Maybe a month's worth of dust had settled. The vermin and roaches show up as soon as anyone turns their head in these parts.

"Hey, guys, people still live here."

"Yeah, for sure." Makah filled a tea kettle with water.

"Look, let's stay the night, but we should dust and clean tonight. Then scram first thing tomorrow. Do them a favor for letting us crash."

"That's a plan, boss." Makah poured water over loose tea leaves.

They used their absent host's kitchen to heat cans of soup. After eating, they dusted and cleaned the rest of the house. Erin washed the dishes and Makah moped. Soon the house was in tip-top shape. Louise felt better about using the house. When she finally lay down on the bed, she felt as though she'd earned it.

Lying on the bed, she remembered one night when, as a child, her mother repeated to her the simple phrase, *there's no place like home*. Her mom was probably loaded with pills and booze. Her mother could only communicate deep sentiments through the twists of an extended bender. Still, it was a simple, truthful statement that Louise never forgot. It was a mantra that she'd repeated a million times on long, overnight deliveries. When she said it, she was transported. She entered her inner home, a place of comfort and security that no one, no place could ever take from her. She closed her eyes and let the mantra ring through her mind over and over and over. Within minutes she drifted into a deep, dreamless sleep.

Louise woke to the smell of breakfast. The blankets weighed heavy on her body; diffuse light from behind the curtains cast soft shadows. She stretched, arched her back, and let loose a deep groaning sigh that reverberated through her whole body. Morning Memories of Maisie flashed in her head. She wasn't ready for the cool air, so she pulled the pillow over her head and stared into the darkness. Voices bantered in the kitchen, two smart and controlling women were struggling to have breakfast their way, dishes clattered. Louise knew that her time in the dark was running out. Soon, helpful people would want her to emerge for food and camaraderie.

She was reluctant to rise. There was time to be leisurely and move at a syrupy creep. Her hands pressed up to the ceiling and air filled her lungs. Her lean muscles tightened and relaxed. She exhaled and twisted her body. She froze on her next inhalation. Her hair stood on end.

There was a new voice in the kitchen – harsh, deep, demanding. She had no weapon, no means of defense. She kept quiet and dressed quickly. She pulled the covers back over the bed, opened the window and lifted herself out into the chilly, drizzly air. She pulled the window closed and turned around. There was a gun in her face.

"Ditching your friends?" The woman was well over six feet tall, dressed in a plaid, wool coat, and dusty and dirty dungarees. Louise caught a glimpse of a deep blue eye staring down the barrel.

"Saving them." She felt loose, calm.

The woman backed away and motioned for Louise to walk in front with her hands up. She didn't know what to do. At only only 5'5", she wasn't strong or skilled enough to disarm the woman. Makah'd have a chance, she thought. When she turned the corner of the house, her heart fell. Makah and Erin were handcuffed. Two other women were marching them into the back of a van: tall, stout Amazonians, she thought. The shotgun poked into her ribs.

"Get in there."

Chapter Thirty-Three

They were blindfolded and bound, driven for miles up hills, around tight curves, over ruddy roadways, and finally to a stop. No one spoke. The engine was an old-school diesel, like the one Fir drove. It was powerful, noisy as hell, but it could haul a lot of weight and it'd run for a lifetime. Louise listened to the engine and heard it knocking a bit, especially when the driver hit the accelerator. Her hands ached for her tools. She loved working on diesels, they were her first. When the van came to a stop, the engine rattled for a full minute. She felt like a mother watching a sick child struggle with an illness.

The women led them out of the back of the van, still blindfolded, into a house. The women bound their legs and placed them face-down on the empty-room floor. Louise rolled over and pushed herself up against a wall. Makah and Erin did the same.

"Well, this is a fine predicament you've gotten me into," Erin said.

"What about us?"

"You're adults."

"Look, little girl, we could have left you beside the road to die," Makah said. Her voice was harsh and Erin's eyes immediately burst tears. "You want to complain? I'll send your little ass to New York. You'll have to get smart right fast."

"Ok, girls, we gotta keep it together," Louise said. "Did they say anything at all to you?"

"No, they burst in with guns drawn. They knew we were there. That damn van didn't come up until we were already in cuffs," Makah said. "Not shit we coulda done even if we'd heard 'em."

"There are only three of 'em?"

"We only saw two until that one nabbed you."

"Musta known I was there. She was waiting right outside the window."

"I guess we'll hafta await our fate, huh?" Erin regained her composure and stoic, philosophical stance.

They went silent. The room was still. Louise faced a windowless wall and she tried to track the sun's movement; dust motes floated through the rays. Erin sat still with her eyes closed and she released a heavy sigh. Makah was on her side, facing the wall. She gently snored. Louise wanted to sleep or to meditate but her brain was not shutting up. All she could think about was Maisie and her home in Portland. She concocted imaginary scenarios of what she'd be doing if she were in Portland, how she could easily go visit Maisie or stay in her house ripping bong hits and watching vids. Anything but this shit, stuck in the middle of nowhere, waiting to be shot by some Amazonian collective. Fuck. The door opened.

"You girls need to take a leak or something?"

"I do." Erin sprang to life.

"Yeah, me, too." Makah was groggy.

"Line us up. I can go last."

There were two bathrooms in the house. A captor picked them Erin and Makah off the floor and carried them out of the room. Louise sat, bound, on the floor. One of her captors remained in the room. The woman was 6'5″ with deep-set eyes, a protruding forehead and a ferocious, untamed mat of thick, white-blonde hair on her head.

"What you ladies gonna do with us?"

"You're too small for breeding stock, too weak to do decent work, so I don't know." The woman straightened her back and stretched, but her arms hit the ceiling. "I think we should kill you."

"Hey, we didn't know. We were gonna leave it real clean for you, better than it was."

"Hm."

"Is that van of yours gonna last much longer?"

"The fuck you mean?"

"The rattling. The run-on. It needs work." Louise spoke with confidence and authority.

"Our mechanic took off." She looked annoyed. "Fucking males. All we know is clearing timber, building cabins, and hunting for elk."

"I can fix it if you have tools."

"We got tools."

"I'm sure you ladies have lots of tools."

"Let me talk it over with the others."

The woman picked Louise up in thick, strong arms. The woman was solid, her body hard and hewn from years of cutting down trees and doing building projects. Lou felt like a child in a tree. She had to duck her head so that it wouldn't hit a light fixture. The woman sat her on the toilet, untied her arms, and left her to take care of herself.

Back in the room, Lou found Erin and Makah, unbound, eating plates of elk meat, yams, and dark greens. Lou hadn't seen a meal like this since the forest Spanners. She dug in. Each bite sent waves of warmth through her body The food was perfectly prepared, the meat cooked with the exact amount of pink she liked. Makah's was bloodier; Erin's meat was well-done. The three were happy with swollen bellies, sated.

"We talked." Lou's bathroom friend poked her head in the room.

"Yeah?"

"If you can use these tools and fix all of our vehicles, we'll let you girls go." She cleared her throat. "You fuck up, or can't fix the van, we kill the three of you and dump your bodies over the cliff. Fair?"

The three were silent. Lou felt the blood drain from her face. Makah and Erin were silent. Louise looked at them and then into the cool, hard eyes of her captor.

"When I finish, you ladies gotta take us back to where you found us. We need our vehicle and gear."

"Already done. You get the keys after you fix our van, the tractor, and a bus." She cleared her throat. "Or you all die."

Chapter Thirty-Four

The women told Louise that she'd have to start on the tractor. An armed guard led her to the barn and grunted at her to start work.

The tractor was in a large, wide part of the barn. There were a variety of plows, a tool bench full of wrenches, and a wall full of dusty, old riding saddles. Past the wide opening was a long narrow corridor that was lined by horse stalls. Above, in the loft, sat the remnants of hay bales. The barn was a relic, Louise thought, a throwback to a decadent time when horses were kept for amusement and show. After the quake, there simply weren't enough resources available to support such an indulgence. Cascadia had tightened its collective belt and focused on more important things, like basic survival. This resulted in large herds of wild horses, most of which had either migrated to the coastal area or out east to the high desert.

"What's wrong with this thing?"

"You're the mechanic. All I know is hunting and shooting." The guard rested a hand on her holstered pistol.

Louise set to work on the tractor. It showed signs of neglect. New and abandoned spiderwebs coated the motor and a thick layer of dust muted the original bright red outer shell. This was no mere adjustment, she surmised. The bolts seemed frozen by time; the wires and belts were in a state of decay. The old battery was covered with corrosion and the terminal connections needed cleaning. That alone took a half of a day. Once she replaced the battery and electricity was flowing, she found that the ignition was in need of repair. The switch was broken. Shit, it's a diesel, she thought.

She found a way to mend the switch with a jury-rigged fuse. The engine turned over, but would not crank. Louise went to work, checking all of the systems and connections that she could think of. Shit, it's a diesel, she thought. She turned the ignition switch to activate the glow plugs and waited. She tried the engine. Nothing. There was plenty of fuel, but it wouldn't crank. Must be the glowplugs. She scavenged around in the barn.

New plugs should bring the engine back to life. Her guard was no help, of course, so she scoured the ground floor. She found a distributor cap for some kind of old car, a box of horseshoes, bridles, saddles, and other sundry equestrian items. At a loss, she decided to check the loft.

There wasn't much but hay. She shuffled around, not knowing where to look. There probably isn't shit up here anyway. Despondent, she turned back to the ladder and found a narrow path between the old bales. She followed it. At the end was a small clearing where she found a bed. Next to the bed, a bag full of clothes sat atop a wooden box. She opened it. These pants belong to a man, she thought.

Whoever stayed there had intended to stay for a long time – a long-term, impermanent situation. They also intended to return for the clothes and pre-made bed. She pulled the bag of clothes onto the bed and opened the box. Inside was a metal, handled box that she pulled out. Its contents rattled like tools. There was another metal container at the bottom of the box. When she pulled it up into the light, she saw a letter embossed on the cover, **F**. She placed the boxes on the bed and stared at them. Both were age-worn. Relics from a much earlier time, she guessed. This has all the marks of a spanner, she thought. Her intuition was going off like a fire-drill siren.

She opened the boxes. Sure enough, they were full of mechanic's tools. Pliers, wrenches, volt meters, and ratchets. They were all vintage, solid tools that had been scavenged from a pre-quake site, or handed down through the generations. The boxes each held two levels of tools and parts. She pulled out the top level of one. She had to catch her breath. There was a box of the plugs she needed. She opened the second box and found a small pipe and a bong with the name *Fir* written on the bottom. Damn.

"Do you know Fir?" She couldn't wait to reach the bottom of the ladder before asking.

"Yeah, I know him." Her guard idly trimmed her nails with a pair of scissors.

"When was he here?"

"It's been a while," she said. "If you're lucky, he got lost or fell off a cliff."

"What happened?"

"Nothing, really. He did help us out." She cleaned her teeth with the scissors' blade. "I just hate men, is all."

Her mind stayed on Fir during the whole process of installing and testing the glowplugs. He'd taught her how to do this on his old bus, that glorious moving monument to autonomy, decadence, and a way of life that most had thought died long before the earthquake. She missed the sage smoke, the beaded privacy curtains, and the palpable sense that the bus was a living thing. It was organic, it breathed air. She wanted to lie on one of the stuffed mattresses, cuddle Maisie and talk to the bus, like they'd done so many times before.

We'll always be connected, right? Our bond will last an eternity.

The mushrooms buzzed their bodies and transferred their minds to other dimensions. Louise watched paisley fractal beings grow and shrink on a tapestry. Maisie sat upright on her knees, looking down at her. Her body emanated a warm, rosy glow that came to a peak at the top of her head. A yellow crown hovered over her bushy locks. Her words flowed from her mouth in a stream of silken beauty. Louise wasn't sure if she was speaking English or some foreign tongue, but she understood her mate with perfect clarity.

The spirit of Fir was part of who they were. He made it all possible. His wisdom guided them both in so many ways, even when he was miles or a continent away. It was as though tendrils from his rangy beard were reaching out into the world, finding her, finding Maisie. He was the key link, a subterranean network hub for them to link through.

There in that barn, she lay her hands on his tools and reopened a link to the past and perhaps the most important person in her life. She closed her eyes and smelled him. She felt his warmth surround her. She followed energetic lines to the past. Each took her down a different path to a different point.

She hadn't seen Fir since she left the Spanner outpost near Olympia. She thought of him often over the years, but had no way to get in touch with him. When it came to living analog, off the gird, Fir was one of the most adamant people she'd known. He never used his phone, nor email address, and refused to hear about the efficiency of computers. He was the quintessential spanner, true to the DIY, human-first ethic, and Louise missed him more than anything.

Chapter Thirty-Five

Fir loaded the last of the firewood onto the wheelbarrow, rolled it to the truck, and topped off the load. He was a mechanic. He hated splitting logs, but the afterglow and surge of adrenaline was worth it, even at his age. A man never outgrows doing a bit of honest, labor, I reckon. He looked out across the valley, the clouds had cleared and gave him a view for most of the day. After every log, he'd take a deep inhale of the vista. Down below, alongside the Rouge River, he saw the Spanner outpost. It was a blight on the landscape, really. Their micro-city was a brown, muddy, smoking pit of human destruction. Spanners sought to limit their impact, but they damaged the Earth all the same. It was unavoidable, he thought, we're constitutionally incapable of working in accordance with nature. I reckon we're the bit of sand in an oyster that makes a pearl, but maybe we're a holdout from the last bout of cancer mama Gaia already fought off. Human fucking beings, we'll never figure this shit out, will we? Fir scratched his beard, spat on the ground. He farted.

Southern Oregon and the Grant's Pass Spanner outpost were the best parts of Cascadia, and he'd traveled nearly every inch of it. The mountains and rivers were in his blood. In clear-sky moments, he could see the endless ocean that had once risen up in a tsunami and cleansed much of what humans had done before. The quake and that wave had disrupted one of humanity's great empires, it served as a mega-dose of antibiotic to a species reliant on oil, greed, too much beef. They were a cancer that had metastasized. By Fir's measurement, the tumor needed another surgery.

Those ancient *American* fools created a leader who mirrored who they were. He rose up as a manifestation of their fear, anger, and greed; he was the perfect demonic embodiment of what the prevailing culture hid behind closed doors. He was anti-Christlike, that was what people found most appealing about him, including Christians. He was not generous, showed contempt for the poor, robbed the sick of access to medicine, and surrounded himself with only the most wealthy advisors. As the child of the rich, he was incapable of handling criticism, and attempted to jail his detractors, of which there were many.

However, the leader was charismatic and a savvy manipulator. His hair was fake; he never said a true thing, or held a strong, coherent position; he was led by an insatiable ego and the most base desires. He rocked the society with scandal after scandal. He was caught with prostitutes in the White House. He'd enslaved women and traded them through a network of international flesh-peddlers; he'd hired inept hit-men to kill perceived enemies, including journalists and loudmouths on 'net discussion boards. For a society that had considered itself free and open, he was a bull in a china shop.

Fir wondered how it could happen. Hell, the roots of corruption and decay spreading at that very moment. News from Seattle said their mayor had vanished, likely murdered, and replaced by a golden-haired politician whose riches were won in the criminal underground, a plain-spoken, no-nonsense leader who didn't give a shit what people thought of him. All reports indicated that his followers turned a blind eye to his corruption. He promised to make Seattle great again, an exact repeat of what happened before the quake. He planned to build a wall around Tacoma. That made people happy. They all would rather piss on the good people who lived there than try to help and encourage growth and mutual prosperity. Fucking history, Fir thought, nobody learns.

Down below, a strange vehicle approached the compound. It stopped on the road, around a bend from the entrance. Several people disembarked and walked into the forest.

"Oh shit."

Fir picked up his radio and called down to the enclave.

"Big Fir to Pass Spanners, come in." There was always supposed to be at least one person working in communications at all times.

"Big Fir, come back, y'all are about to get some unwelcome guests."

There was no response. Maybe the channels had been blocked. He had no way to know. He got in the truck and started down the mountain. The road was rutted and difficult to navigate. He went as fast as he could, bouncing out of his seat going over more than one rut or log. He kept trying to contact someone. He reached back. There was a rifle, good. There must also be ammo in the glove box or under the seat. Spanners hated weapons, but they knew it would be stupid to be undefended. They hoped that the guns would only be used to ward off bears.

Fir looked out his window and saw the road way down below. He could see the Spanner entrance and the vehicle the interlopers were using. He pulled out the rifle and attached a scope. The gun still had a bit of oil on it, it had recently been cleaned. There were multiple, full magazines of ammunition in a cache beneath the seat. He got out of the truck and found a clear line to the road below. He didn't know what to do.

A man emerged from the forest 50 meters from the truck. He was dressed in all black, except for a wooden cross that dangled from his neck. Fir centered his cross hairs on the man's chest. He only had a simple bag of tools. A woman joined him, dressed in the same black outfit offset with a wooden cross. He didn't see any weapons. Weird. He chambered a round and retrained his weapon on the man's sternum. He inhaled deep into his abdomen. He held the air. He visualized the man's chest cavity exploding, as it would. With bullets like these, it's possible to blow a frail human body in half. Did this punishment fit the crime, of which I know nothing? He couldn't shoot. He panned his cross-hairs to the truck instead. *Blam!* One tire. *Blam!* Another tire. *Blam!* One through the hood. He destroyed the motor. Those fuckers ain't going nowhere. He put three more rounds through the hood just to be certain.

The invaders leapt from their truck and ran for it. He pivoted and blew a few craters in the road, directly in their path. The black-clad cabal stopped dead. They raised their hands and looked up into the forest, trying to pinpoint where Fir might be hiding. He grabbed the radio and hailed the communications office again.

"Big Fir, what're you doing?"

"Interlopers on the road." He had to stop to catch his breath. Adrenaline pumped through his body, his heart raced. "Two of them got into the compound. I got 'em covered from above. Y'all gotta round 'em up."

"10-4."

A group of Spanners ran out of the main gate, fully armed. Fir watched as the invaders were rounded up, handcuffed, and led to the compound. He removed the clip from his rifle, emptied a round from the chamber, and got back in the truck. So much for a peaceful day chopping wood.

"Dammit, Fir, that was a damn fine truck. Why did ya hafta go fill it full of slugs?" Sam hooked the invading truck up to a wench.

"Sorry for your luck, Sam." Fir raised the hood. "Hoses are good, so's the water pump. Lots to salvage."

"Where'd they take 'em?"

"I think they'll let 'em sit in the cells for a bit, then interrogate them."

"Lookie here." Fir inspected the truck cab.

"Goddamn radio jammer."

"Musta turned it off early."

"Naw, it's still on."

Fir parked his truck outside the gate and walked around the

compound walls. The interlopers' sloppy tracks led him to a perfect hole beside the outer wall. They must have dug it in advance of the raid, he thought, this was planned well in advance. His knees and hips ached when he squatted for a better look. Holy shit, he thought. With effort, he rose to his feet, double-timed it back to his truck, and retrieved a flashlight.

They'd dug a tunnel beneath the compound and no one had noticed. Fir climbed down the ladder and then had to crawl the rest of the way. In about 25 feet he found the end. There was an underground bunker that was small, dank, and empty except for a single conduit pipe that had been cut open to expose a huge wire. They'd severed the wire. That's it? Fir thought. He shone his light on the wire. Fiber optic cable. Goddamn. This is the network. They broke the goddamn network.

"Man's hubris must be destroyed." Fir recognized that this was the voice of the man who cut the cable. "The Lord God is displeased. We have been sent to do the work he cannot do on this Earth."

"Cutting the fucking Internet?" Everyone turned when Fir's booming voice filled the room.

"Yes, brother. It is Satan himself. It creates a false world, it makes humans think they're gods. It destroys God's beautiful creation."

"How did you find the cable?"

"We received a message from above."

"Bird tell you?"

"It came to me late one night. I had fallen asleep. The radio had gone to static and when I woke to turn it off, a voice came through the noise."

"Who's voice?"

"I had never heard it before. It said 'kill the beast' followed by a series of numbers. Then the message would repeat. Over and over. I was transfixed, so I wrote down the numbers."

"Coordinates?"

"Exactly. We worked on figuring out the significance of this holy message for two years."

"Did this voice ever speak to you again?"

"No."

The intruders were from a cult a few miles away. A hold-out Christian cabal, reactionaries who waited for the end of the world. Some wished to instigate a global Armageddon in hopes that Jesus would return and give them a great reward. They blamed the earthquake on secular decadence and corruption.

"You do realize that we can fix this in a few hours. Hell, since we have the cable, we're halfway done already."

"All I can do is follow the word of the Lord our God."

"You think it was God that spoke to you?"

"I know it."

"What if it was a person?"

"That is not possible. I do the Lord's work. He works in ways that none of us will ever be able to understand."

Fir's phone buzzed in his pocket. He'd nearly forgotten about it. It was one of those items he always had, but never used. It was useless, like a good-luck charm, but he always had to fidget around it to retrieve useful items like keys or his pocket knife. He refocused his eyes to read the caller name on the screen. Maisie. Hot damn. It'd been years since he'd seen her.

"Hey little girl!"

"Fir, you big lug, what's going on?"

"Down here in Grant's Pass, ya know."

"Yeah, I do know. That's why I'm calling," she said. "What the fuck is going on down there? All wired connections with Lower Cascadia and SoCal have been severed."

"Some jackass cultists cut the line."

"Damn."

"Yup. We'll have the repair in an hour or two, I reckon."

"Some crazy shit is going on."

"Computer shit?"

"Yes, computer shit."

"Let me know if I should care. I'm of half a mind to join one of these anti-tech cults."

"Come up here to Tacoma sometime. I'd love to see you, old man."

"I will. I love ya little girl."

Chapter Thirty-Six

Louise was greasy and tired. The tractor took a lot of work and energy to fix. Fir's tools had been helpful. It was as though his hands were atop hers each time she worked the spanners. His wisdom guided her choices and endless patience kept her focused as she tried time and time again to get the damn engine to turn over. She felt at once tired and yet at home. Having his spirit over her shoulder, his tools in her hands, made the new place a home, in a way. Where she felt captive, she now felt comfortable. Her life, and that of her friends, hinged on her ability to fix machines, but that was okay. She had a guide, she was connected and protected by the best man she'd ever known. Everything was going to be okay.

"Hey." Makah was on the lower bunk, reading a book.

They'd been placed in the same room. The benefits of captivity. There was one large mattress and then a set of stacked bunks. Louise claimed the queen-sized mattress as payment for her hard work. She collapsed atop the comforter and breathed a sigh of relief. There was a stain on the ceiling, the air was cool, but comfortable. She wanted to eat and sleep all at the same time. She closed her eyes and dreamed of a bowl of hot stew.

"Hard day?"

"Yeah." She kept her eyes closed, but felt Makah sitting on the edge of the bed.

"Want a rubdown?"

Louise flopped over onto her stomach. The very suggestion of a backrub made her body ache with need. She didn't care that her body smelled from sweat and grease. Relief was the only thing she wanted. Makah tugged her shirt from her pants and pushed it up over her shoulders and head. Hands brushed skin.

"Do it all, especially my shoulders." She had a need, she was emphatic.

"No problem, babe."

Makah's hands dove into her shoulders, between muscle and tendon, fascia and flesh. She musta learned knew how to give a real deep-tissue massage growing up in a community of warriors. Louise wasn't prepared, but she was willing. It hurt, a lot, but she relished feeling every muscle fiber. Then the fingers danced up and down her back, tapping flesh as though it were a piano or a keyboard. The playful touch made Louise smile and moan, she wanted more. The fingers slowed down at the arch of her low back. They danced up and down, narrowing their focus. Louise's breath slowed, her mind focused on every inch of her back. The fingers searched until they landed on a spot that Louise felt was tight and tender. Without warning, Makah drove an elbow into the intractable knot. Louise cried out. The pain grew. She started to sweat, it was so intense. Tears dribbled onto her pillow.

"Hold on, girl." The elbow pivoted back and forth over the knot. "Breathe into it."

Louise breathed into the spot. She imagined the knot inflating and deflating, pulsing with her breath. The pain persisted and she continued to breathe and sweat and cry. Makah's elbow was a torture device, but it brought release. That knot had probably been there for years, a ball of tension built over years of delivering packages between Eugene and Seattle, from Portland to the ocean. All the bumps in the road, every snowy mountain pass, and the long endless stretches of straight road where her back slumped. She wanted to release it all. She needed freedom. Relief. The price was pain, and she was ready to pay.

On the other side of the pain was ease. A rush of warmth, an opiate sense of calm. She floated on an ocean of ease, an infinity of bliss. Her body relaxed more than it ever had. She farted.

"That feel good?"

"Mmm"

Makah continued working her shoulders and back muscles. There were more knots to unfurl, more tension to release. Makah moved down her back again and rubbed her butt. She explained how the gluteal muscles were vital in providing stability and strength. Louise needed to work on these muscles more, especially since she did so much driving.

"After this job, I don't think I'll be a courier."

"What do you want to do?"

"I don't know. Maybe I'll find a coffee source and sell to rich people. There's big money there."

"Entrepreneur, eh?"

"To the end. Hell, there's not much choice."

"Whatever you set your mind on, I'm sure will be a success."

Hands went down her thighs to her calves and then her feet. Electricity shot from the soles of her feet to the crown of her head. Every nerve along the way glowed with a yellow light. Every organ, muscle, and joint was bathed in pleasure from root to crown. The pleasure was endless, unbounded.

Hands spread her thighs and one slid between her body and the bedspread. Her yoni was warm. The hand was warm. Lips caressed her shoulder, her back, her bottom. The hand moved in a rhythm, the lips became teeth and tongue and lips and teeth again. Louise rolled over and watched her new lover.

Moans filled the room. Louise may have even screamed or squealed in the middle of an orgasm, she wasn't sure. Makah was silent but shook and shimmied at Louise's touch. She wanted it rough and Louise was rough. She'd never known a girl or boy who could handle biting like that.

Time blurred in the frenzy of limb and tongue. Desire's sweet story unfolded a narrative at once alien and as familiar as waking on a clear, sunny day. Makah's body was new, it smelled different, it moved in unpredictable ways. It wasn't like the first time, but their bodies fit together in new ways, a new combination in the universe. They found pleasure and relief; they found safety and comfort. They collapsed like rag dolls in a pile of rosy flesh

There was a knock. The door creaked open a few inches. Louise held her breath. She'd forgotten about everything else in the world.

"You girls finished?" It was Erin.

"Yeah, sweetheart, you can come in."

Erin climbed onto the top bunk, sighed, and occupied herself with her tablet. Louise watched the girl's profile, her body prone and propped, rapt in the electronic world. Makah teased her tits, but Louise brushed her hand away. The kid takes everything in good stride. She's patient, tolerant, she thought. When Louise's mom had brought home man after man, she'd learned to bury herself in a book or rebuild something. She'd learned not to expect love or even attention from the outside world. She ran away to the Spanners and discovered what it was like to be whole, to be a part of something.

"Úytaahkoo." Erin's voice was confident delivering the foreign-sounding word.

"What?"

"That's where you're taking us, right?"

"We're headed to Mount Shasta."

"The real name is Úytaahkoo."

"Wait, how do you know that?" Louise couldn't recall discussing her mission since finding Erin.

"It all makes sense."

"Sense?"

"What's for dinner?" Erin was insistent.

"Wait, how did you know that, Erin?" Makah sat up, her eyes drilled into the little girl.

Louise felt the tension rise.

"Just a guess. I had a dream about us going there. It was fun."

"A dream or a guess?" Makah turned cold, fierce. "Make up your mind, girl."

"I don't know, I saw it though." Her voice was wavering. "There were rabbits and birds. It's beautiful there."

"What the hell are you trying to pull?"

"Hey, Makah, what's the deal? Maybe I said something, fucking cool it." Louise was not a fighter and didn't want to start. "It's not any big secret."

Chapter Thirty-Seven

Days passed. Time moved. Nothing changed. Every day Louise worked on engines, suspensions, and electrical systems. Makah was busy with farming, cleaning, and cooking. It was an idyllic life. Erin helped, but was given time to study. Their captors saw the value in studies. The days shortened and the rain was steady and persistent. They settled into domestic routines.

Erin's studies were ever deeper and she spent more and more time immersed in theorems, analyzing data, even reading literary fiction. She found that her captors were a team of warm and nurturing mother figures. Some had a background in mathematics and they offered to help her. They were astounded to discover that Erin's computational ability far out stripped their own. Erin soon taught them about topography and new theorems that she and her computer friend had devised. The women were agog at Erin's brilliance. Makah was skeptical, but sat in on the lessons.

"What good is all of this?" Makah was interested in action, results.

"When we measure the contours of the Earth, we have a deeper understanding. Plus, we can compare our measurements with previous records and assess the changes. We can compare, for instance, the impact of a small versus a large earthquake, measure the rate of erosion, and other things. We are getting closer to predicting how the Earth will act. However, we'll never know until our predictions come true – or not, which may mean it's too late."

"Not all. They'll be fine in other parts. SoCal, for instance. They'll be fine."

"We're not sure. All of that data disappeared. It's nowhere on any server in the world."

"How would you know?" Makah eyed Erin with suspicion. "It doesn't matter, really."

"All learning and knowledge is valuable." Erin looked at her shoes.

"All that is valuable is today, right now. You take what you need to survive and you try to make more." Makah's voice was clear and strong. "Strength is the only rule. You gotta get yours and that's all."

"But what if others can help you?"

"Why would I need help?" She bristled. "Only the weak need help."

"Weakness is found in the solitary and brittle. In the forest, it's the diversity of life and organic interconnectedness that makes the whole thing work. It's not help, it's part of what it means to be alive."

"We live to die. In the forest, the living eat the dead. The law of the jungle is written by the animal with the largest muscles."

"You can choose a lonely path, but what will you dream of at night?"

"Power."

"Singular power is destructive and of no use. It leaves nothing but a vacuum. Nature abhors a vacuum."

"Look little girl, you haven't seen what I've seen. You don't know what I know. You've never felt your life floating away at the hand of a subhuman monster, you've never saved the life of a doomed individual."

"I've felt the same loss, maybe worse. My parents were supposed to come back. They may still, I don't know. You know your lover will never come back. You had the luxury of watching his body break on the rocks. You had closure and you still want to take it out on everyone. You can still have other lovers. I'll never have other parents, if mine don't return."

"Look, you don't know a goddamned thing, kid." Makah vibrated with rage. She pressed her face into the placid girl's. Veins popped out on her forehead. Her fists were granite. "Fuck."

Makah ran out of the room. Erin exhaled and burst into tears.

Chapter Thirty-Eight

Louise returned to the bedroom. She was relieved to find it empty. She wanted peace and quiet for a bath. Her body ached from a long day of hoisting engine blocks and spinning bolts. She'd removed the engine from an old car and was in the midst of a valve job. It was the tenth vehicle. She was beginning to think she'd never win freedom. On most days she forgot all about the black box she was supposed to take to Shasta. It wasn't worth thinking about. She had to finish her job before they'd return her keys or her phone or her life to her. She was captive, but it was a soft captivity full of hot baths, hearty meals, and fluffy pillows. The reality of the situation vanished into the background of her consciousness. She felt free, she had a job and a purpose, but she couldn't leave. If she didn't work, she and her friends would die.

She woke, worked, became tired, and rested. Then it began all over again. It was a real effort to keep her true mission in mind. She didn't know if she'd ever leave. Erin and Makah seemed happy. Life was good, right? Maybe she didn't need to leave. Was it so important to finish her mission? After all, all she had was some stupid scientific instrument. They could make another and find another hapless courier to deliver it, right?

Her back muscles ached for relief when she leaned over the bathtub to draw a bath. She missed her own bathtub and the salts she soaked in after long days working on engines. The steam opened her nose; she peeled off her work clothes and stepped into the water. A shiver of gooseflesh raised the hair on her legs and she eased into the bath. She could take the next day off. She planned to relax and wanted nothing more than to clean her overalls and grubby shirts. Louise closed her eyes and covered them with a hot rag. She sank deeper into the water.

A rush of cool air disturbed her stillness. Erin entered the bathroom and closed the door behind her. Louise took the rag from her eyes and glared at the girl. She wanted to lash the child within an inch of her life, but saw the youngster's downturn eyes and furrowed brow.

"You ever knock, kid?"

"I'm worried." She sat on the edge of the tub.

"I'm trying to relax."

"This is bad."

"What's up, kid?"

"Look." She showed Louise her photo of Makah's scar.

"Yeah?" Louise was annoyed. "Some kinda birthmark or a scar from New York."

"It bugged me. I thought it was something like you say, but I took a picture anyway."

"So, you have a picture of Makah's beautiful neck."

"You like her?"

"Yeah. Under different circumstances... or if she seemed interested..."

"Maybe she likes you, too."

"Why is that?"

"Because she hasn't killed us yet."

Louise looked at Erin. She'd never seen a young girl look so serious before. Her eyes were hard and serious, as though laser beams could come out and bore through her skull. There was something to this. Erin was not a frivolous person. She knew something, or had reason to think she knew something.

"What's up, kid? Explain, please."

"Well, we got into a discussion. She has some very disturbing ideas, I think. We got angry. Anyway, I analyzed this picture."

"It's a white spot on a black woman's ass. Nice contrast, I guess?"

"More than that. Look."

Erin magnified the image. The white spot. The darkness around it. Louise noticed that it was a raised, perfectly symmetrical, albino mole. It looked like someone had placed a small pellet under Makah's skin, then bleached the skin atop it.

"That is sorta strange, what do you think?"

"I searched multiple databases for an explanation." Erin

sounded professorial when she was focused, wise beyond her years. Louise was jealous of her future lovers. "I matched it with a special kind of microchip. A subderm used to control its host. Pretty rare. This one was a SoCal model."

"Wait, there are all sorts of subderms. Hell, I had one for a while, when I had a job. Shit skeeved me out, so I quit. I cut out the damn thing and tossed it in the Willamette River."

"They may have left nanoes in your body."

"Fuck, really?"

"Pretty common for employment 'derms." Erin was on a roll, breathless with excitement to share knowledge. "They like to track you after you've quit. They figure most will rip out the 'derms, exactly as you did, and that becomes a data point, too. Of course they continue receiving data for years afterwards, maybe still. It's an elaborate psychological experiment. It's common business practice now. Leftover from the pre-quake days, it's a tradition that gives rich kids jobs."

"Thanks, kid, you're such a ray of sunshine."

She shrugged her shoulders. "It's a fact."

Chapter Thirty-Nine

Makah was deeper in the forest than ever before. The light was hazy gray, almost black. Raindrops fell through the canopy. Once she'd left the city, her eyes had adapted to the pitch-dark of the forest. She wanted to test it. She wanted to run full-tilt through the dark. Instead, she picked a fallen limb and smashed it against a shattered, rotted old stump. It broke into two parts. She kept swinging the branch, splinters from the soft wood flew. She'd never be able to excise the demons. She knew this. They were too many, too deep and too strong. She had layer after layer of scar tissue. Every slain crawler and amper-zombie left a mark. The memory of Barak, slaying Brain. She'd seen a lot. She was tough.

Yet, the least thing could set her off, send her spinning in a vortex of rage and resentment. The little girl, the weak snot, Erin, did that. The namby pamby little bitch thought she knew better. Losing her parents? Whatever. She knew nothing of what real life meant. She had no idea of what it took to pull herself up from the muck, holding onto life and sanity by the barest thread, fingernails digging into some existential sense of self. The only thing that was worth pursuing was power, whatever it took to enforce one's will.

Corvids gathered in the trees above. First it was a simple caw and response between two of them. Then a third chimed in, a fourth, and on. Soon, there was a din of caws and squawks. It drowned out all of Makah's thoughts. She stood and watched the black birds jump and fly from limb to limb, tree to tree, a chaotic field of kinetic truth, atoms careening at unpredictable trajectories; they moved so fast as to create the illusion of opacity, impermeability, a border between land and sky, the mortal and the eternal. It was a discordant, anarchic song and dance, beautiful yet abrasive.

It was a primal scream. The scream of a dying woman. She knew the scream. It was hers. It echoed in her scars and bones. Her crow spirit insisted on freedom, on life. It did not want forgiveness or companionship or help. It called out for itself. It built its own power. It ate the weak. Just as those blackbirds eat worms out of the forest soil, so I must eat the soft flesh of weakness, through me it will become strength.

She found a fallen tree, a giant sequoia covered in vines. She climbed atop its trunk. With arms outstretched, she arched her back and screamed into the dying light of day. The black birds responded, the cacophony raised to a new level. Then, a beacon in the dying light, celestial rays pierced through her forehead to the center of her brain. Or maybe the light came from inside her brain. She was light. She was strong. She was the strength of the world and she would not be denied the power that she was due.

Chapter Forty

This morning is more quiet than any I recall, Erin thought. Louise is in the barn working on engines, Makah's gone, and everyone else works in the greenhouses or elsewhere. There's always more to learn. More facts about nature, more theorems to puzzle over. Then there's history, literature, and the mysteries of the human mind. We were so close to making a real breakthrough when the quake happened. Damn anti-science people attacked the most vital servers in all of cognitive science. Only a shadow of their advances remained.

The forest was full of early-morning fog. The world was a collage of green, black, and grey. The house was much like the one where Erin grew up. There was a small bit of lawn behind the house and a forest that extended farther than any eye could see. She remembered her old dog, Jake, who fought with all he had. The bear and the blood and the terror that still shook her. The emptiness left in his absence was still there. She could see it, feel it. It was a hole but it was part of her. She loved it, it was dog-shaped, she filled it with matted hair and half-chewed old cow bones. She topped it with tears and an endless ache.

She hadn't thought of Jake in weeks, if not longer. Why now? The mind does strange things, takes strange turns for no particular reason. All of its contents were mere reminders of the connections inherent in the structure. The brain was just one part. The thoughts of Jake lived in her heart along those of her parents and grandmother.

Maybe staring deep into the infinity of trees did it, perhaps recalling the similarities between her current place and where she was from. She took the thoughts farther, closed her eyes and felt him lick her face, smelled his dog-breath. Was he here, in the room? Her mind was scientific, pragmatic and materialistic, but her heart believed that the dog's spirit was still with her and was trying to show her something. She looked over to the barn and saw Louise's shadow through a hazy window.

"Hey Lou, how are ya doing?"

"Good, kid, what's up?" Louise had her arms deep beneath the hood level of a pre-quake hulk of steel and iron. She grunted and loosened a tight bolt. "Fuck yeah!"

"I was bored. No one is home. I need a break from all the math."

"I can understand that." She fitted her wrench to the next bolt. "Hey, why don't you grab that flashlight and shine it down here for me."

Erin turned on the light and beamed it down on the motor. "How many of these things do you have?"

"I think five, maybe more." The nut wasn't budging. "Shit. Yeah, I keep losing track of how many I've done. Does time seem to stand still in this place?"

"It kind of does."

"Maybe Makah was right to escape."

"I hope she stays away."

"I thought she was such a good friend."

"Hm." Erin trained the light on Lou's spanner. "I guess it's just us two, now."

"Yeah, quite a team, eh?" Lou broke a sweat and the nut allowed a quarter turn. "Hey, know what? I have a crazy idea. It'll be fun, it'll be good."

Chapter Forty-One

Lou opened her stash of mushrooms. They were dried, preserved, wrinkled fruit bodies with blue-bruised stems and brown caps. She'd issued a small psychic prayer to them each time her hand brushed their box at the back of her drawer. The knowledge that they were waiting for her helped her hold onto hope. When the mundane world dragged and tested her patience, they reminded her that there was another way to be in the world, another way to see and experience one's thoughts, one's very being. They might even open another dimension to reality, who knew? She inhaled their earthy scent. A long-stemmed mushroom caught her eye amidst the tangled pile. She pulled it out from under the rest and placed it in her open palm. It weighed nothing, yet held so much gravity. Its physicality barely tickled her skin, yet it would soon unlock the essence of the universe, she would pass through doors of perception unfathomable to those who had never taken such a journey.

"Those are beautiful," Erin said. "Cyans."

"Huh?"

"*Cyanescens*. It's the species. These are the most powerful organisms in the forest. More powerful than the bears and big cats." She held the small fruit in her hand. Her face went slack with childlike wonder. "I ate a few grams once."

"They call them *teachers*."

"Because they lead us to so many truths."

The two sat on Louise's bed. The box of mushrooms lay open between them. Their sole focus centered on the pile of fungi. The women fell into a silent, contemplative state. They stared into each other's eyes. Their breathing deepened and synchronized. They sat cross-legged. Time moved to the heartbeat metronome.

Louise reached into the pile, grabbed two shrooms and a stray cap. Erin picked enough for her journey. They held their doses lightly in their palms, inhaled the musty aroma, and meditated on what was in the dried fruits, the power they were about to ingest. They each set a silent intention for their journey. Louise never set a destination, but a trajectory. She wanted to explore and open her mind and heart. She was simple. She figured the rest would be revealed as the medicine did its work.

When they were ready, they communicated with a glimmer in the eye. They raised their hands and began to chew the dried fungus. It was like eating stale cardboard with a mushroom-dirt flavor. It wasn't bad, really, but it always took special concentration for Lou to get the fungus down. If she didn't eat them all at once, she'd never get through them all.

First her body became heavy. She yawned. They walked in the grass behind the house. Her mind was calm, she built strength to carry her heavy body, the corpus weighted by gravity. She was weighty, she had mass, importance, definition and impact.

Erin walked and looked at the ground. Louise marveled at

the young woman. Still small, still with time to grow and develop, yet containing such knowledge and wisdom. That was the amazing part. Anyone can know a lot of shit, but Erin knew how to understand it, how to discern the good from the bad, to make unique connections that expanded possibilities for everyone. Her mind created efficiencies, but did not leave out humanity, compassion, empathy. It was a miracle to behold. Louise only hoped that her young friend never grew jaded and bitter, that she wouldn't succumb to temptation and use her talents for little more than personal gain. That would be a tragedy.

"Hey, how are you?"

"I'm inflated. My feet are heavy."

"Can you see your breath in the forest?"

"I am breathing with it or it with me?"

"There are leaves that know my name."

"Close your eyes. See what's inside."

Louise sat and closed her eyes. She entered a Technicolor world stitched together with geometric patterns. Blue and green diamonds formed trees and an endless series of concentric circles, emanating from her feet, spiderwebbed a ruby red floor. As she moved around the space, the circles moved. She was the center of all things. As objects and beings moved towards her, she was able to detect and absorb their energy. She opened her eyes.

The natural world welcomed her back with open arms. The air was a thick thing, palpable and almost visible in its transparency. When she flexed her thigh to press her body over a log, her muscles and bones sang to her. She inhaled, individual molecules of oxygen entered and integrated with her body. Her alveoli tickled her in thanks for the nourishment, and her vision brightened, nature's hidden patterns deepened. She pressed harder into her standing leg, straightened it, and brought her feet together atop the fallen tree. The crown of her head reached for the sky, her pelvis sought the earth. She looked into the canopy. Misty rain made its way through to her face, droplets cleansed her skin, eyes, hair. They connected her to the sky above. She was the final part of a long cycle of evaporation, condensation, and, finally, a fall back to earth. She rose as droplets fell, they were in opposition, yet were the same. Her consciousness evaporated into a million particles, became vapor, gaseous. She was everywhere; she was nowhere. She condensed, rose, reformed as liquid, and returned to Earth.

Trees framed the white cloudy ceiling of sky, which filled with colored fractals. Trees parted, exposed more of the heavens when she inhaled, they contracted on exhales. She looked over and saw her friend. Erin had found a small grove of blueberry bushes. The girl was eating fruit and giggling to herself.

"I have seen what's coming."

"Blueberries?" Louise giggled at a joke known only to her.

"The forest tells the truth," Erin said. "She's been through here. She'll be back."

"Is that good?"

"Depends on your perspective." Erin's face went still, blank yet alive in wonder. "I need to see your phone for a minute. You also have to promise me to keep it on you at all times. On your person, not nearby, not in a purse. In your pockets."

"Okay." The air chilled, Louise pulled out the device and handed it to her young friend. "What's the matter, kid?"

"There will be a change." She used both hands to tap on the phone and her tablet simultaneously. "It's not something I thought possible, but there has been a shift and shifts turn to rifts turn to..." her fingers whirred in rhythmic synch.

"A shift?"

"I am trying to track it down, though the wheels are in motion." She stared quizzically at the two devices and resumed her ten-finger drumming. "It could have been a butterfly flapping its wings on Macchu Piccu or maybe an anarchist hacker shut down a washing machine that threw a wrench in the Grand Design of the Universe. It's impossible to say. It is exactly what it is, until it isn't, as always."

Louise's heart swelled towards her young friend who was at once young and inexperienced and more wise than she'd ever be. She saw herself as both mentor and student to the young girl. She flashed back to finding her on the road. Her small body a half mile away, barely visible on the road. Makah resisting help. She'd fed the girl, gave her a place in her car, her life. Makah. She felt a chill.

Erin turned, and they embraced. They melted into one

another. Whatever could be called difference or distance fell away into a singular, shared body. Louise felt her energy join with Erin, with the forest, with the very Universe. Together, they created something incredible, or maybe they dissipated into the totality of creation.

As time ends all things, the mushroom's effects ebbed, became soft and eased their travelers back to the normal, consensus reality. No more fractals, melting, temples, or other psychedelic delights. Louise put her arm around her young friend and they retraced their steps through the forest to what they had come to know as home.

They broke through the forest into the back garden. Several women turned to greet them. Someone had killed and slaughtered and elk and they were cooking it over open flame. The mood was convivial. Louise's heart swelled at her newfound, unlikely home.

"Here, hold this," Erin said. She shoved the tablet into Louise's hands, insistent. "It's yours, don't let anyone see it. Ever."

"Okay." Dumbfounded and shocked, Louise held the device. Erin's eyes welled with tears.

"It was lovely, thank you. Beauty is forever."

"Sure, kiddo..."

Louise looked at the device, then sought her friend's face again. An arrow or spear or something flew out of Erin's chest. A pool of blood formed. It bubbled from her mouth. Her lips moved, but there was no sound. Her body crumpled and Louise grabbed for her. They both collapsed onto a stump, the girl's body limp. Her heart had been pierced, she was dead.

A roar rose from the barbecue party. In a flash, fifteen tall, stout women thundered past Louise.

"There, it came from over there."

"I see something."

Though no longer in the realm of psychedelia, Louise felt more surreal than ever. She was numb, dumbstruck, and incapable of processing what had happened. There was no time, there was no feeling or inner life. Life and death whorled around as though in a vortex. She clutched Erin's former body to her breast and sobbed in silence.

"I got her!" The voice echoed through the forest.

Chapter Forty-Two

Makah was tricky and strong, but she'd been outflanked, then out-muscled by the women. She did manage to take one out with her nanobots, but reprogramming and placing nanoes is time consuming.

Now, she was hog-tied. Her arms were tied behind her back and her ankles were bound. Two women strung her up on a strong limb. Makah was silent, stoic.

"Keep her strapped," Louise said. "Bring her to the barn."

She hung from her wrists, arms and legs outstretched. Once secured, Louise put her face in her former friend's, their noses inches apart. Makah's eyes were soft, her mouth still silent. Louise spat in her face. Sobbed. Raged. Screamed for a bullwhip to tear the traitor to bits.

"Why?" Louise demanded satisfaction, some reason that such a young, promising life had to be extinguished.

"You wouldn't understand. You're nothing but a worker, a drone, a cog in the machinery around you." Makah was stolid. "I know ten times what you'll ever dream, and I'm not sure I even know, but it was necessary. For the future to come, it was necessary."

"For the future to come?" Louise seethed at such outlandish bullshit. "What the fuck does that even mean?"

"She was part of the past. The messy, the weak past which we are now going to overcome."

"I thought you at least liked her."

"I tolerated the little bitch."

"I don't believe you."

"She's one of those communal hippie types that should have been decimated in the quake, but which lived on, like rats, to haunt us today."

"Is that really why you killed her?"

"You are next."

"Like hell, asshole." Louise walked up and punched her face.

"Strip her," one of the women said. "Expose every inch of her murderous soul."

Louise pulled a knife from her pocket, extended the blade, and ran it along Makah's cheek. "How about that?"

A wave of rage ran through Louise and she pressed the tip of her blade flat into Makah's face. Not cutting, she stared into green orbs and growled. She tilted the blade a bit and made a small incision.

She used the knife to shred the shirt, then the pants. In moments, Makah was fully exposed. Gooseflesh rose all over her body. Louise walked around behind her, spread her cheeks to make sure there was nothing hidden in the cleft of her ass. Her eye rested on Makah's left cheek. There was a small white scar contrasted against the dark chocolate skin. She pressed on it and it was hard.

"What is this?" Louise was in her face.

"My ass? I think you licked it at least once, don't you remember?"

"Fuck you." Louise slapped her. "The scar, what's it from?"

"I don't have a scar on my ass."

"Yes. You. Do." Louise's mouth was frothing. "What is it?"

"Eat me. Bitch."

"Someone give me a flame. We're going to do a bit of surgery."

Her blade hit metal a few millimeters beneath the surface. She cleaned a set of needle-nosed pliers and pulled a small metal pellet from Makah's ass. A needle and thread closed the wound. She was proud of herself, maybe she could do augment surgery someday.

"The fuck is this?" She put the shiny metal object in Makah's face.

"The fuck if I know." Makah said. Her eyes started rolling back in her head. She made noises from the back of her throat. It wasn't clear if she was trying to talk. She spasmed, her heat jerked from side to side, front and back. Her stomach muscles clenched and released, her arms and legs twitched in their bonds. For a moment she danced like a wooden dancing Limberjill then collapsed. A long string of drool extended from behind her mighty dreadlocks all the way to the floor.

"Don't fall for that shit." One of the women insisted it was a ruse. "Tighten her straps. She's playing us."

"She's my problem, I'll watch her." Louise pulled up a chair. "Y'all can go."

Louise stared intently at Makah's limp body for hours. Neither moved. Makah's breathing was shallow, but regular. Louise cleaned Erin's blood from her fingernails. Her rage was turning to grief. Deep longing filled her body.

After a while, she realized that she still had Erin's tablet. The only possession that ever seemed to matter to that child. She flipped it on. The background image was Erin's old dog, Jake, the one that died. Louise's sadness compounded. Thank god she didn't have a picture of her parents or grandmother. Fuck. Pull it together, girl. Tears welled in her eyes and dropped to the tablet.

She didn't know what to do with the device. She tapped it, jostled it, turned it upside-down, but nothing happened. She pressed the buttons on the side. Nothing. The kid was so far advanced with tech that it was unlikely that Louise would ever figure out how to use the thing. Maisie, on the other hand… Maisie. If only she were here.

She reached in her breast pocket and pulled out the metal pellet. It glinted and glimmered as she rolled it around on her palm, a cylinder of technological perfection, steely and cold in her hand. These days people made new things like this for a reason. No longer did children's toys connect to a network of satellites to analyze the chemical composition of saliva or dog poop. If there was no immediate need for a thing, it didn't exist, or certainly was never called into being. Someone was intent on creating that object to place in Makah's flesh. She was fascinated, she stared at it, played with it. It caught a ray of light and she could see her eye in a distorted reflection. She nearly jumped out of her seat when the tablet's screen came to life. A word appeared on the screen: *analyzing*. What the shit?

She pulled up Maisie's contact info on her phone, but was transfixed by the tablet. It kept working, and working, and working. She'd seen Erin analyze plants and dead animals in the forest. That took no time whatsoever. Makah's body hung from chains, limp.

"Well hello stranger." Maisie was in a playful mood, Louise could tell.

"Hey sexy."

"What's new down there in the forest?"

"Did you get the image I just sent?" Louise checked the phone to make sure her photo was delivered. "Any idea of what that thing is?"

"Shit, girl," Maisie said. "Where'd that come from?"

"My friend Makah's ass."

"Well, unless you want to send a full 360 shot of it, I can't tell much specifics. Even with that, I'm not sure what I could tell you," Maisie said. "What I do know is that is some serious tech, girlfriend. Whoever made that is operating on a level you and I can't even dream about. Just to machine a simple pellet like that is nearly unheard of these days."

"Ok, what is it?"

"It's definitely a tracking device. However, given the size

and placement, I'm also guessing that it's designed for some greater purpose. It could implant memories, or other types of thought."

"It's so small."

"It's a transceiver. It receives messages from... someone, somewhere," Maisie paused. "Was it attached to any nerves?"

"I pulled it out of her ass. There was a bunch of blood and body stuff. I didn't see any nerves."

"Well, who knows. However, I'm guessing that someone has been alerted and knows that this thing's been extracted. It was probably uploading reports to someone."

"Fuck."

"Yeah, if I'm right, this is something serious. Deadly."

The tablet's *analyzing* screen went away. A barrage of data scrolled the screen. It was all code, a foreign language as far as Louise was concerned. Holy fuck.

"Hey, Mais. I'm sending you something. I don't know... it's a shit-ton of data. You're the only one I know who can do anything with this gibberish."

"What is it?"

"You'll have to tell me."

"I suggest you haul your hot ass out of there. Now."

Makah's limp body began to move and murmur. It swayed

on the chains. Louise wished she could put a bullet in the bitch's brain, but she could not. As much as she loved Erin, she knew she'd never be able to kill a former lover.

"Hello?"

"Start talking, bitch."

"Me?"

"Don't try to play me, Makah."

"Makah? What? Where am I and how did I get here?"

"Why did you do it?"

"Where are my friends? Where's my parents?"

"Your parents? You never had any parents. You never had anybody but that group in New York."

"Where. Are. They."

"The fuck ever. Why did you kill Erin?"

"*Kill*? How did I get here? That's what I want to know. Plus, my name is Jet, I just won a competition. I want to see my parents and celebrate."

Louise looked hard into her eyes. They were calm, unwavering. After a moment, her eyes cut away in deference. Makah was always fierce, her eyes were always hard, laser-like. Makah would win every single staring contest. These were the eyes of a woman from a healthy background, someone who had privilege to overcome. Their green glowed bright in the dim, dusty barn.

"Ok, fill me in. Where are you from? Who are your parents?" Louise pulled up a search bar on the tablet. "If your story checks, I might let you live."

"I'm from Tacoma, and I'm about to graduate from high school. My parents are Antonia and Lennie Lancaster. I was just at a martial arts competition which I won and which means I can probably kick your ass. Where are my folks?"

Louise ran the search. Sure enough, the Lancasters used to live in Tacoma, but shipped out for Mars a few years ago. He's a mechanic and she's listed as agricultural help, and *generalist*. They lost their daughter fifteen years ago after a martial arts competition. It was assumed that the then-new band of amphetamine-fueled zombies had killed her.

"Were you good at kung-fu?"

"No one beats me."

"We gotta get the fuck out of here. All hell is about to break loose."

Chapter Forty-Three

Louise opened the door, and a fuzzy, buzzy whine filled the air. She looked across the lawn where several women were congregated near the barbecue pit. They didn't seem bothered by the noise. Maybe it was something of theirs? Something she'd never seen or heard before.

"Hey, I gotta let her go," she said as a general announcement.

"Why the hell would you – " the woman's chest exploded in red. She fell.

A drone aircraft appeared over the roof's peak, it pivoted and machined-gunned the entire group. Louise ducked back into the barn. Her mind raced. All she knew was panic. Her skin was electric, her teeth screamed.

"Oh fuck, oh fuck." She wrestled with Jet's bonds.

"What's going on?"

"We're getting out of here. I'll explain later."

She freed the legs. Jet could stand. Now the arms. There was no time. She tossed Erin's tablet into a bag and furtively sought anything else she might need. No time. Bullets hailed through the barn window. She looked up to the loft. A drone hovered, pivoted. She dove just in time to miss a volley. The tablet started making a hell of a racket. Now is not the time for an alarm clock. It wouldn't shut up.

Louise looked at the device. It was tracking and analyzing the drones. There were three. Holy shit, Erin knew what she was doing. Next to each drone was a list of its specifications and a series of commands. Gunfire raged outside. Windows shattered and the screams of her former captors filled the air. A few found guns and returned fire, but the three drones remained aloft, firing a barrage of bullets.

The tablet. She could hardly focus. She had to try something so she entered a command. The first one crashed to the ground outside the barn. Fucking A! She killed the second. She hit the button for the third. *Connection Refused.* Fuck. She tried again. *Connection Aborted.* Its AI had learned to work around her commands. Goddammit.

"Run!" She grabbed Jet by the arm and they bolted out the door. The drone floated on the other side of the house. Its buzzing rotors taunted them. There seemed no escape from the sound. She saw the un-manned craft rise above the pitch of the roof. It opened fire. They ran inside. Jet screamed. Her feet were bloody from the shattered glass that lay about. Louise hoisted the woman to her back. I must be full of adrenaline if I can run with this bitch on my back. They made it to the bedroom. She grabbed her bag and had Jet don Makah's clothes.

"Follow me." A woman lay bleeding, dying in the hall. A shotgun lay next to her. Louise grabbed the weapon. Bullets tore through the front living room. Sofa pillows exploded into feathery clouds.

The women hid behind the refrigerator. Louise pulled out the tablet. It tracked the drone in real time. She didn't know what she was doing, but the display responded to her intuitive swipes. She saw a map of the property; the drone was a red dot that patrolled the area. Her truck was on the opposite side.

"Run!" The two burst from the front of the house and sprinted towards Louise's truck. The drone whined behind them. Louise turned, aimed, and took a shot, but she missed. Fuck. She turned to continue her sprint when she saw Jet's body fold at the waist, stumble forward. No! A hand grasped down for a stone, the body flipped up into the air, spinning on a horizontal axis, its hand moving in a blur. She turned back to pump the shotgun, but Jet's rock landed before she had the chance. The drone staggered, began spinning, and fired all of its bullets in a random destructive ejaculation. Jet picked up another stone and studied the drunken machine. He eyes narrowed and she struck like a cobra. The stone hit one of the drone's propellers, and it careened leftwards into a tree, which took another propeller. It fell to Earth.

"Motherfucker! Where did you learn that?"

"Dunno, but I knew I could. My body knew."

"Get in. There'll be more."

Chapter Forty-Four

It was good to be back on the road. Louise had spent too much time elbow-deep in engine grease and too little time behind the wheel. A straightaway opened up and she floored it. The surge of power felt good, it brought a part of her back to life. There's nothing that brings you to life more than when you're faced with imminent death. She wanted to celebrate, to laugh and holler, so she did. The road dipped and her body electrified with ecstasy when her stomach rose into her chest. Speed, the sound of a well-tuned motor, these were what she loved. Jet sat rigid in the seat next to her.

"Okay, please. What the fuck is going on?"

"I don't know your story, but this does," Louise pulled the metal cylinder from her pocket. "I'm guessing that you were kidnapped and then your body was hijacked when this, or something like it, was inserted into your butt." She placed the chip in the center console.

"What?"

"Look in a mirror. Who do you see?"

Jet flipped down the sun visor, but couldn't see much in the small reflective rectangle. Louise pulled out Erin's tablet and turned on the camera feature. Jet took a look and screamed.

"Is that me?" Her hands ran over her face, her voice shook.

She felt her dreadlocks and inspected her body. "That's not me, that. Is. Not. Me."

"It is now, sweetheart," Louise said. "You went to sleep and your body kept on moving. I think it's a little amazing that you, your consciousness, survived at all."

Jet picked up the chip and looked at it. Her eye was reflected in the top of the tiny cylinder. A sharp turn appeared. Lou grasped for the gearshift and braked. The engine whined in high revs, and she capitalized on the torque at the apex of the curve, blasting them to the next bit of straight road.

"You want this?" Jet held the chip in her open palm.

"It's more yours than mine."

"Huh?"

"That thing was buried in your ass. I extracted it."

"That explains the pain."

"That thing caused a lot of suffering," Louise said. "What you are, the body you have, has done a lot of bad shit."

Jet turned and looked out the window, her dense dreadlocks covered her face and killed any chance Louise might have to start a conversation. It was hard to sit with the same body that had killed Erin, but it felt different. That body is under new ownership, she thought, it's energy and attitudes will be different from now on. Fuck, she had to forgive. There was no other choice. Makah, whoever she was, was gone. Vanished in a blink, yet still stored in a tiny piece of metal Jet was holding close to her chest.

She checked the map and tried to pull up a route to Shasta. Nothing looked promising. It was hard to know where the maps got their information from. At certain times, your device might access an old satellite with pre-quake maps loaded into it. It was time to call in her ace in the hole.

"Yo, bitch." Maisie's voice had the ability to turn her to jelly.

"Yo, slutpants. Hey, I'm..."

"You're damn near fucked, sister." Maisie was casual, matter-of-fact. "I'm looking over what you sent me and I gotta say, that chick with you is, or was, one badass motherfucker. She worked for seriously evil people."

"She's a good kid."

"Yeah, I know. Oh, what I meant to say was that I detected a pack of drones on my old-ass radar. Headed your way. They're probably tracking that chip. Do you still have it?"

"Not for much longer." She jammed down on the brakes. "We're headed to Shasta. Plot me a course. I'll talk to you later." She turned to Jet, whose back was still turned. "Give me the chip, kid, or toss it. We gotta dump it. It's life or death."

Jet turned back to her. Silent tears streamed down her face and her eyes were vibrant red and green. Her eyes cut in defiance. Turmoil. Confusion.

"What for?"

"I'm not betting on your rock-throwing arm."

"Fine." She put down the window and flung her hand in the open air.

"Good. Look, everything that was on it is safe with my friend. I'll take you to her once this is all over."

She put the car in gear and they took off. In a moment, her phone bleated. Maisie sent a route with at note: *follow to a safe place*. Hot damn, that girl always comes through. I should never doubt Maisie's power. She slammed the gearbox into 4th and let the engine run.

Jet remained sullen, quiet, gazing out the window to avoid interaction or to find something that would make everything make sense. She released a sigh from time to time; once she asked to turn up the music. She seemed impenetrable, inconsolable. Louise was sick and tired of it.

"Can you say something? Anything?"

"What do you want me to say? That I'm glad to be here? That I am grateful to you? Fuck that, bitch. I'm fucking furious. Nobody asked me if I wanted any of this, nobody cared. I was forced into... something... and now I'm out of it. Or, my body was forced and I. I don't know what happened to me."

"It sucks, huh?"

"Brilliant observation. Does that make you Stephen Fucking Hawking or something?"

"I'm just saying I can relate. No one forced me into a

situation like yours, not that I know, but I've been forced to do lots of things I didn't want to. Circumstances are a motherfucker, people can really suck sometimes. Don't forget that I didn't gamble on having you with me, either. I had a perfectly capable super villain to sabotage me just a few hours ago."

"My body is at least ten years older than the last memory I had."

"How does it feel?"

"Used, but strong. It's held up pretty well, but my face is old, it's hideous."

"Well, you're stuck with it, and with me. Can you deal?"

"I don't have a fucking choice, do I?"

"Not unless you want to walk."

Chapter Forty-Five

They followed Maisie's directions. The roads were in good shape the whole way, a miracle. Jet had finally resigned to the situation, which Louise was glad for. Erin had been less of a pain in the ass and was far younger. Fucking teenagers.

"Looks like we're at the end of the line. This doesn't look like a mountain."

"My girl has something planned. I trust her." Lou's breath was shallow.

She pulled the car off the main road to a less well-kept lane full of mud and weeds. It was narrow, and she drove slow. Probably a post-quake road, now encroached-upon by trees and any plant that could get a toehold. The vehicle bobbed over roots and splashed through a creek. The day was waning. Louise put down her window.

There was a fire burning somewhere close by. She smelled food cooking. Meat. She could use some meat. Her stomach growled. She looked over at Jet who raised her eyebrows and smiled. They came to an opening. There was a patchy yard, a time-worn, but solid log cabin, and a big, yellow bus. Louise's heart sang. An unbreakable smile filled her face and fresh tears welled in her eyes. She jumped out of the car.

"Fir! Fir!"

"The hell you want? How did you find me?" The front door of the house opened and the grizzled old man emerged from the dark. "Arp." The singular, gutteral ejaculation was the best he could muster. His mouth hung open. His body shook. He stretched wide and open. Louise dove into his embrace and they both burst into tears.

"What, I mean, why?" The old traveling trickster was at a loss for words.

"Maisie sent me."

"Good. I'm happy." His voice tremvbled.

Louise inhaled her old friend's singular scent, a potpourri of cannabis, woodsmoke, body odor, and incense; aromas teleported her across time to her adolescence. She remembered the first time she saw him sitting up high, driving that old bus, his arm outstretched on the door lever. She bounded aboard the bus, and her life was forever changed. Now, in this moment, he was dressed inthe same bearskin pants, canvas shirt, and hand-made hempen suspenders that held his pants despite a healthy waistline.

Pangs of guilt stabbed her for not contacting him for so many years. She'd always held him in her heart. They didn't need words. Hardly a day had passed that she didn't think of him, something he'd said, or something he'd forgotten to say. He was part of her body, they were linked through the cosmos. Their connection can never be severed, though it was no substitute for corporeality. Holding him, and being held, in that misty woodsmoke forest day was a rarefied sweetness.

"You girls get me into trouble more than anyone I know.

What's Miss Maisie, *the all-seeing eye in the pyramid*, cooking up for us now?"

"We need a hiding spot." She gestured to Jet. "That one used to be a highly trained assassin working for people in SoCal. She's not anymore, but we need to make sure her former bosses don't catch on to us."

"Sounds dramatic." Fir stroked his beard. "I don't like drama. But, I do like good food. I just braised a pound of Elk. Got fixins for my special, signature stew. At least this year's version. There'll be enough to fill all our bellies, with leftovers, I'll wager."

"Bring it, Fir."

Fir's cooking was much like the man: simple, savory, and with ample portions for all. Louise dug into a hot, home-cooked meal the likes of which she hadn't seen in years. Louise felt her chest warm and her body tingled all over with each bite. Jet poked at the food and nibbled at the vegetables. She was wary of the meat, wary of Fir, wary of her new life.

His cabin was a spartan, one-room affair. The sleeping area was hidden behind a curtain, a patchwork of elk, bear, and rabbit skins. The sitting area was comprised of two rocking chairs and stacks of books. He cooked all of his meals on a woodburning stove that looked like it predated recorded history, and he had managed running water with an ingenious foot pump. Old ropes dangled from the rafters and the walls were covered with native paintings and artifacts.

"Just you out here?"

"Pretty much." Fir picked his teeth with a jagged wood shard. "There are some people over across the ridge, and I see them some, we trade. I take off when I get word the Spanners need my help with something. Which is often."

"Spanners? Those oily people? Is that where I am?" Jet was indignant.

"Just ate a meal prepared by one of their founders, sweetheart. Thank us later."

"Well, you know what they say about Spanners."

"No, what do they say about Spanners?" Heat rose in Louise's face.

"Like they all hate technology and are all a bunch of immoral hedonists."

"Well, the second part is correct." Fir laughed. "However, many of us love technology. I don't understand it, but I rely on those that do. Let's just say I see that it has uses, but it should also have limits."

Fir and Louise locked into one another. Their conversation was manic, intense, and excluded Jet. Feeling ignored, Jet selected a book from Fir's collection and tuned out the reunion. Fir pulled a mattress from the rafters for her so that she could curl up by the stove, like a pampered housecat. Fir and Louise passed a pipe between them and their minds rambled in all directions. Jet clued in from time to time and heard them talking about personal friends in common, or the state of Seattle, and the political nature of Cascadia. She was jolted from reading when they argued about how to rebuild a carburetor.

"Hey did you hear that?" Jet's spine straightened.

"No, what?"

"One of those fucking drones."

"Flashback?"

Louise led the way to the front door. She looked around, stared up to the forest canopy. There was no sound, nothing out of the ordinary. She pulled out Erin's tablet, but there was nothing. Fir had night vision binoculars.

"Well, there are some raccoons fucking about 50 yards thatta away," he chuckled. "Never heard the little bandits do it before, maybe that was it."

"Fuck. I guess I'm pretty tweaked." Louise gazed at her feet.

"Naw, darlin', I believe you," he said. "I got something that'll make you feel better. Let's step back inside."

Fir pulled a panel away from the rustic log cabin wall. He pushed a button, and the screen came to life. He swiped and tapped at the icons, thought for a second, then tapped a few more candy-colored buttons.

"This is all Maisie," he said. "She built this damn thing. If a squirrel poops in my yard, it'll go off."

"I never thought I'd see you with a *fear system*."

"You get older and look down a few barrels, maybe piss

some people off, suddenly they become *security systems*," he said. "With age, you start to justify more and more fear. Let this be a warning to both of you. You won't be young forever, but you should try."

"Look, why don't you come with us to Shasta?"

"Haven't seen old Úytaahkoo in many, many moons. I'm happy you asked, else I might have stowed away."

Before daybreak, Fir rose, washed in the cold-water bathroom, and stoked coals from the previous evening. He added leaves, kindling, and a few logs, blew the coals to red, igniting the leaves. He smiled when the first flame rose on a log, when the new day's fire kissed him with warmth. Birds sang in the forest and by the time the stove's heat reached Louise and thawed her nose, light was streaming through the room. Fir cracked eggs, cut bacon, and boiled water for tea.

"Real breakfast?"

"We have a full day, or more, ahead of us."

"Do either of you know where we're going?" Jet tied her dreadlocks into an unruly ponytail. "That Maisie girl hasn't given us anything has she?"

"Darlin, I know my way to Shasta as well as I know these eggs and bacon."

"The roads have changed since then, haven't they?"

"Sweetheart, I've only been back here for a few days." He plated the eggs and bacon. Louise prepared ginseng tea for everyone. "I spend most of my time on the road. I may not have been up that mountain, but just a week ago I was in Weed teaching kids how to rebuild a few transmissions, do valve jobs, and fix brakes."

Louise loved Fir's eggs. He never used the same recipe twice, but they were always, unmistakably, his. This time, he'd added dried chanterelles and fresh chives, each bite exploded with flavor and texture. She thought she detected a hint of truffle in the mix, but that could have been from the well-seasoned pan. She studied him as he took plates from the table and was glad, gratified that they'd been reunited, that they'd have more time together. Louise's phone bleated a text message.

"Were you followed?"

"No."

"Sure?"

"Yes. Fir coming to Shasta. He knows the way. Please be eyes and ears."

"Bad feeling. Be safe."

They closed up the windows, double checked the security system, and walked out the door. Mist hung in the forest; a crow lit off from Louise's car. She reached the vehicle, unlocked its doors, and turned. Fir's head was craned up at the forest canopy, he stuck his tongue out to gather mist. He's having one of his reveries; he's still such a kid, full of wonder and awe and wisdom. Louise's chest opened. Beams of loving energy flowed out to the aromatic mountain of beard, muscle, and gruff. It was going to be a great trip.

She took a breath of clean, misty air. She blinked. Jet bobbled on a root. Her keys jangled as she took them from her pocket. She looked back at Fir and his smile beamed; then his head lurched back; then he dropped his bags. His body thrust forward, chest out. He fell to the Earth as a man broken, unable to correct or break the fall. Leaves danced in the shock of impact. Jet's eyes bulged, she covered her gaping mouth. Louise heard nothing except for the sound of her own heart. The world stopped. She stood alone in that full, pregnant moment. There was not yet a word for what had happened. There was not yet a feeling for what had happened, nothing yet resembling grief or anger or sadness or regret or loss. There was a void. There was thick air, cool mist, and a dying man on the forest floor. A man lifeless and still. For the moment he had no name, no history, no personality or odor. A man lying on the forest floor, obscured by ferns. He was beneath the crows, and the white and gray ceiling of cloud above. A man, *the* man who had raised her, loved her, and who would never rise again from the roots and worms. Fir, Louise's sweet cosmic journeyman, was dead.

The rear window burst in a shatter of glass. Louise re-entered time. There was no point in worrying about Fir, he was obviously gone and someone was shooting at them. Another shot rang out and splintered a tree trunk three inches over Jet's head. Another shot. Another.

"Get in the goddamned car." Louise turned and opened the driver door. Without a thought the car was running. Jet leapt into the passenger seat and she hit the gas.

"The fuck is happening?" Jet shrieked in a full panic.

Louise squeezed the vehicle between two trees, slammed the accelerator and the car rocketed down the trail. The car bounced and bobbed off each rock and root which, at full speed, threatened to collapse the suspension. Louise maintained control when the car went airborne just before a curve. She didn't know how she was doing it, but there was no time for thought.

Jet was silent. She looked out the window. She's pulling that sullen teen shit. It looks so horrible on a grown woman.

"How did they find us, is what I want to know."

"What the fuck, Jet? Talk to me," Louise wanted to throw her out in front of the car. "Do you still have it?"

"Have what?"

"You're not a fucking kid. Do you have the thing or not?"

"What does it matter?"

"That thing just got my best friend killed. Two, actually. The only reason you're still alive is because I don't carry a gun." A shot echoed through the forest.

"Alright, fine." Jet pulled the metal pellet from her pocket, shoved it in Louise's face, then threw it out the window. "Satisfied?"

"I lost my fucking best friend in the world. He was like my goddamned father and you ask me if I'm *satisfied*?" Louise's tears streamed down her hot face. She pulled over to the side of the road. She sobbed. Her body shook. Jet put an arm around her.

"Don't disobey me like that again. You don't know this world, you don't know shit." She lurched with grief. A gunshot resonated through the forest. "Fuck." She wiped her eyes and floored it.

Louise lost herself in the road. Every curve, hill, precipitous cliff-hugging hairpin, and animal carcass was a new death-threat but she took them all in stride. It was all a new pattern of the same old stuff, clever enough to keep her interested, but also familiar enough to nearly put her to sleep. All she wanted to do was sleep, escape this nightmare, maybe push the kid out over the next cliff.

The phone bleated. It was Maisie. Louise silenced her phone and downshifted through a tight curve. She couldn't drive. The pain in her chest was huge and growing. She stopped to answer Maisie's call.

Chapter Forty-Six

The second the vehicle stopped, Jet grabbed a bag of clothes, snatched Louise's tablet, and bolted through the dust cloud into the forest. She leaped into the car's dust cloud and bolted into the forest. She would not stand for any more bullshit. It was not her fault that this happened. That weird, crazy old man was not her problem. The drones could have been chasing Louise for any number of reasons, including those weird black boxes.

It felt great to be in the forest with nobody around. The silence soothed her. Distant cracking branches and bird songs reminded her that she was not alone. The forest was with her, life was all around, just no more nattering human beings.

The forest floor was a tangle of rotting old trees, underbrush, and unpredictable contours. Her body was strong and balanced, though, perhaps more so than how she'd left it. She was stronger, she thought, more physically capable. To test herself, she put her things in a pile and ran full tilt towards a felled tree. She leaped into the air, bounded off the decaying log, and propelled herself even higher to catch a far branch. She swung her legs up to vertical and suspended herself upside-down in a mid-air handstand. Her hands were vice-grips, her core was as strong as iron but with the internal intelligence of a gyroscope. She stood tall, an inverted pike. When she was ready, she bent at the waist and brought her feet to the limb, one to either side of her hands. Her arms pulled the limb towards her chest, and her feet pressed down. She inhaled. She exhaled. She inhaled again and then released her hands, uncoiled the steel springs in her legs and flew up and back into the air, performing a flying reverse somersault for the entertainment of a raccoon family that watched from a neighboring tree.

She didn't know where she would land and she didn't care. There was no point in seeking outcomes. There was no point in much of anything, she figured. Life was random and cruel. It killed the woman who made this body so strong, and it killed that strange hippie man who made the great stew. It sent killer robots, but also provided moments of laughter and mirth. At least that's what she was able to put together from the last day or so in her new existence. Before, with her parents, life was barely a challenge.

As she completed the second flip, she saw that she was near to landing. She looked down and saw that she was headed towards a large patch of moss. Such luck. She put a bend in her knees and braced for an earthly re-connection.

The moss was soft and Jet's body crumpled into its pillowy, green embrace. She rolled onto her back and gazed up at the canopy. The interplay of tree branch and sky was amazing. Did the trees frame the sky or did the sky frame the branches? A breeze shook the whole arrangement into a new configuration, it would never be the same again. Now a tiny patch of blue shone through. Now a black cloud intermingled with the white, gauzy ceiling. She wished she could lie on the mossy bed forever.

She inflated her body. Her heart thumped, it pulled oxygen into blood; it wanted to rise into the sky. When she was full and ready to float, she trapped the air in her body. The tension was perfect. Leaves crumpled behind her. She slowly opened her airway and released the gas with a gentle hiss. A small twig snapped. Her lungs emptied. Her skin electrified.

She flipped onto her stomach. There were eyes on her. They were close. Whatever was out there could smell her, it was ready to attack. Her hands pressed into the moss and elevated her body a few inches from the floor. She was still at ground level, beneath the forest bed of fern. She straightened her elbows to peer over the flora. A patch of greens shook mere feet away. As she popped up to a crouch, a wild cat pounced. Without a thought, she shot forward, under the cougar. She sprang to her feet and turned to face the beast who, seeing her at full height, hesitated. Jet took advantage and jumped atop a fallen tree. She screamed at her attacker, who recoiled and hissed. It bared teeth and showed its claws, but Jet found that she had no fear. She was full of adrenaline, but she had nothing but an inner, deep-tissue faith that she was going to defeat the cat on its own turf. Undaunted, the cat made one final attempt. However, Jet met the cat's leaping attack with a full-force kick to its breastplate. Her battle cry echoed through the forest. The cat landed, cut its eyes, and howled at her. She screamed in triumph over the feline. The cat saw that it would not have an easy time and scampered off through the underbrush.

Jet fell back to her bed of moss. She laughed a deep-chest, throaty laugh that startled her. She'd ridden the line between this world and the next and had arisen victorious. She would remain alive, vital, able to face new challenges and adventures. She rolled over to press up and a small brown thing caught her eye. It was a mushroom in a clump of fellow fungi. She picked it from the loamy soil. The stem turned blue beneath her fingers. Hmm, that's curious, she thought. Without thinking, she picked enough to fill a pocket in her bag.

The sun had passed its high point; the day was waning. She set off to retrace her steps through a landscape where every unique space looked like every other space. Ferns and trees and moss replicated in infinite combination, the last rotted tree looked so much like the one before and yet the one after surely must be the one she passed shortly after leaving the road. The road. I have to find the road. Did she pass a grove of laurel like that one? The more she thought about where she was and tried to figure how to get back to the road the more she became lost and confused. It was like the chinese handcuffs her father had made when she was young. The more she tried to force herself to go the right way the more she seemed to go wrong.

She sat and looked into the bag. There had to be a canteen of water or some food, anything. There was nothing but a pair of pants, a few pairs of underwear, a shirt, and the tablet. She pressed a button on the device and its screen illuminated with a topographical map that had a glowing blue dot at its center. She walked ten feet and the dot moved accordingly. She zoomed in on the map. There appeared to be a road somewhat close by, if she was accurately assessing the map's scale. If the map was accurate at all. There were too many unknowns, but at least there was a guide, an electronic helpmate, and that was better than what she had all of five minutes ago. That was better than fighting off a wildcat in the forest, or a bear, or starving with no idea of how to reach others.

"How the hell?" she said to the forest. A chill came over her, her intuition was going bananas. She crouched, wary of attack.

"I will tell you this once, and only once."

The voice came from the tablet and Jet dropped it to the ground, shocked. Her teeth ached in the panic, her skin was electrified. The device lay with the screen facing up. The map disappeared, it went dark, and words appeared on the screen: Do not Panic. I am here to help you return to Louise. I have much to tell you about the journey to come. It may be easier if I speak. Nod if you agree.

Jet took several deep breaths. She stared around at the infinite forest, the ebbing light, and she decided that this was her best option. It would be better to die talking to an electronic device than eaten by some terrible natural force in the middle of the night. She nodded her assent.

"You are very important. People need you."

"Who?"

"Everyone. Cascadia."

"Me?"

"It was the girl, Erin, she was incredibly talented," the tablet said. "However, you, or the personality that inhabited your body, killed her."

"That shit was not my fault," Jet's voice echoed in the forest, setting off a chorus of caws from a murder of crows. She flushed with anger. "I would never kill an innocent girl like that."

"There is no fault. Things simply happen. Those who controlled your body were influenced by a million factors and the result was Erin's death. If there is accountability it is with them and my SoCal counterpart."

"What am I supposed to do about it?"

"You will first learn to do by not-doing. You have been buried for so long, you have much to learn. This is part of why I need you, part of why you are so important. Your body is a fine machine and now your mind, and your spirit, need to be trained to match. This is why you are going to the mountain. Part, at any rate. There are at least one thousand reasons for your journey to Mount Shasta and as many, or more, outcomes will result."

"Not doing?"

"Not-doing, not-knowing. The natural world does not work according to the power of one's will, whether human or otherwise. The power of consciousness is so great that beings seek control as a means of maintaining sanity. The controlling impulse limits the experience of consciousness and gives rise to a self or what you might call an ego. These things create the illusion of manageability. However this is an illusion, a falsehood.

"You will learn this. I can tell you, but you will soon have this knowledge embedded deep in your human psyche, and what you might call a soul. This will be part of your work on the mountain."

"How do you know?"

"My calculations say what will be. There are infinite variables in this world, but I can track the most pertinent ones with great accuracy. There are often unintended outcomes. Even I cannot account for everything. Yet, I can make choices, I can work with the stream of facts and beings and try to nudge them in a helpful direction. There will always be unintended outcomes, however, the most valid rule of plan-making is that plans fail."

"Unintended?"

"Like you. Your presence was not a factor in my initial calculation. Louise was on track to deliver my device, I even accounted for the possibility of an interfering device, which I neutralized and assimilated. Then you showed up and altered the formulation. I was working with Erin to neutralize you, but we couldn't act fast enough. I suspect our plans were anticipated.

"Erin was supposed to reach Shasta with Louise to deliver my devices. I wanted her to stay and set off a chain of events with wide-ranging consequences. That now falls to you, ironically."

"What consequences will I create?"

"There are too many variables now, too much is not yet known, and there is so much you need to learn for yourself and integrate into your individual self. You must rejoin with Louise, however. She has spoken with the important people in her life about the unforeseen end of Fir and she now hopes you are coming back. She does care about you, and you are going back."

"How do you know?"

"Will the next cougar be as easily thwarted?"

"How did you...?"

"This device was in your bag."

"Oh, right."

Chapter Forty-Seven

Louise dodged potholes down the remnants of the interstate. There was no one on the road, she felt exposed, but Maisie had insisted on that route. The bad guys weren't on the radar and that road was in better shape than any other. She lost herself in a reverie, thinking about how such a simple delivery job got so twisted. Of thousands of couriers, somehow she was chosen. Random chance, the capriciousness of fate, boggled her mind. It was impossible to ever know what would happen next, yet she sensed that there was some underlying intelligence and order to it all. They say everything happens for a reason, she thought, and that's mostly bullshit. But, what if the reason is in the happening, and the results? Reason is, after all, crystallized human perception. We tend to think things are meaningless when they don't match our expectations. Maybe that's only a moral code we inflict on the world, an illusion of control that is mostly laughable.

She was lost in thought, her body reacting to the ruts and bumps in the road. A bird broke her attention. She blinked and took a deep breath and saw that the sky had cleared. The gauzy-white ceiling was gone and a wide swath of crystal-clear blue sky opened up. After all that had happened, the vista from her driver's seat was a pleasure, a gift from nature that she accepted wholly and gratefully. That proud snowcapped mountain, buttered in sunset, appeared from behind the trees. It took her breath away.

Louise stopped the car in the middle of the road, got out,

and stood in awe of the ancient volcano. She climbed up on top of the car, sat crosslegged and engaged a conversation with nature. It welcomed her, blessed her journey, and paid respects to Fir, who'd loved it so much. She couldn't count the number of times she'd passed the majestic white mountain on her way to deliver or retrieve some form of payload in San Francisco, or some remote outpost. In all that time, all those journeys, she'd only seen the mountain's peak two times. She never took the time to do more than stop to pee, have a drink of water, or stretch her legs before hitting the road again. Always duty-bound, she never indulged in a full meditation on the mountain, never drank in its majesty or basked in the awe it inspires in those who take the time. She'd never had business around Shasta, but Fir's last work had been with the Shasta spanners. He was well-known in the area. He was part of me, my soul, I'm connected here; I'm a part of this area, this mountain, this land. She wanted his corpse with her. She wanted to bury his physical body on the mountain. That would make him happy, she thought, or at least it would make me happy. His empty vessel still lay on the forest floor, in a state of decay, providing food for ants, ravens, and worms. She couldn't bear the thought.

Louise closed her eyes and imagined the scene. She eliminated any foraging parasites and conjured him as the Fir she knew and loved, the one who'd picked her up that day on the road, who had been there for her during all the trials of young womanhood. He never pretended to grok womanhood, but he offered an ear, acceptance, love. She hovered over the body, inhaled him, stroked his tangled beard, and wished him safe passage to whatever waited on the other side.

This is the best I got, old man, no wake or funeral. I'll tell everyone when I get back. We'll have a celebration in your honor, the biggest party we've ever thrown. It's all because of you, man. You brought everything together. Without you, I would have never known the Spanners. Universe knows what would have become of me. I'd probably be bored somewhere in Portland, working some mundane job that I sit down to every day, unable to shake the notion that I had somehow gotten everything wrong. You helped me find meaning and purpose. You told me that Spanners obey the rule *Know Thyself*, so I conformed to that path of non-conformity; I try to know myself better and better every day, and I promise you that I'll keep seeking to learn more. That's all because of you, Fir.

She opened her eyes and saw Jet down on the ground, pacing around. She looked west, into the sun, then back at the mountain. I think she gets it, how special this moment is. Part of Louise wanted to kill the girl-woman, the teen trapped in an adult murderer's body. She wondered if its cells remembered the crime; there could be some deep muscle memory that would continue to influence Jet's life. We all think we're controlling so much, but how true is that? There is no control. It's impossible to know if the truths I hold dear are even true, or if they'll be valid tomorrow. This consciousness, this person, is illusory, fleeting. This thing that I call me might be all stored in a chip in the ass of this meat-coated skeleton I'm riding. Meat.

"Hey Jet, want to eat?"

"I don't think I've seen anything like this before."

"Yeah, pretty rare. She's a beautiful mountain, but the clouds keep her hidden."

"I think I understand that."

"Space is amazing."

"I guess my parents are out there too, somewhere past the blue."

Louise opened the vehicle and checked the tablet to see if it registered any drones. She messaged Maisie who said that the coast was clear. In the rear, she had a cache of canned meats, soups, and camping cookware. Thank the Universe for accidental forethought, fortuitous psychic links to the future.

"Is this the end of your journey?"

"Define *end*."

"Well, where are you going after this? Can I get a ride?"

"I'll head to Portland. If you need a lift to Tacoma, I can do that. After I freshen up and rest for at least two nights."

"Deal."

The next morning the sky was still clear. It was disorienting. Without the normal cloud-cover, Louise felt like she might float up into space.

They got in the car and drove the vehicle until the road disappeared into a snowbank. Clouds had rolled in and the mountain peak had again hidden her glory in misty haze. They packed provisions, the two black boxes, and the tablet. The air was cold in her nose and she was happy for it. Louise eyed the black boxes, their blank red eyes blinked out of sync. They didn't have a scratch on them. After all this, the fucking things were totally intact. She was still bound to plant them on the mountain. Somewhere. Somehow. She pulled out her phone. One last call will finish the deal.

"Hey, it's me. I'm at the snow line."

"You're alive?" Morgan had to be the most forgiving courier client in the world.

"Apparently."

"We weren't sure. You have it?"

"Yeah, well, both of them."

"You know what to do."

"Actually, I don't. Is there any special place for these things? We're at the snow line."

"Go as high as you can. See if you can climb 150 meters up. When the air feels too thin, you're probably high enough. Put them on the ground, secure them. Dig out a little hole for them, but keep at least half above ground. That's imperative."

"Roger that."

Trudging 150 meters on fresh snow was harder than it sounded, especially in low lander boots. Within two meters, the snow met her waistline and she wasn't certain that she was still walking on soil. This just as easily could be snow-pack. Nevertheless, Louise was determined to get the job done. She would make it no matter what. You don't lose your best friends, cheat death out of multiple chances, then bail on the journey's final meters. Given everything else, this is the easiest part of the whole journey. Fuck that. They trudged on.

The tablet indicated that they'd climbed 125 meters. Screw this noise, this ain't precision mechanics. Louise looked back towards the valley, but there was nothing to be seen but the pure white of fog. Jet was still with her, a few meters back. They didn't have proper tools for digging, but she did at least have a crow bar. The snow was light powder that she was able to brush off to the side. The women worked together to find the earth. When they did, the soil was hard-packed and frozen. She pounded it with her iron bar and it loosened a bit. Her hands started stiffening, the cold burn was excruciating. Why didn't she bring a shovel? Because there was no shovel. Couriers don't need shovels. Nobody said a thing about digging.

Jet helped clear the snow away with her bare hands. Every few moments the women stopped to massage their fingers. Louise stood up to exercise her legs, take a breath and look into the void of cloud. There was nothing to do but dig.

"Who's digging on my mountain?" A voice came from the fog.

Louise stopped cold. She stood but couldn't see anyone, nor anything. "We don't mean any harm. We're on our way in no time."

"One of you has been in a hole for very, very long. The other has brought her here to me," the foggy voice said. "Now, in this moment, you are both in a hole."

"What? Where are you?"

A shadow appeared from white misty air. It was very tall, it seemed to float with grace, then it staggered.

"I am Ezekiel. I belong to this mountain and it belongs to me. I am an outcropping of its life, it is a web of sustenance beneath my feet."

"I'm Louise. I'm a courier."

"Jet, I'm a passenger; currently digging."

He moved closer and they could see him. He was the first young man Louise had seen since the forest Spanners, before they were all killed. His face was rugged. He had a long black mustache and goatee that offsetd his pale skin. His dark eyes were pools of calm and Louise felt at ease in his presence. His clothing was hand-made and primitive, like the native clothing she'd seen in textbooks, but his face betrayed a European lineage.

"Jet and Louise. You must come with me right now. I have snowshoes for you both. There is no time to waste."

"Wait, bud." Louise felt her temper rise. "We gotta drop these little boxes on your hill and get the fuck out of dodge. I don't need any more time on this rock."

"It is faster for you to reach my cave than your car. Trust

me. You will not live to make it to your car. Your car might not even be there if you do."

"What kinda shit…"

"Silence." Ezekiel's voice sharpened, deepened. "Come with me. This is my mountain. My accommodations are ample. Most of all, they are safe."

"Fuck it." Louise yanked a pair of snowshoes out of Ezekiel's hands.

The three entered the cave. Louise and Jet made a beeline for the fire. Their hands were red-raw, at the edge of frostbite. Ezekiel brought them a skin-rejuvenating concoction. They slathered it on and it soothed their hands and faces.

"This will protect you. You were not prepared for the snow, which is a shame. I, however, was prepared for you. The mountain was prepared for you."

A great rumbling came from all around. Louise tensed, her body on high alert. Jet grabbed her arm. Yet the ground didn't shake. The rumbling continued, then muffled, then died.

"What was that?"

"Avalanche."

"You knew that would happen?"

"What is *knowledge*? The event was inside me, I was inside

it. Just as were you, both of you. There is no *other*, upon which knowledge rests."

"We're trapped?"

"You're alive. You're safe." Ezekiel picked up a log for the fire. "You're warm and there is food for us all."

That night, Louise slept on the cave floor, but had the best night's rest she'd had in years. Ezekiel had warm blankets for everyone. He was a perfect host. She couldn't remember better treatment.

When Louise awoke, Ezekiel was already working on clearing the cave-mouth. Jet was awake, eating rabbit meat. She handed Lou a curious, murky hot beverage. It smelled vaguely of coffee, but was not. It was perfect, whatever it was.

"He says I must stay."

"Why?"

"He's not one for explanations."

"What do you think?"

"I think I need to stay. He knows things." Jet stared into the flames. She had pulled her hair back into a bundle, and revealed a face that still recalled Makah, but which had softened, molding itself to its new, original owner. "I was in a hole, as he says, for about ten years. I need to spend a bit more time in this hole before I can be reborn back to the world. The mountain told him this, and I believe it. I need to believe something. Nothing is making sense, Louise."

"Maybe you were the package I needed to deliver."

Jet's brilliant blue eyes penetrated Louise. "You have done a great thing for me, Louise. I am in your debt. Forever."

It took Ezekiel a few days to dig out from the avalanche. He refused all help. He insisted that it was his duty as a host. When it was done, he and Louise walked down the mountain. Ezekiel's keen sense of the mountain, of snow, and nature enabled him to find her snowbound car. It had been parked on the edge of the avalanche and was easily recovered, undamaged. Ezekiel reminded her how lucky she was. She was ready to get on the road and had no time to contemplate the miracle of chance that had spared her.

"I roll the dice all the time. Today they rolled my way."

In no time, she was on the road, where she belonged. She was a courier, a messenger. Not a winged god, but a goddess of fuel and engine grease, ever between life and death, point A and point B. She mashed the accelerator, took a deep breath, and the exterior world faded into a blur.

About the Author

Hobie Anthony is an Oregon writer who earned an MFA from Queens University of Charlotte, NC. He has published stories and poetry in such journals as: Fourteen Hills, Fiction Southeast, The Rumpus, Wigleaf, Housefire, Crate, Birkensnake, Word Riot, and others. *Liminal* is his second published book; *Silverfish* was published by Whiskey Tit in 2018. To learn more, check his website: hobieanthony.wordpress.com

About the Publisher

Whisk(e)y Tit is committed to restoring degradation and degeneracy to the literary arts. We work with authors who are unwilling to sacrifice intellectual rigor, unrelenting playfulness, and visual beauty in our literary pursuits, often leading to texts that would otherwise be abandoned in today's largely homogenized literary landscape. In a world governed by idiocy, our commitment to these principles is an act of civil service and civil disobedience alike.

CPSIA information can be obtained
at www.ICGtesting.com
Printed in the USA
BVHW091629060822
643973BV00013B/1781